From the USA
SOLOMON K
Dane Maddock

A treasure lost in the desert. A notorious unsolved murder. A contest where the stakes are life and death.
When treasure hunters Dane Maddock and Bones Bonebrake travel to the Mojave Desert to help launch an adventure race, they make a baffling discovery- a dungeon room hidden high in the desert hills, and beyond, a previously undiscovered network of caverns that seem to go on forever. But someone will kill to protect the secrets that are hidden there.

When an attempt is made on Maddock's life, the assassin's trail sets the former Navy SEALs on a search for one of the greatest legends of the southwest. But to find it, they must unmask the notorious Black Dahlia killer!

PRAISE FOR DAVID WOOD
AND THE DANE MADDOCK ADVENTURES

"*Contest* is an adrenaline-fueled thrill ride!" Alan Baxter, author of Hidden City

"With the thoroughly enjoyable way Mr. Wood has mixed speculative history with our modern day pursuit of truth, he has created a story that thrills and makes one think beyond the boundaries of mere fiction and enter the world of *why not*?" David Lynn Golemon, Author of *Ancients, Event, Legend,* and *Leviathan*

"A twisty tale of adventure and intrigue that never lets up and never lets go!" Robert Masello, author of Bestiary and *Blood and Ice*

"Dane and Bones.... Together they're unstoppable. Rip roaring action from start to finish. Wit and humor throughout. Just one question - how soon until the next one? Because I can't wait." Graham Brown, author of *Shadows of the Midnight Sun*

"What an adventure! A great read that provides lots of action, and thoughtful insight as well, into strange realms that are sometimes best left unexplored." Paul Kemprecos, author of *Cool Blue Tomb* and *the NUMA Files*

"Let there be no confusion: David Wood is the next Clive Cussler. Once you start reading, you won't be able to stop until the last mystery plays out in the final line." Edward G. Talbot, author of *2012: The Fifth World*

"I like my thrillers with lots of explosions, global locations and a mystery where I learn something new. Wood delivers! Recommended as a fast paced, kick ass read." J.F. Penn, author of *Desecration*

"A page-turning yarn blending high action, Biblical speculation, ancient secrets, and nasty creatures. Indiana Jones better watch his back!" Jeremy Robinson, author of *SecondWorld*

"Hits all the marks that a blockbuster should. With elements of mystery, lost technology and a mythical city, this book reads like vintage Clive Cussler. His best yet!" - Rick Jones, Author of *The Crypts of Eden*

"David Wood has done it again. Within seconds of opening the book, I was hooked. Intrigue, suspense,monsters, and treasure hunters. What more could you want? David's knocked it out of the park with this one!" -Nick Thacker, author of *The Enigma Strain*

CONTEST

A DANE MADDOCK ADVENTURE
DAVID WOOD

ADRENALINE PRESS

Contest- ©2019 by David Wood

The Dane Maddock Adventures™

All rights reserved

Published by Adrenaline Press
www.adrenaline.press

Adrenaline Press is an imprint of Gryphonwood Press
www.gryphonwoodpress.com

Edited by Melissa Bowersock

ISBN: 978-1-950920-01-3

This is a work of fiction. All characters, locations, and events are products of the authors' imaginations or are used fictitiously or for the purpose of satire.

BOOKS BY DAVID WOOD

THE DANE MADDOCK ADVENTURES
Dourado
Cibola
Quest
Icefall
Buccaneer
Atlantis
Ark
Xibalba
Loch
Solomon Key
Contest

DANE AND BONES ORIGINS
Freedom
Hell Ship
Splashdown
Dead Ice
Liberty
Electra
Amber
Justice
Treasure of the Dead
Bloodstorm

DANE MADDOCK UNIVERSE
Berserk
Maug
Elementals
Cavern
Devil's Face
Herald
Brainwash
The Tomb
Destination: Rio

Destination: Luxor
Destination: Sofia
Aztlan (short story)
Urban Legend (short story)

JADE IHARA ADVENTURES (WITH SEAN ELLIS)
Oracle
Changeling
Exile

MYRMIDON FILES (WITH SEAN ELLIS)
Destiny
Mystic

BONES BONEBRAKE ADVENTURES
Primitive
The Book of Bones
Skin and Bones
Venom

JAKE CROWLEY ADVENTURES (WITH ALAN BAXTER)
Blood Codex
Anubis Key
Revenant

BROCK STONE ADVENTURES
Arena of Souls
Track of the Beast (forthcoming)

SAM ASTON INVESTIGATIONS (WITH ALAN BAXTER)
Primordial
Overlord

STAND-ALONE NOVELS
Into the Woods (with David S. Wood)
The Zombie-Driven Life
You Suck
Callsign: Queen (with Jeremy Robinson)
Dark Rite (with Alan Baxter)

DAVID WOOD WRITING AS DAVID DEBORD

THE ABSENT GODS TRILOGY
The Silver Serpent
Keeper of the Mists
The Gates of Iron

The Impostor Prince (with Ryan A. Span)
Neptune's Key

PROLOGUE

October 7, 1949
The Mojave Desert

The sun beat down on the back of Jean's neck as the little red sports car zipped along the sun-baked road. The wind swept her hair back and the setting sun's last rays colored her skin a delicate shade of orange. Jean had given up on trying to keep her hair tied and had just let it fly. She'd fix it when they stopped to fill up. Evelyn Knight was on the radio, crooning a love ballad. It was perfect.

Jean looked over at Kirk, who flashed her an easy smile. "What's a buzzin, cousin?" he asked.

She rolled her eyes. "Don't call me that. It sounds so wrong."

"Come on, dolly. It's just a saying."

Jean frowned. "I understand idioms. I just don't care for one that sounds so incestuous."

"Don't flip your wig." Amusement sparkled in his dark eyes, and the breeze ruffled his thick black hair. He really was a dreamboat. "You are having a good time aren't you?"

"Aces," she said, and immediately felt foolish using the vernacular. Kirk was a writer, a man of words. She didn't want him to think she was just another chucklehead. "I still can't get over this car."

"What do you mean?"

"Well, the steering wheel is on the wrong side, for a start. And it only has the two seats."

"It's a Jaguar XK120," he said proudly. "Imported it from England. They race these over there, you know? Leslie Johnson just won a biggie back in August."

"Wow. That's amazing." Jean had no interest in automobile racing, but she tried to put some sincerity into her words. "How fast can it go?"

"I'll show you." Kirk stepped on the gas. The engine roared and the car surged forward.

Jean knew she ought to be frightened, but she found the experience exhilarating. The parched landscape flashed by in a blur of tan and green. She threw back her head and laughed. After a few minutes, Kirk slowed down to a normal speed.

"What did you think? Amazing, wasn't it?"

"I loved it!" It was the simple truth. She'd found it utterly exhilarating.

"I love *you*," he replied.

Jean gasped. She searched his eyes for a sign of laughter, but there was none.

"Kirk, we've only known each other for three weeks." And what a three weeks it had been! They'd met on the set of *Cursed Treasure*, where she'd been working as an extra. She'd taken him for an actor, given his good looks, but he said he was a writer and also worked behind the scenes in some unspecified capacity. The first time their eyes had met, she felt as though he could see right through her. He hadn't smiled, only a quirk of an eyebrow acknowledged her existence, but she'd been smitten from that moment. The courtship had moved rapidly. As a dancer, model, and actress she was accustomed to receiving attention from men, but not from someone like Kirk. He was handsome, self-assured, and by all appearances, rich. What was more, he didn't seem to mind that she was divorced.

"Not just three weeks. Three *wonderful* weeks, baby," he said. "Tell me you don't feel the same."

She hesitated. "I don't want you to think I'm some Able Grable." Too many men assumed that a divorced woman was always open for business.

"I know you're not. You're a classy dame, else I wouldn't be with you." He reached over and gave her hand a squeeze. His leather driving gloves were surprisingly supple. She looked down and noticed a dark patch on the thumb.

"Oops. You've got a stain."

He jerked his hand away like he'd been bitten by a snake. His eyes went wide for a moment, but then the easy smile was back.

"Sorry. I just love these gloves. Guess I'll need to buy a new pair."

"Maybe you can buy some when we get where we're going." She paused. He still hadn't told her his plan. "Where are we going, anyway? You've been quite secretive about this whole thing." She reached out and gave his shoulder a playful thump. "Is there something you're not telling me?"

Kirk laughed. "As a matter of fact, there is. Something very important."

Her heart lurched. "Oh God. You're married, aren't you?"

He laughed even harder. "No, no. I only meant that I'm not going to tell you where we're going or what we're doing this weekend. It's a surprise. You don't want me to give it all away now that we're almost there, do you?"

"Oh. So we're almost there? That's a clue." She opened the glove box.

"What are you doing?" Kirk snapped. He slammed the box closed.

"I was looking for a map." Try as she would, Jean couldn't keep the hurt from her voice. "I wanted to see if I could guess where we were going. I thought it would be fun. A little game, you know?"

Kirk sighed, the sudden flash of anger already faded. "I'm sorry, Jeanie. I've got all the paperwork for the car in there and I was afraid it would blow away. I'm just so touchy about this new car and everything related to it." He swallowed hard, his voice trembled. "I just like you so much and I wanted this to be a perfect trip. Now I've gone and ruined it."

Jean relaxed. She leaned over and rested her head on his shoulder. "I shouldn't have nosed around. Let's just forget it ever happened, okay? I'll let you have your little surprise."

"Thank you. You're too good for me." Kirk sounded like he truly meant it. "Speaking of surprises, I've got one for you that you can open now. Just be careful not to drop it. It's delicate." He reached under the seat, took out a small white gift box, and handed it to her.

Jean's heart raced. She could tell just by the fancy box that it was expensive. The last gift her ex-husband had given her was a new frying pan wrapped in the funny pages. She untied the ribbon that held the box closed. Anticipation flooding her senses, she slowly, almost reverentially, removed the lid and extracted the layer of cotton batting. When she saw what lay inside, she let out a little gasp.

It was a glass flower, rendered in exquisite detail, its leafy stem topped by a many-petaled bloom. The sun sparkled off its indigo surface, each facet reflecting a tiny sliver of light.

"I don't know what to say," she breathed. "It's gorgeous."

"A lot of guys give a lady flowers," Kirk said, "but those don't last. This one you can keep for the rest of your life, and it will be just as perfect as it was the day I gave it to you."

Tears welled in her eyes, a torrent of emotions surged through her. She leaned over and kissed him on the cheek.

"I love you, too."

"Finally! It only took a fancy gift to get you to say it back to me." He winked to show he was kidding.

"Don't be like that." She took another long look at the obsidian flower. "What is it? What variety, I mean?"

"It's a dahlia."

Jean's stomach dropped. A thousand images flashed through her mind. Newspaper headlines. Haunting photographs of a beautiful young woman. An unsolved murder. "You gave me a black dahlia?"

Kirk slapped himself on the forehead. "Jeez, Jeannie, I didn't even think of that. I read that the dahlia symbolizes dignity and elegance. And when you give it to someone as a gift, it's a symbol of a commitment and bond that lasts forever." As he said the last, he reached out and brushed her cheek. She couldn't help but shiver. "If it bothers you, I'll get you something else."

"No, I was just being silly. The Black Dahlia murder has been in the news so often, that's where my mind immediately went. I'm so sorry if I made it seem like I don't love your gift. It's the most amazing thing anyone has ever given me."

On the radio, Vaughn Monroe's *Red Roses for a Blue Lady* blared from the speakers.

"I should have gone with red." Kirk let out a little laugh and then his expression grew serious. "That Black Dahlia thing is something, isn't it?"

"I guess that's one way of putting it. It's crazy that he hasn't been caught."

"He's smart. Too smart for the cops, anyway."

"I'll betcha the boys on *Dragnet* could catch him," she said, referencing the popular radio drama.

"Maybe. The real police certainly don't seem to have a clue. They haven't even put two-and-two together when it's staring them in the face."

"What do you mean? Do you know who it is?" She almost added in a joke about her glass flower, but didn't want to hurt his feelings again.

"I think he's the same guy as the Cleveland killer."

That gave her pause. "Same as the what?"

Kirk frowned, puzzled. "You haven't heard about the Cleveland Torso Murderer? The Mad Butcher of Kingsbury Run?"

Jeanie shook her head.

"He killed thirteen people. Dismembered them, cut them in half, just like the Black Dahlia killer. And he was too smart for the police, too."

"I take it they didn't catch him?"

"Eliot Ness himself tried and couldn't track him down. The murders eventually stopped on their own."

The sun had slipped below the horizon, darkness

crept up on them. Jean shivered, suddenly cold.

"So, you think he packed his things and moved to Los Angeles?" Jean knew it was idle speculation, but the thought frightened her.

Kirk nodded. "The killings were ten years ago. I think he drifted west. I'll bet there are all sorts of bodies lying between Ohio and California just waiting to be discovered."

"Are you interested in this sort of thing? Serial killers? Dead women?" she teased.

"I'm a writer, so I'm naturally curious. I just wonder why he was never caught. I don't believe a killer like him could ever stop killing." He glanced at her and his expression softened. "I'm scaring you. I didn't mean to. Sorry for the morbid turn of conversation."

"Not scared. It's just a weird thing to think about."

He slowed the Jaguar and turned onto a dirt road. Really, it was more of a faint track in the sand.

"Where are we going?"

"This is the surprise! I'm going to show you something amazing! Something no one but me knows about."

Jean lapsed into silence, watched as the moon's silvery glow replaced the sun's golden light. They rode on, the twin headlight beams illuminating the dirt, sand, and cactus.

"I don't see a road anymore," she said.

"There is no road. I found this place myself. No one can know that there's anything back here but desert."

Perhaps it was the unsettling conversation they'd just had, or maybe it was the speakers playing a Dick Haymes tune, a song about telling little white lies beneath the light of the moon, but she found herself growing anxious. She had suspected he was taking her to the Salton Sea, but she'd been wrong. What could there possibly be out here in the middle of the desert that would be worth showing her?

She was about to ask him to turn the car around when Kirk parked the car and cut the engine. "We'll walk from here. It's not far. I know a shortcut."

A wave of uncertainty rolled over her. What could Kirk possibly want to show her out here in the desert?

"I'm not dressed for hiking."

"It will be fine. I promise." Kirk came around to the passenger side. He opened her door with a flourish, and offered his hand. "I'll take care of you."

Unable to resist his charms, she allowed him to help her out of the car and escort her into the darkness. After a short walk, they came to a halt on a ledge overlooking a valley.

"There it is. Isn't she magnificent?"

Down below, sheltered by a giant sand dune, a dark shape thrust up from the sand. It was so out of place here that it took a minute for her mind to process what she was seeing.

"Is that a sailing ship?"

"Yes! Can you believe it?"

She shook her head, surprise and wonder rendering her mute.

They stood there, holding hands, as their eyes adjusted to the dim moonlight. As they gazed at it, the details of the ship became visible. It sat half in and half out of the water, its bow angled upward slightly. The sails were long gone, but bits of rigging clung to the masts.

"Oh, Kirk. This is..." She couldn't find the words.

"Come on. I'll show you inside."

"Is it safe?"

"Of course. I've been here several times. I've even brought a few friends. Not someone special, like you, though. Just friends," he hurriedly added.

Curiosity overcoming caution, she climbed out of the car, took his hand, and allowed him to lead her toward the bow.

"We'll have to crawl through this hole," he said. "Trust me. It's worth it. Ladies first?"

"You lead the way and I'll follow."

"Fair enough." Kirk dropped down on his hands

and knees and slipped through the opening. A moment later she heard a metallic click, and a flickering light danced inside the old ship. His fancy cigarette lighter, she wagered. "You coming in, doll?"

"On my way." She hitched up her skirt, crawled through, and slid down a pile of sand to the deck below. She stood and brushed the sand from her knees before allowing Kirk to help her to her feet.

"Atta girl!" He slipped his arm around her waist. "Come on. The thing I want to show you is just through this doorway.

What she saw took her breath, and not in a good way. Bodies hung suspended by chains from the walls. More accurately, the upper torsos hung there. They'd all been cut in half above the waist. Their lower halves lay in heaps in the sand that covered the deck. Her first thought was this was a slave ship, but these bodies were not hundreds of years old, mummified by the desert air. These were much more recent. Women in contemporary dresses, the corners of their mouths sliced into horrifying, clownish smiles.

"Just like the Black Dahlia," she whispered.

And then she understood.

She turned, but before she could try to escape, Kirk seized her roughly by the hair and flung her to the ground.

"It's you!"

Kirk smiled, drawing a knife from somewhere beneath his jacket. "You were right about the flower, Jeanie. I did give it to you on purpose. I had it made as soon as the newspapers coined that stupid nickname. I gave it to all of them, too." He waved the knife in the direction of the hanging bodies. "I told you the flower would keep for the rest of your life. Of course, a real dahlia would have lasted that long." He made a show of checking his watch. "I try to make it last, but most of my girls don't hang in there for very long. A shame, really."

Jean's throat seemed to clamp shut. She couldn't breathe. As she gazed up at this man whom she thought she knew, she wondered how she had never seen the madness in his eyes. Her bladder released and she didn't care.

"You…" she managed. "You said you loved me."

"Oh, I do, Jeanie. I love you more than you could ever know."

He reached for her and Jean screamed.

But she knew there was no one to hear her.

CHAPTER 1

The Tango Cat was a Hollywood dive bar that could hardly claim the address, although the adjective fit like a glove. Steven Segar chose the cleanest of the empty tables, tested the chair to make sure it would support his weight, and sat down. Album covers, scuffed and worn, adorned the walls, along with signed photos of the musicians who had paid the bar a visit. None of them had been framed.

"Can I get you anything, sir?" A young bottle blonde with a spray tan and the biggest eyelashes Steven Segar had ever seen, approached. Her name tag read KYRSTIN. Even her name was full-on Southern California.

"No, not yet. Still waiting for my friend." He stumbled over the last word.

Smiling, the girl gave a nod and then froze. Her eyes narrowed, and she pressed a red lacquered fingernail thoughtfully to her chin. "Say, haven't I seen you before?" She pursed her lips, the strain of deep thought reflected in her brown eyes.

Here we go, he thought. After three decades in the film industry, he had come to expect it. He rocked back in his chair, rested his arms on his belly, and smiled.

"Yes?" He wondered if she'd want an autograph. People seldom wanted autographs these days, just selfies.

Her eyes went wide. "I remember! You're Bekki's granddad. You sat at the bar on her first day of work and kept ordering mixed drinks that didn't exist. You were so funny!"

"No," Segar said flatly. "I am afraid I do not have grandchildren."

"Oh. Sorry. You look just like him. I think it's the…" Her voice trailed off as she cupped her hand over her belly. "The belt buckle," she said hurriedly. "He had one just like that."

"Oh, Clint Eastwood gave this to me. We did a film together a while back."

"Clint Eastwood? The guy who did the films with the orangutan? My dad loves him. Anyway, just give me a shout when your friend gets here. What does he look like? I'll keep an eye out for him."

"He's tall and skinny with long, stringy hair and overlarge teeth. He prefers military-style camouflage clothing, but he never served."

"Sounds like an interesting fellow," Kyrstin said, inching away.

"Don't forget my cowboy hat, even though I'm not cowboy." A tall, angular man stepped around the waitress and dropped his hat onto the table. "Stevie here thinks you have to hail from the Southwest in order to wear one of these." The man flashed a too-white smile. "I grew up on a dairy farm. I think that makes me a 'cow boy' but it pisses him off to no end. Icing on the cake."

He wasn't wrong. Everything about Terry Gold pissed Segar off.

"All right, then," Kyrstin said. "Can I start you guys off with some drinks?"

"I'm sure Stevie would like something pretentious," the tall man said. "Do you have anything with Tibetan gonad berries?"

"Goji berries," Segar corrected. "I'll have one of your local craft beers. Your choice. Bring me a chilled glass, but I'll pour it myself. And Terry here will have something pedestrian. Your cheapest light beer will do. You might consider saying 'dilly dilly' when you bring it out."

"Light beer on draft is great, and I'll have an order of cheese fries," the man called Terry said.

"I'm sorry, but we don't have cheese fries on the menu," Kyrstin said.

Gold smirked. "Do you have cheeseburgers and fries on the menu?"

She nodded. Her brow knotted in puzzlement.

"Then I'll take an order of fries, and throw a couple slices of cheese on them while they're still nice and hot." Terry gave her a wink. "Don't worry, sweetheart. I'm a generous tipper."

"Fries and two slices of cheese. I'll have it right out."

"That's disgusting," Segar said as the girl walked away. "You should try eating healthy. I can send you a copy of my diet regimen, not that I have any reason to wish you to live longer."

Gold laced his fingers behind his neck, rocked back in his chair, and propped his feet on the table. "Oh, Seagull, I have missed you."

Segar tried to maintain his calm exterior, but the nickname, juvenile as it was, always seemed to get a reaction out of him. He was certain it was a thinly veiled jibe at the size of his nose, though Gold denied it.

The two had hated each other for practically their entire careers. When Terry Gold had been a young, popular rocker, he'd provided the soundtrack for one of Segar's first action films. His price had been a supporting role in the film. It had been a disaster. Besides being a terrible actor, Gold had a lousy work ethic and took pleasure in needling his fellow cast members at every turn. What some actors called their "method," Gold called "pretentiousness" or worse, and had made it his mission to cut people down to size where and when he deemed it necessary. It had been a nightmare. By the end, security had to be on hand every time the two men shared a scene.

"I wish I could say the same, Nugget. I'm surprised you don't have a semi-automatic rifle slung across your back. Getting soft in your old age?"

Chuckling, Gold took his feet off the table, let his chair fall back onto all four legs, and scooted up to the table. "I'm carrying concealed," he said softly. "But you know I don't have a permit for this state, so I'll trust you not to rat me out. You're a douche, Segar, but you were never a rat."

"Never fear. Your secret is safe with me."

"I'm amazed *you* don't carry," Gold said. "Famous guy like you, people might think you've got money. You must make at least a couple of bucks off your B-movie action flicks. So what if they go direct to the WalMart clearance bin?"

"At least I'm still distributed. You're down to selling your music off your website and at county fairs. You must feel right at home performing in those rodeo arenas." Segar smiled, knowing he'd scored a point. "Besides, I don't need a weapon, as you very well know."

Gold took a toothpick, thick with lint, out of his breast pocket and stuck it in the corner of his mouth.

"Hey, I charted on iTunes, bitch. Amazon, too!" He waggled his eyebrows. "But how about we discuss your famous martial arts career? Ray Rogain sent me an interesting video. Want to see it?"

Segar tensed, felt his cheeks burning. Rogain was part of the new generation of what Segar termed "hybrid celebrities." Moderately famous in several disparate corners of the entertainment world, the cumulative effect making them a major player. In his role as a commentator, Rogain was well-connected in the martial arts community, and very well might have gotten a copy of the video in question.

"Not really." He tried to keep his tone casual, but already, cracks were forming in the bubble of serenity with which he'd surrounded himself upon entering.

Gold laughed. "Relax, Seagull. I'm not going to show anyone. The last thing anyone wants to see is their favorite action hero getting choked out by a seventy-year-old judo instructor."

"Sixty," Segar corrected.

"Did you ever manage to get that yellow stain out of your gi?" Gold threw back his head and cackled. "I guess that foolproof escape you always bragged about wasn't so foolproof after all."

"The guy had been treated for testicular cancer." Segar swallowed the bile rising in his throat. "He had them removed, so…"

Gold was racked with an onset of silent laughter. His shoulder heaved and he struggled to catch his breath. "You mean," he huffed, hand pressed to his chest, "that all this time," another gulp of air, "it was just grabbing them by the…"

"By the *nuggets*," Segar finished. That cut down on the laughter a little bit. Gold hated the nickname Nugget. Segar found that odd. The man had named his son Platinum Record. What was so bad about Terry Nugget when you had a Platinum R. Gold in the family? "I had some other options for escape," he explained, "but I didn't want to hurt the old man."

Kyrstin returned with their drinks. Gold caught his breath, wiped the corners of his eyes with his napkins.

"Your fries will be out in a minute," Kyrstin said.

"Cheese fries," Gold corrected.

She rolled her eyes, let out an impatient sigh, and hurried away.

"You know she's going to spit in your food, don't you?"

Gold shrugged. "She probably just got into some bad avocados."

Segar laughed and hated himself for it.

Gold took two large gulps, let out a wet belch, and patted himself on the chest. "That hits the spot."

Segar sipped his beer, savored the taste. It was bitter with just the right hint of citrus. He held it in his mouth for a few seconds, swallowed, and took another drink.

Their opening salvos exhausted, the men sat there drinking in silence until Kyrstin returned with Gold's version of cheese fries. He offered one to Segar, a wicked sparkle in his eye.

"I'm not hungry," Segar said, "especially not for that. Now, why did you insist on meeting with me?"

"I'm dipping my toe into television. Reality television to be precise. And I want you to partner with me."

Segar's lips moved but surprise rendered him mute. How could the man even think they could work together?

Gold mistook his silence for interest and kept talking. "I was thinking back on our... rivalry, and I came up with the idea for a show that will put our shared interests and best attributes on display. It'll be a contest. Not that gladiator crap and Spartan crap."

"I hate that stuff," Segar said. "Those things are for gymnasts and gym rats. There's no real-world application. If a bad hombre accosts you in a dark alley, you won't be making your escape Tarzan-style over a swimming pool and onto a spinning platform."

"Why are you always going up dark alleys, Segar? What is that about?" Gold chuckled, took another drink. "But seriously, I agree with you. If you're out in the wilderness and a bear attacks." He spread his hands as if the rest were obvious.

Segar found himself intrigued. The chance to best Terry Gold was hard to pass up. "What is the contest? And there better not be a companion soundtrack."

"No, nothing like that." Gold waved a fry at him. "I want to make it something where neither of us has much advantage. I mean, I'll always be a notch above you thanks to good genes, but there's nothing we can do about that."

Segar folded his arms and waited, his drink forgotten. He didn't want to seem too interested.

"A couple of interests you and I share," Gold went on, "are the outdoors, and unsolved mysteries. I know this dude, total bookworm, message board trawler, deep dive into newspaper archives kind of guy. Finds all sorts of bits and pieces that never made it onto the web in any form. He has uncovered a mystery that he believes can be solved. He's collected enough clues to point us in the right direction. We each take a small team and a camera guy and head off in the wilderness. We keep it super simple to hold costs down."

"So, this is 'searching for lost treasure' series? Along the way we talk about the mystery, throw in local color, that sort of thing?"

"It's that with added layers. You and I are outdoorsmen. We'll talk about survival skills, about ecology, respect for nature. So many audiences we can target."

"I'm more than an outdoorsman. I'm a warrior and a poet. I'm spirit brother to the wolf and…"

"Come on, Segar, are you interested or not?"

Segar nodded. He doubted they'd actually find any lost treasure, but the idea was solid, even if it was hatched from the addled mind of Terry Gold. "What does the winner get?"

"Bragging rights and a donation in his name to the charity of his choice. Makes us look better that way." Gold had finished off the cheese and now drowned his remaining fries in ketchup. "The rest of the proceeds we split right down the middle. I've already started pitching it." He removed a folded sheet of paper from his pocket and slid it across the table. "That's the first official offer, but we've got strong interest from at least three other parties."

Segar unfolded the paper and his eyebrows shot up. It wasn't box office hit money, but for this sort of program it was a solid offer. And he liked the concept. It wasn't something demeaning, like living in a shared house, or taking a road trip together. This was a challenge. A contest of skills and intelligence. He'd like to see one of these YouTube celebrities or hipsters with man buns take on a challenge like this.

"I hate to admit this," Gold went on, "but I literally can't do this without you. If it's not a contest between the two of us, nobody's interested."

He had pressed the right button. Segar drained his beer in three gulps, folded the paper and tucked it into his pocket.

"All right, Gold. I will resurrect your dead career. You'll be my Lazarus."

They shook hands. Gold leaned in so close Segar could smell the cheap beer on his breath.

"I gotta tell you, Seagull. After all these years, I

cannot wait to kick your ass on a streaming network."

CHAPTER 2

The sun baked the parched canyon and scorched the back of Dane Maddock's neck. As someone who lived in southern Florida, he was well-accustomed to the heat, and although the lack of humidity was a plus, he missed the breeze that would be blowing in off the Gulf of Mexico right about now. Boxed in by parched hills, the canyon that was home to Grizzly Grant's "UFO Ranch" was an oven. It baked the group of forty or so who stood waiting for instructions.

"I still can't believe I let you talk me into this," Maddock said to the tall, broad-shouldered Cherokee standing beside him.

"Quit your bitching, Maddock. You've been an emo kid ever since we got back from Africa. I'm sick of it."

Bones Bonebrake had been his best friend since their early days in the Navy SEALs and he seldom pulled punches, literally or figuratively.

"True," Maddock admitted. His ears burned, and not from the sun. He'd been betrayed by someone close to him. Even now it hurt and angered him in equal measure. "I do need a break, but did it have to be this?" His sweeping gesture took in their surroundings. Parched earth, stunted palms, yucca growing stubbornly around red rocks worn smooth by wind. "Couldn't you have taken me to, I don't know, Vegas?"

Bones turned angry eyes on Maddock, folded his powerful arms, and stared down at him in disapproval.

"Are you freaking kidding me? How many times have Matt and Willis and I asked you to go to Vegas with us? And you always make the same excuse."

"I know. I'm not a Vegas kind of guy. Well, right now I'm willing to give it a try. Air-conditioned casino, cold drinks..."

"Hot chicks..." For a moment, a faraway gaze clouded Bones' dark eyes. Then he gave his head a quick shake. "Jeez, Maddock. Here I am having a good time and you go and put the Mandalay Bay swimming pool in my head. Thanks for that."

Maddock chuckled. He knew that, as much as Bones loved Las Vegas, he lived for the out-of-doors, and was perfectly content right here. The fact that there were more than a few fit, athletic-looking women in the group didn't hurt.

"This is an awesome vacation. We get to hang out at Grizzly's Hollywood movie ranch for as long as we like, for free. Might even meet some actresses."

"We're a few hours from Hollywood, Bones. I don't think we'll be meeting many celebrities out here."

Bones shook his head. "Always the killjoy."

"Bones! Maddock! So glad you guys could make it!" A handsome man with wavy brown hair and intense, dark eyes approached. He was clad in a short-sleeved khaki shirt, olive shorts, and hiking boots. A machete hung from a sheath on his belt, although they weren't exactly surrounded by jungle. The man hurried over and shook their hands.

"Grizzly," Bones greeted. "Good to see you, bro."

Don "Grizzly" Grant was a cryptozoologist and former television host. He'd recently joined Maddock and Bones on an adventure in Scotland, and their discoveries had led to a modest rebound in his career. He was back on television, albeit in the form of a short-run series on a subscription-based network.

"Good to see you guys, as well. What have you been up to? Capture Bigfoot yet?"

"No, but we found King Solomon's Mines," Bones said.

Maddock flashed him a warning glance. That particular bit of information had been passed on to government agencies through their friend Tam Broderick. It was supposed to be kept on the down-low.

"The hell you did," Grizzly said.

Bones faked a smile. "Yeah, just kidding. We've been keeping busy, though."

"Grizzly, this is quite a production you've got going on here," Maddock said, changing the subject. "I'm impressed." Flattery always worked on Grizzly.

"Thanks. I wanted Jo Slater to co-host it with me, but she's apparently too busy getting her own show back up and running."

Like Grizzly, Slater was a television host whose subject matter covered the unexplained. Maddock didn't know her personally, but she and Bones had once gone off together on a search for the Skunk Ape.

"Have you talked to her?" Bones asked, a note of hopefulness in his voice. Slater also happened to be intelligent, confident, and attractive.

Grizzly shook his head. "Word is, she's down in the Antarctic on some top-secret project."

"I'll take the heat here over the Antarctic cold any day," Maddock said, shivering involuntarily. He and Bones had been to the Antarctic and he didn't miss it one bit. He looked around at the parched, brown hills, speckled with low growing clumps of green. Various obstacles had been constructed around the property. He saw cargo nets, climbing ropes, even a mock-up of an old west town. Doubtless, the surrounding hills hid many more. "Branching out from cryptid hunting, I take it?"

Grizzly nodded. "There's a lot of competition in my niche and programming is becoming diluted. New programs like mine aren't getting much traction. Everyone's busy binge-watching Ancient Aliens and watching those guys on Oak Island trapped in a perpetual cycle of fail."

Bones cleared his throat at the mention of the home of the legendary treasure pit. Little did the hosts of that show know, but the treasure of Oak Island had been discovered a few years earlier.

Grizzly went on. "There are so many channels, streaming networks, any assclown can host a legends and conspiracies show."

"That is so true," Bones said.

Maddock didn't laugh, but neither did he manage to fully suppress a grin. Grizzly took no notice.

"I need to start developing the Grizzly Grant brand. And what do people think of when they hear the name Grizzly?"

"Bear attacks," Bones said.

"Far-fetched theories that lack evidentiary support?" Maddock offered.

As usual, their quips bounced right off of him.

"That's right! Adventure! So, I've started the Grizzly Grant Celebrity Adventure Challenge! Teams of celebrities compete in adventure races. Different celebs every week."

Bones elbowed Maddock at the mention of celebrities.

"I'll host it, of course. It'll be a Battle of the Network Stars for the modern day." Grizzly paused, gazed out at the horizon. "We could turn Salton into another Palm Springs."

"There he goes again." A woman clad in shorts, hiking boots, and a Grant Productions t-shirt stepped up alongside Grizzly. "The short story, which you'll never get from this guy, is this. We start with the television show, which will serve as a marketing tool for the competitive races we'll sponsor all around the country and hopefully the world. We're also laying the groundwork for UFO Ranch to serve as a filming site for Hollywood productions."

"How do you do that?" Grizzly asked. "You're like a human Cliff's Notes."

"It's called brevity."

Grizzly shook his head, then introduced the woman as Rosie Rivera, his second in-command. She was an attractive woman, athletic, short black hair and brown eyes that were just a bit too large for her face. She shook hands with each of them in turn. Her grip was strong, unsurprising since she had the build of a fitness buff.

"Good to meet you. Call me Riv."

"Riv is short for Rivera?" Bones asked.

"Good guess, but wrong." Riv pulled up the sleeve of her t-shirt to reveal a tattoo of Rosie the Riveter, the iconic symbol of women who worked in the manufacturing industry during World War II.

"Badass!" Bones said.

"Thanks. Always loved Rosie. I never was a girly-girl, you know?" She glanced at Grizzly for a split-second, but Maddock saw the ghost of a grin flicker at the corners of her mouth, then disappear just as quickly. Perhaps the two were more than just coworkers. "Thank you for coming, by the way," Riv said. "We needed at least a few highly capable people for our test run, and Grizzly said there were none better than you two. He numbers you guys among his best friends."

Maddock was a little surprised at that but pleased. Despite his rough edges Grizzly was a good guy with a thirst for adventure. He and Bones assured Riv that they were delighted to take part.

"I have to ask," Maddock said, "what, exactly, is a UFO ranch?"

Grizzly laughed. "That's a very long story."

"No, it isn't," Riv said. "The original owner of the land sighted UFOs on the property."

"That is not the whole story," Grizzly protested.

"Exactly. It's the important part."

"You'd better keep her around," Maddock said to Grizzly. "You two seem to balance each other out pretty well."

Just then, a tall man of middle years nudged past Maddock. He wore khakis, starched and pressed, and hiking boots.

"Mister Grant. There you are," he said.

"What can I do for you, Shipman? And I've told you before, you can call me Grizzly."

Deep lines formed in Shipman's brow. Evidently, he didn't care for the nickname. "I spotted a rattler sunning herself beside the path that leads to your," he paused, cleared his throat, "your eating challenge." He grimaced.

"I tried to gently shoo it away, but it was not in the mood to be trifled with."

"Thank you," Grizzly said. "We'll make sure the contestants don't disturb it."

Shipman gave a curt nod, then turned and stalked away.

"Who the hell was that?" Bones asked.

"That's Bryce Shipman. He used to own this place and is having a hard time letting go."

"What's his deal?" Bones said. "Why is he still hanging around if you own the place?"

"We only purchased a portion of his property. He's still our neighbor. As far as why he's hanging around?" Riv shrugged. "It's a television show and Grizzly is a celebrity." Maddock could hear the air quotes in her voice. "Some people are fascinated by the entertainment industry."

"Hoping to be discovered?" Bones joked.

"He's an author. Probably thinks he'll get the chance to pitch to a producer." Riv checked her watch. "Three minutes to welcome, Grizz."

"Great! You guys follow me."

A small crowd had gathered in front a small stage. Behind it, a banner read WELCOME TO THE GRIZZLY GRANT CELEBRITY ADVENTURE CHALLENGE. Corporate logos, sponsors of the race, ran along the top and bottom.

Maddock scanned the assemblage. It was an interesting mix. Bones had been right. The racers included a couple of minor celebrities whom Maddock recognized from movies, and a few more beautiful people who might also work in entertainment. Others wore t-shirts that marked them as connected to various event sponsors, mostly nutritional supplement manufacturers and fitness centers.

Grizzly clipped on a wireless microphone and mounted the stage.

"Welcome to the Grizzly Grant Survival Challenge!" He paused for the obligatory polite round of applause. "Today you will be put to the ultimate test of endurance competition."

"If he means enduring an endless stream of hyperbole, he's right," mumbled the young woman to Maddock's right. She was pale, with short, inky black hair. She wore a pair of bright red, oversized secretary-style glasses, cargo shorts, and a t-shirt that read *Keep Earth Clean. It isn't Uranus.* She didn't look like an adventure racer, but Maddock knew appearances could deceive. In any case, she seemed to have Grizzly's measure.

"You will face a series of obstacles and challenges that will test your strength, speed, endurance, and mental dexterity," Grizzly went on.

"You're in trouble, Bones," Maddock said.

"Screw you, Maddock."

"Our objective today is to test the course," Grizzly said. "I have, of course, completed it myself. It was easy for me, but we need to find out how ordinary people will respond to the challenge. That's where all of you come in."

Ragged laughter didn't quite mask the obscenity uttered by the woman in the red glasses.

"Sounds simple enough," Bones said. "Can't be worse than Hell Week."

"What is Hell Week?" the woman next to him asked. "I'm Lilith, by the way."

"I'm Maddock, this is Bones. Hell Week is the most grueling segment of Navy SEAL training. We're veterans."

Lilith rolled her eyes. "Just what the world needs. More toxic masculinity. Just tell me you didn't bring guns."

"I've got a gun with me," Bones began, "but not the kind you..."

"Just don't, Bones," Maddock said.

Grizzly now invited a local businessman named Orry Rockwell to join him on stage. From the quiet murmurs all around, Maddock assumed the man was a big deal.

Orry Rockwell was a fit-looking man in his late thirties, and he was dressed to race. He brushed back his dirty blond hair and made an embarrassed wave to the crowd as the applause died down.

"Thanks for that, but you might want to take back your applause once I lay my guilt trip on you." He winked as the crowd laughed. "If you've spent much time in this area you know that, on a windy day, you don't need a map to find the Salton Sea. Only your nose." More laughter. "And that's why I'm here today. For decades the Salton Sea was a thriving town and a popular tourist destination. It's also the only remaining wetland in southern California. And it's nearly dead."

Maddock knew the story. Created by accident in 1905 when the Colorado River overwhelmed a series of gates and dikes designed to contain it and poured into the Salton Sink area. Engineers at the time lacked the technology to quickly address the problem, so the flooding continued for two years. It formed a pair of new rivers, submerged Native American lands, a railroad siding, and the town of Salton as it formed what is now known as the Salton Sea.

"You're all familiar with the story. Due to its location, its lack of fresh inflow, and lack of drainage, the sea has essentially become a septic tank for agricultural runoff. The tilapia sportsmen once caught by the dozen now die off in massive numbers. Their carcasses rot on the shores in such great quantities that they foul the air all around the sea, but their numbers are so abundant that they keep reproducing, only to die in the polluted sea. Birds come here for desperately needed water, but they, too, keep dying."

Lilith hissed a stream of curses under her breath. Maddock made out a few choice words, but most were incoherent. He agreed with the sentiment. He loved the sea and the creatures that made their home in it.

"Sonny Bono worked hard to bring the Salton Sea crisis into the public eye and to put pressure on the government to make changes, but his efforts died with him. Now it's up to us." Rockwell glanced down, a pained expression passing over his face. "There are a lot of people out there who think the sea should be drained and forgotten about. They say it was created by accident, that it was never meant to exist."

"Palm Springs." Lilith uttered the name like a curse.

"I say it doesn't matter how it was created. It's here. Cleaning up the Salton Sea is the right thing to do. My people are working very hard to bring attention and resources to bear on this crisis, but I need your help. I implore you to use your platforms and your connections to bring attention to our cause. And we wouldn't say no to a donation, either." He grinned and winked. "Thank you and enjoy the race."

"At least he kept it short," Bones said.

"He happens to be a brilliant man," Lilith said.

"Smart enough not to bore us to death."

Grizzly reminded everyone to keep themselves hydrated and assured them that staff members would be posted along the course in case participants ran into trouble. Next, he thanked his sponsors, all of whom had at least one representative taking part in the event. Next, he divided them into teams of six.

The composition of Maddock and Bones' team was a bit uneven. Jashawn Powell was a former college football player who now worked as a representative for a nutritional supplement company. Dakota and Spenser Saroyan were a brother-sister team, mid to late twenties, both blue eyed blondes. Dakota, the brother, was tall and slim, his sister, Spenser compact and curvy. They were clad in crisp athletic wear and expensive looking shoes, and wore top of the line GoPro cameras strapped to their heads. Everything in their wardrobes had a logo prominently displayed.

Jashawn explained that the two were influencers who, in his words, "got free stuff by threatening to trash businesses online." He went on to say that there were plenty of legitimate influencers out there, but Dakota and Spenser were the spoiled offspring of a Hollywood power broker and one of his mistresses. For them, influencing was just a way to avoid getting real jobs. The final member of their team was Lilith, who seemed no happier about the arrangement than Bones.

"What's up, squad?" Dakota wore a golden retriever smile as he shook hands with his new teammates. When he reached Bones, he pressed his palms together and made a slight bow. "Namaste, my brother. I'm sorry for what we did to your land."

Bones made several attempts to reply but couldn't seem to find the words. Maddock and Jashawn trembled with suppressed mirth.

"You are a very large man," Spenser said, eying Bones as if he were a freak show exhibit.

"You have no idea," Bones said with a wink.

"Would anybody like some raw water before we start?" Dakota asked, holding up a bottle of ever so slightly green-tinted liquid.

"What the hell is that?" Bones asked.

"It's water free of all the unnecessary crap the government does to it."

"You mean like cleaning it and adding fluoride," Jashawn said.

Dakota's smile somehow grew wider. "See? He knows what I'm talking about!"

His sister let out a tired groan. "Dakota, you did just listen to the talk about the Salton Sea?"

"Yeah, but that's not where I got this water."

"Where *did* you get that?" Maddock asked.

"It's my own label. I mean, I'm not like, officially in production yet, but I've got my own label." He tapped the sticker on the bottle. The label, obviously made on an ink jet printer, read *Dakota Springs*. "I just scoop it out of a little stream that runs behind my house. Unadulterated, just like nature intended."

Bones raised a finger. "Have you ever heard of a guy named Inigo Montoya?"

"I think you mean Vizzini," Lilith corrected. "He

was the one who didn't know what the word meant."

To Maddock's relief, rather than bicker with the woman, Bones thought for a moment, then nodded. "Good call."

Dakota frowned, then his eyes lit up. "*The Princess Bride!* I loved that movie!" He held his bottle aloft. "Last chance. Anybody for a drink?" When no one replied, he shrugged. "Time to chug. Your loss, amigos."

As the young man gulped the polluted water, Maddock turned to Bones.

"The over/under on time to hurl is nineteen minutes."

Bones chuckled. "That kid? I'll bet he doesn't last ten."

CHAPTER 3

Bones was wrong. Dakota lasted twenty-two minutes before losing his raw water, along with the remnants of a breakfast burrito, just outside the entrance to the cave complex. This unexpected obstacle was not popular with the other race participants, who ignored his assurances that his body was merely cleansing itself. When his body decided to start cleansing itself from the other end, he decided he'd had enough. A staff member drove him back to the ranch house.

"He didn't quite make it down the post-apocalyptic highway," Bones said to Maddock as they clambered across a pile of car tires. "Too bad. He'd have made a good warlord's jester in the world to come."

"Come on. That's my brother you're talking about," Spenser huffed. The young woman had kept pace with them through the obstacles so far without a word of complaint, although she did have the annoying habit of occasionally talking to her "subscribers" via the GoPro. "He's a dummy, but he's my dummy."

"I'd trade him in for something you can take off-road. He's not on your level." Bones offered the girl a hand as she clambered down a pile of old tires. She declined.

"I'm okay," she said. "I appreciate it, but I want to see how far I can make it on my own."

"Respect," Bones said. He eyed the girl anew. Behind the stereotypical Southern California looks lurked a resilience he hadn't expected from the young woman.

"She's not your type," Maddock said as they watched Spenser vanish in a cloud of smoke that poured from a burning truck.

"What makes you think I'd be into her?"

"Fair point. She's female and has a pulse."

Bones frowned. "That's not fair. I also require that a woman have an even number of legs. But she's cool, though. Better than her brother. I think there's some raw material there to work with."

"Better raw material than raw water."

Bones quirked an eyebrow. "That almost made me grin. But you keep trying. You'll make a funny joke someday." He gave his friend a condescending pat on the shoulder and Maddock shoved him away.

"Let's get moving," Maddock said. "Lilith's not going to make it over that wall on her own."

"Like she'd really accept the help."

True to form, Lilith refused assistance despite being physically unable to scale the wall in front of them.

"I'll get it," she said after making it two thirds of the way to the top before sliding back down the rope.

"Maybe if she had some raw water," Jashawn mumbled.

Spenser flashed him an affronted look, then turned to Bones. "I think you should do something."

Bones cocked his head to the side. "Why me? I'm probably the last person in this group she'd accept help from." Lilith was prickly around everyone, but him more so than the others.

"Exactly," Spenser said. "Sucks for you, funny for the rest of us."

"Put it to a vote," Jashawn said. He quickly raised his hand, followed immediately by Maddock and Spenser. "You're it, Bones."

"I vote no," Bones said.

"That makes it unanimous." Maddock smiled and inclined his head in the direction of Lilith, who was sizing up the wall for another go.

"You guys suck."

Bones took a moment to steel himself, then sidled up to Lilith. He stood, head high, arms folded, gazing ahead, eyes slightly unfocused. Mimicking the wise Indian from a western flick was one of two ways a Native American was guaranteed to get a white person's full attention. Sleeping with a white man's wife was the other way, but that wasn't an option here.

Lilith was staring at the wall with the air of a fighter who knows she's beaten but can't find it in herself to admit defeat.

"Here's the deal," he said quietly, not meeting her eye. "There's a lot of things I know nothing about. Something I do know, from professional experience, is that obstacle courses sometimes require teamwork, and there's nothing wrong with it."

"I want to do it myself."

"Look, I could make a speech but that's not my style. All the determination in the world won't give you the upper body strength to climb over that wall. That's reality. You signed up for a team event, and your selfishness is holding everyone else back. So, either you let us help you or I pick your ass up and throw you over."

Lilith rounded on him, fists clenched. Hot anger flashed in her eyes. "Selfishness?"

"And stubbornness."

She stood like a statue for five shocked seconds, then all the tension fled from her and she let out a laugh.

"Okay, I get it. I need to be a good teammate. But for the record, if you ever pick me up without my consent, I'll murder you in your sleep."

Bones nodded in approval. "I'm liking you better every minute."

The wall traversed, they next climbed a steep hill. Their feet ground the dry earth into fine powder, their footsteps stirred it up into a cloud of dust that coated their tongues and filled their nostrils. The hill was followed by another and then another. By the time they reached the next obstacle, crossing a makeshift pond on a big, rolling log, he was ready to tank the challenged just to get a dip in the water.

Fortunately, the staff had coolers on hand. The tepid water was like the nectar of the gods. Between the strenuous activity and the desert climate, it seemed impossible to keep hydrated.

Bones barely made it across the log without falling in. It was a bittersweet victory. No one else on his team managed the feat. Spenser made it almost all the way across before falling on top of Maddock, who was taking his time wading out of the pool. She managed to talk him into giving her a piggyback ride, and Bones was happy to see a genuine smile on his friend's face. The dude had been a complete sad sack of late.

Next up was the camouflage challenge, in which contestants coated every inch of their exposed flesh in mud, which nearly proved to be Spenser's undoing. She had put a lot of work into her look and didn't want it ruined when they were only partway through the course.

"It's not that I mind getting dirty, but I accepted sponsorship money from cosmetics companies and I'm not sure it's ethical to cover it up."

"It's the rules," Lilith said. "While you're coating yourself in mud, be sure to mention that your sponsors also sell mud masks."

Spenser apparently knew good advice when she heard it, because she dived right in, both into the mud and her narrative. As she covered her arms, legs, and face in the brown goo, she described the benefits of mud for the skin, and plugged a few of her sponsors' products by name.

"I can't decide if this is hot or not," Jashawn said to Maddock and Bones.

"The mud doesn't do it for me," Maddock said, "but I like a girl who can think on her feet."

"This is turning out to be the weirdest obstacle course I've ever run," Bones said.

"I don't think it's the course," Maddock said as they trotted toward the next challenge.

"No, what is it then?"

"Have you ever run a course with civilians in tow?" Maddock asked.

"Fair point," Bones conceded. "At least we've got Jashawn. He seems to be a cut above."

"You know, I thought so, too." Maddock slowed to a walk.

"Did something change your mind?" Bones asked.

"Look at that." Maddock pointed to the next obstacle, a cargo net. The young man had gotten tangled in the net and now hung upside down. Spenser and Lilith were trying to help but seemed to instead be interfering with his efforts to right himself.

"I guess we should help him out," Maddock said.

Bones closed his eyes and let out a groan. "Civilians."

CHAPTER 4

Three quarters of the way through the race, Bones had had his fill of hills. They'd crawled through dark caverns, then climbed a hill, navigated the post-apocalyptic street, then climbed some hills, crawled through mud, and climbed some more hills, ran through a series of obstacles carrying a condom filled with water, and climbed some more hills. Theirs was the third team off the starting line that day, so the path was well worn. The soft earth crumbled and gave way with every step they took.

"It's like running on the beach, vertically," Spenser said.

"I know what my feedback is going to be," Bones grumbled as they topped a rise and saw another path winding away into the parched hills. "Rename it the Grizzly Grant Hill Climbing and Oh Yeah a Couple of Obstacles Challenge."

He found a kindred spirit in Lilith, who turned their ascent and descent of the next hill into her own personal Festivus, airing a long list of grievances against their host.

"He's a clueless windbag. Riv is the brains of the outfit. Don Grant is nothing but a pretty face."

Bones had to remind himself that Grizzly's given name was Don, not Donald, for reasons likely known only to his parents.

"He is kind of cute," Spenser said. "Although I prefer blonds." She winked at Maddock, who pretended not to notice, but Bones could see his friend's ears go red with embarrassment.

"I'm just glad he's getting away from the pseudo-science crap," Lilith continued. "Did you know that jackass claims to have found the Loch Ness monster?"

Bones coughed and hastily changed the subject.

"What do you think is around that rise?" he asked, pointing up ahead.

"Probably another hill," Jashawn said.

"I don't know what you all are complaining about," Maddock said. "It's a beautiful day, and I promise you this course could be much worse."

"Yeah," Bones said. "At least nobody's shooting at us."

They rounded a turn to find themselves in the middle of a film set—the old west town they'd seen before. Shots rang out and Jashawn hit the dirt with a shout of surprise.

"They're just blanks," Bones said. "What's up with the village? We just run through?"

"Without getting shot." Spenser pointed at the sensor strapped around her ankle. Each participant had been issued one as a means of timing them through obstacles and tracking their location should they become lost.

"Bonus points if we find the treasure room," Lilith added.

"I don't know, Maddock," Bones said with exaggerated uncertainty. "This is unlike anything we've ever done before."

"The voices you're hearing in the background," Spenser said loudly to her GoPro, "are a couple of old Army dudes who never miss a chance to remind us all that they've done obstacle courses before."

"Navy," Bones said. "Anyway, I'm just saying we should all follow Maddock's lead."

"That," Spenser said, "is the smartest thing you've said all day."

Maddock took the point and Bones brought up the rear. He admired the way Maddock instinctively flowed into a command mindset. It came instinctively, effortlessly. Leadership was in the man's DNA. He kept them all alive through the village, keeping them behind cover as they moved off the main road and into a bombed-out church.

"We're getting farther from the way out," Jashawn said.

"Treasure always comes at a price," Maddock said. It was a quote from his father, who had been a treasure buff in his day. Pirate treasure, to be specific. "They'll want to put it somewhere we'll have to expose ourselves to fire in order to get it. My money is on the altar. Or what's left of it." He pointed to a pile of broken marble slabs. "Under there."

"On it." Jashawn took off at a dead sprint. Gunshots rang out from an invisible sniper somewhere nearby, but he was too fast. He dove behind the pile of rubble and began moving chunks aside.

"No!" Maddock shouted. "That's not what I mean."

"Found it! It's a..." A loud boom drowned out his words. Red lights flashed and a cloud of vapor poured out of the box Jashawn held.

"It's a booby trap," Maddock said. "I was talking about the trapdoor set in the step right below the altar. See the handle?"

"How did we miss that?" Lilith asked. "It's so obvious once you pointed it out."

"I don't know," Maddock said. "It's almost as if I'd done it before."

I think that's the way to the next obstacle." Spenser pointed along a narrow path that ran off to their left.

"There's definitely a path there," Maddock said, "but it's not well worn. I doubt that's the way the other teams went."

"Fresh footprints," Bones said. "Just one man, though. Not a whole group."

"How do you know it's a man?" Lilith chided.

Bones sighed. She wasn't wrong, but why did she have to needle him about every little thing? "Sorry, a man, or a chick in size elevens. That better?"

Before Lilith could reply, a voice called out to them. "I beg your pardon. This is private property!" A figure appeared down the narrow trail, stalking toward them.

Lilith cursed. "It's Shipman. What is he doing up here?"

"Just stay on the trail," Shipman called.

"We were just leaving," Maddock called back. "Let's get out of here," he said to the others.

"Want me to scare him, just for fun?" Bones offered.

"No. He's a jerk, but if he wants to be that protective of his land, it's no sweat off our backs."

"Like anybody could sweat in this desert air," Bones complained as they jogged off.

The remainder of the race went off with few hitches. Lilith demanded to know if the crickets they were expected to eat had been killed humanely and if they were gluten-free. Those bumps aside, the challenges proved to be fun. There was a shooting contest, in which both Bones and Maddock both claimed victory, and a spear-throwing contest in which Spenser came out on top. Bones was still working that one out. The final descent was down a water slide and into a frigid pool. They emerged, shivering, to a round of applause from staff members and from the racers who had already completed the course. A single camera crew ducked in and out of the crowd, chatting with participants.

"Well? What did you think?" Grizzly asked. He had taken up a spot just inside the beer garden gate, knowing everyone would have to pass directly by him if they wanted to get to the good stuff.

"It was actually pretty cool," Bones said, truthfully. He decided to omit the feedback about the many, many hills.

Grizzly blinked, then looked at Maddock. "Really?"

"It was great," Maddock said. "Maybe a bit too many hills for your average celebrity."

"Oh, the hills won't be part of the show. That'll be for the competitive, iron man type races. Which is why I needed you guys."

Bones nodded, forced a smile, and tried to ignore his screaming hamstrings. "That's just… really great."

A couple of beers improved everyone's mood. Even Lilith chilled out and joined in the good-natured ribbing of Dakota, who had rejoined them. The young man was interested in hearing about everything he had missed. When they got to their encounter with Shipman, Grizzly interrupted them.

"Wait a minute. Where did this happen?"

"The ridge before Everest," Lilith said.

"Yeah, Everest. The gigantic sandhill we climbed for no particular reason," Bones said to the ceiling.

"That's nowhere near the property line," Grizzly said. "He didn't have any business up here."

"And he's a creep," Lilith added. "Riv says he's always checking her out."

"Really?" Grizzly sat up straight. "She didn't say anything about that to me."

Lilith's face went scarlet. "Well, I don't know if she said 'always,' but…" The remainder of her sentence died a swift death in a swig of beer.

Grizzly was not placated. He turned and glared in what Bones presumed was the direction of Shipman's property. "This place," he mumbled. "It's just so weird."

"What do you mean?" Maddock asked.

Grizzly sighed. "That's a long story." Before he could tell it, Orry Rockwell arrived at the beer garden. He was soaking wet from his slide into the pool, and bits of mud clung to his hair, but he was all smiles.

"Grizzly," Rockwell said, offering his hand to shake. "Fantastic race. Very well done." Without being asked, Lilith went to fetch him a beer while he sank into the chair she had vacated. "I like what you've got going here. Just difficult enough to make it a challenge, but not so difficult as to put the casual racers off."

"Thanks," Grizzly said. He picked up his tablet, which was lying on the table, opened an app, and began to scroll. "You've got some nice scores here, Rockwell.

Especially that shooting score. You're third out of the entire field so far."

"Better to be lucky than good," Rockwell said.

"I'd say it's more than luck when the only people who topped you are a couple of Navy SEALs." His eyes flitted to Maddock and Bones.

"But who came in first?" Bones said.

Grizzly looked down at his tablet again and grinned. "Oh, my!" he said in a fair imitation of George Takei. "This is going to cause quite the scandal when the scores appear on the website tomorrow." He closed the tablet.

"You're really not going to tell us?" Bones asked. "Screw you, Grizzly."

"Is that any way to talk to the man who's providing free beer?" Lilith sat a beer on the table in front of Rockwell, then pulled up a chair next to him. Maddock scooted over to make room, which put him elbow-to-elbow with Spenser. The young woman didn't appear to mind.

"Where did you learn to shoot?" Grizzly asked.

"Utah." While Rockwell took a gulp of beer, the others waited for him to elaborate, but no more details were forthcoming.

"Cool story, bro," Bones said. Even Rockwell laughed.

"He doesn't like to talk about it," Lilith said, "because a lot of the same people who support our environmental initiatives are extremely anti-gun. It's best to keep his wild west upbringing on the down low."

"Makes sense," Maddock said. "How are things going with the cleanup efforts?"

"We've had some setbacks. Environmental issues are always a difficult sell, but Salton comes with its own particular set of challenges."

"Such as?" Bones asked.

"As the sea grew more polluted and the fish kills grew larger, tourism dried up, and the real estate market collapsed. The people who live here now tend to be lower income. There's a lot of property crime—larceny, smash and grab robberies, minor drug possession. Nothing terrible, but the numbers look big in print. People in Palm Springs and some of the other wealthy communities nearby would prefer it if the Salton Sea simply dried up and blew away."

"But that's exactly what would happen," Maddock said, a knowing look on his face. "I'm sure Coachella would love to be covered in the occasional alkaline cloud."

Rockwell nodded. "We already have problems with the air quality here. Dust particles from the desert, pesticide mist, smoke from crop burns, pollution from Mexican maquiladoras. The rates of respiratory issues are extremely high in this area."

"Good thing you chose this place to hold a race," Jashawn mumbled.

"But the desert winds whipping across a dried-up Salton Sea for decades to come or even longer?" Rockwell chuckled, sipped his beer. "You've hit it on the head, Maddock. It always comes down to money, and we have to make people see that the Salton Sea alive is worth more than she is dead."

Bones leaned over and whispered to Spenser. "You wouldn't know it from looking at him, but Maddock is actually really smart."

"What's his story, anyway? How is he still single?" she asked.

"He just got dumped. By a dude."

Spenser rolled her eyes. "Try again."

Bones suppressed a grin. He had the feeling this girl loved a tale filled with drama and heartbreak. "He has the worst luck with women of any guy I know."

"What do you mean?" Spenser whispered; any interest in the Salton Sea conversation had evaporated.

"Well, he was married, but she died several years back."

"Oh." Spenser's expression turned to an odd mix of sadness and curiosity. "Any kids?"

Bones shook his head. "Anyhow, since then, nothing's worked out for him."

"Why not?"

"Different reasons. One of them couldn't handle how dangerous our job is."

"You're still in the SEALs?" she asked.

"No, that was a long time ago. We're marine archaeologists, treasure hunters. That's how we know Grizzly."

"Really?" Spenser was now eying Maddock like a prime cut of eggplant, or whatever the hell her crowd ate instead of a nice chunk of beef. "Are you any good at it?"

Bones gave his best indifferent shrug and rocked back in his chair. "We do all right."

"So, what about the other women who didn't work out? Any common denominators there?"

"A couple of them were real… you don't want me to say the word, do you?" When Spenser shook her head, he went on. "Then there was another one where life just got in the way. It was too bad, really, but I don't think it was meant to be. This probably sounds stupid, but Maddock's a puzzle that only one person can solve."

"And who would that be?"

Bones shrugged. "The right woman, whoever she is."

As Spenser turned and smoothly inserted herself into Maddock and Rockwell's conversation, Jashawn leaned over to Bones and spoke in a low voice.

"Playing wingman for your buddy?"

"It's always fun to send a woman Maddock's way. He'll twist himself into knots trying to behave like a respectful gentleman, and end up overthinking everything. It's good for a few laughs."

Jashawn eyed the pair speculatively. While Dakota pitched the idea for raw water to Rockwell, Maddock and Spenser were sharing what appeared to be a pleasant conversation about the Salton Sea.

"You know something? I get the feeling she's got a lot more drive and determination than her brother. And she appears very interested at the moment."

"I think you're right. And Maddock's too polite to just shut her down." He turned to Jashawn and grinned. "Which is why this is going to be an excellent prank."

They clinked glasses and sat back to watch the show.

CHAPTER 5

That night they gathered in the great room of the main ranch house. Light from the crackling fire in the kiva fireplace danced on the adobe walls and tiled floors. Maddock sat on a thick bearskin rug and sipped a Dos Equis. The desert air had cooled considerably after sundown, and a cool breeze blew in through the open windows. Bones had stuffed himself into a hand-crafted rocking chair and sat gazing at the fire, a contented smile on his face. Grizzly and Riv were ensconced on the big leather sofa, the former drinking a cup of coffee, the latter crunching numbers on her laptop. Lilith had departed with Rockwell after the race, and Jashawn had left after dinner. It was too bad. Maddock and Bones had enjoyed the young man's company.

"I brought you a refill." Spenser appeared at his side and handed him another beer. In hopes of some positive social media buzz, Grizzly had invited her and her brother to stay at his ranch house for a few days.

"Thanks," he said as she sat down beside him. Once she'd dropped her on-camera persona, she proved to be clever, with a dry sense of humor. Much different from his first impression. Obviously, he'd been too quick to judge. "What happened to your brother?"

Spenser rolled her eyes. "Rockwell had reservations about his raw water idea, so Dakota chugged a whole bottle to prove it's safe. The results were predictable."

"Loco que una cabra," Riv murmured.

Maddock was familiar with the idiom, which translated to "crazier than a goat."

"Why hasn't someone explained the science to him?" Maddock asked.

Spenser feigned offense, but laughter shone in her big blue eyes. "Is that how little you think of me? I've been telling him since the first time his dumb ass tried to drink water from what he thought was a puddle but was actually an overflowing septic tank."

Maddock winced. "You can't be serious. He couldn't possibly function if he were that dim."

Spencer leaned in so close that a strand of her hair brushed across his cheek. "Next time you see him," she said quietly, "take a look at his hands. On the left, he's written 'breathe in,' on the right, 'breathe out.' Just in case he forgets."

Maddock laughed. "I thought it was bad that Bones has to make an L with his thumb and forefinger so he can remember which hand he…"

"Please don't finish that sentence," Riv said without looking up from her laptop.

"Naughty boy got scolded by the teacher," Spenser said softly.

The back of Maddock's neck felt suddenly hot. He gave a little jerk and sat up straight, jostling her in the process. "Sorry. Back cramp," he invented.

That was a mistake.

"In that case, you should let me work on you." She didn't wait for him to agree. Moving as if made of liquid, Spenser slipped her body between Maddock and the wall against which he'd been leaning moments before. "I am the back-rub goddess." She began gently kneading his trapezius muscle, working it with the tips of her fingers and thumbs. "I actually have a degree in kinesiology and I'm a licensed massage therapist. I figure I should have a career to fall back on in case the social media bubble ever bursts."

"I didn't know that about you," Maddock said.

"As much as I hate to admit it, I keep it quiet. Things like getting an education and working for a living wouldn't play well with a lot of our followers."

"Why not?"

"We're selling a fantasy. Most of our subscribers can't afford most of the places we visit or the products we market. We're selling the fantasy of a carefree life of leisure. Got to give the consumers the product they're after."

As she worked her knuckles down his erector spinae muscles, Maddock closed his eyes and allowed himself to relax and enjoy what was admittedly an excellent back rub. Grizzly and Bones were discussing legends of ghost sightings in the hills around the ranch.

"How is it that you're so smart but your brother drinks sewage water?" Maddock asked.

"Believe it or not, he's not dumb." She lapsed into a few seconds of contemplative silence before elaborating. "Have you ever known someone who is ninety-nine percent amazing, but that other one percent is just mind-numbingly awful?"

Maddock chuckled. "Just broke up with someone like that."

"Did she drink raw water?"

"No, just screwed me over. Twice." That was an understatement.

"Twice? I hope there won't be a third time. Now, stop thinking about your evil ex before you ruin your massage."

"That actually feels pretty amazing," he admitted.

"I know." She paused, waited. "I just quoted Han Solo. Do you not like Star Wars?"

"I do, but I'm more of an Indiana Jones guy," he said as she resumed her work.

"I love Indy!" She began kneading his shoulders with just the right amount of pressure. "I guess it fits since you're a treasure hunter."

"Fortune and glory, kid. Fortune and glory."

"I could have been your greatest adventure," she purred.

"Wait, what?"

"I thought we were swapping quotes from the movies."

"Oh, yeah."

"Speaking of treasure," Grizzly interrupted, "did you know there's a legendary treasure associated with this place?"

"You said you had a long story to tell about the ranch," Maddock said, trying to keep his mind off the warm feeling that was flowing over him as the knots in his back melted away under her studied attention.

"It starts with a guy named Kirk Striker."

Maddock frowned. "I know that name. My dad used to read his adventure novels."

Grizzly nodded. "One and the same. Striker was an author and wannabe Hollywood player back in the 1940s. He made his living off his pulp adventure novels, but every bit of his spare time, and most of his money, was spent trying to cozy up to producers, directors, actors, anyone in the business. I don't know if he was taken seriously or if they tolerated him because he always picked up the tab, but he kept at it for years until, in 1949, they finally made one of his books into a movie called *Treasure Fever*.

"I guess Hollywood success wasn't all it was cracked up to be, because he started making treks out into the desert. I guess he was on some kind of spiritual quest. Finally, he ended up here in these hills."

"Guided here by aliens who could speak inside his brain," Riv said mockingly.

Grizzly didn't bite. "Three UFOs converged over a spot in the hills, and according to Striker, he understood the message they were sending him. That this was the site of the Lost Arch Gold Mine."

"I've never heard of it," Bones said.

"The legend goes something like this. In 1848 a pair of prospectors named Fish and Crocker were searching for water when they stumbled across a rich vein of gold directly beneath a natural arch formed in the basalt. With only a minimal amount of digging they managed to fill their pockets with heavy grains of gold. They couldn't stay there, though, because they were dangerously low on water. They ended up traveling two days to the Colorado River. It was a harrowing journey, by all accounts, with different versions giving different details of the dangers they faced, but they all agree that

Crocker died a few days after the pair reached the river. Without his partner, Fish never managed to find the arch again."

"And it's supposed to be somewhere around here?" Bones asked.

"Legend generally places it in the Turtle Mountains, northeast of here, but Striker must have had his reasons for believing it was here."

"He did, dear," Riv said. "The aliens told him."

"I think he only said that so people wouldn't take him seriously and start poking around out here. As far as anyone knows, he never found the mine, but he lived out the remainder of his life here. The older he got, the more paranoid he became. He claimed to hear the voices of the dead. According to him the men in black were regular visitors to the ranch, too."

"How did he support himself if he didn't find gold?" Spenser asked.

"He was a published author. I guess he lived off his royalties."

"That only happens in movies," Riv said.

Grizzly turned to her and replied in mock annoyance. "Remind me why I keep you around?"

Riv turned her laptop so he could see the spreadsheet she was working on and held it out to him. "Here. Finish this for me."

Grizzly shook his head. "I don't even know what that is."

"And that is why you keep me around." Riv returned to her work, but not before blowing him a kiss.

"Dude, you have met your match," Bones said.

"It happens to all of us sooner or later," Spenser chimed in, though so softly it could only have been meant for Maddock's ears. The attention she'd paid him during the day hadn't really merited any thought when he'd believed her to be a spoiled, vapid rich girl. Now, he was reassessing the entire situation and wasn't quite sure how he felt about it.

"Striker died in 1971 and that's when things got

spooky." Grizzly flashed a warning glance at Riv before continuing. "People were naturally curious about the so-called UFO Ranch, so it became a popular spot for camping and exploration. But then others started hearing cries at night. Some of them encounter men in black, who warned them away from certain spots. Some even disappeared."

"But nobody found the gold mine?" Maddock asked.

Grizzly shook his head. "And then, almost ten years later, Shipman appears out of nowhere and buys all the land that belonged to Striker. A kid, barely out of college."

"So, an adult," Spenser said.

Grizzly nodded. "But a few years younger than you. The point is, no one knows where he got the money. And then he's seen tooling around town in an old Jaguar XK120."

"Trust fund kid?" Bones asked.

"Not as far as anyone knows. But next thing you know, he's quizzing all the old folks in the area about Striker. And not just about the mine. He wanted to know every little thing about him. The tiniest little details about his personality, his behavior. Strange stuff."

"Maybe he believed if he could understand Striker, it could aid him in his search for the mine," Maddock said.

"Probably. It's interesting that Shipman not only bought Striker's land, but he also became an author. He writes murder mysteries about serial killers. I guess his books aren't selling too well anymore. He ended up selling a decent-sized chunk of his land to me."

Riv cleared her throat but did not call attention to her earlier comment about royalties.

"Do you think that's why he's been poking around?" Spenser asked. "Maybe he's found a new clue to the gold mine and he thinks it's located on the land he sold to you."

Grizzly perked up. "I hadn't even considered that."

Riv closed her laptop and let out a tired sigh. "You just had to get him going, didn't you?"

"A treasure hunting show, right here on our own property!" Grizzly's eyes were alight. "No travel expenses. No red tape."

"I'd love to be involved," Spenser said, Maddock's back rub forgotten. "I've always wanted to produce travel adventure videos. Dakota was the one who steered us toward influencing."

"Perfect," Grizzly said. "We could co-host."

Riv put a hand on his arm. "Don, dear, listen to me. What do we do with new ideas?"

Grizzly rolled his eyes. "Write down every little detail so I don't forget, then set it aside until I finish what I'm currently working on."

"I do think it's a good idea," Riv said, "and for exactly the reasons you say. But we haven't even started filming the adventure race series. This is not a great time for you to dive into something new."

"We're just brainstorming, Riv." His grin said he knew he wasn't fooling anyone.

"Maddock and I could do a little scouting around," Bones offered. "Look for clues. Let you know if we think it's worth exploring. Down the road, when you have time," he added hastily under the heat of Riv's stare.

"Sure, if you don't mind us hanging around," Maddock said. He knew what Bones was thinking. Even if there was no treasure, this area promised to be rife with challenging rock faces even for an experienced climber. Just their sort of vacation.

"That's a great idea," Grizzly said. "You three can be my advance scouts!"

"Three?" Maddock asked.

"You and Bones know treasure hunting. Spenser knows production. It's more efficient if she's involved from the start." Grizzly seemed to sense Maddock's reluctance. "It'll be fine. And if you guys don't handle this for me, I'll let it distract me. And then I'll have her highness to answer to. Come on. This could be the project that takes me to the next level."

Maddock chuckled. Although he was a bit too full of himself and not always as fast on the uptake as the average person, the man had an undeniable charm. He was an eternal optimist who wasn't afraid to dream big, and he delivered results with just enough frequency to make you believe the guy just might make it someday.

"All right," he said. "You've got yourself a scouting crew."

CHAPTER 6

The headquarters of Rockwell Industries sat in the middle of Bombay Beach, a virtual ghost town that had once been a thriving tourist destination. Located on the northwest shore of the Salton Sea, only a stone's throw from Joshua Tree National Park, it was now only a mere echo of what it had once been. Salt encrusted hulks of old boats lay on sunbaked earth, well beyond the sea's current shoreline. The remnants of years of fish kills lay in mass graves, their skeletal remains bleached in the sun. A journalist had once dubbed Bombay Beach "A Post-Apocalyptic Nightmare on the Salton Sea," and Lilith couldn't disagree with the assessment.

She drove by abandoned houses, some covered in graffiti, others merely empty. Rockwell had ordered the most dilapidated and potentially dangerous ruins torn down and hauled away. Still, what remained looked like something out of the zombie apocalypse. The place even smelled like rotting flesh. To her left, a door frame was the only thing left standing in a spot once occupied by a local shop. Above the door, someone had painted the words *Buried Alive* in shades of green. The wall of another abandoned building boasted a painting of a bleached skull. And there were more oddities: a piano sitting out in the middle of nowhere, a school bus half-buried in the sand, a seaside building that had collapsed at an odd angle and had crumbled in such a way that it now resembled a shipwreck.

In her time working for Rockwell, Lilith had largely grown immune to the town's eccentric charm, if that's what it could be called. Her boss, however, never ceased to marvel at the strangeness of the place. He liked to compare the town to a modern art exhibit and vowed to preserve its unique features even after he'd restored Salton to its former glory.

Lilith parked her Smart car next to Rockwell's Subaru wagon, then sat for a few seconds, steeling herself. When she was ready, she held her breath, cut the engine, and hurried into the office. Even with all her efforts, the sulfurous odor of the Salton Sea still managed to follow her inside.

"God, this place is so gross," she whispered, wiping her hands on her shirt as if she could brush away the foul air. She stopped when she heard Rockwell's voice inside his office. He frequently arrived early for conference calls with people on the east coast or in Europe.

Headquarters consisted of a front room, a back office, and a modestly appointed meeting room. Lilith hated sitting at what was obviously intended to be a receptionist's desk. She was coordinator of the Salton Restoration Project, but all visitors ever saw was a young woman sitting at a desk outside her boss's office. That sort of first impression was a challenge to overcome. She sat down heavily in her chair. Her eyes fell on the two framed photos on her desk: Amy Pohler as Leslie Knope, and Kate McKinnon as Hillary Clinton. Somehow, they always managed to make her smile.

The door to Rockwell's office opened and he poked his head out.

"So, you did make it before nine. I thought you'd sleep in."

"I'm a professional, Orry. I don't let pleasure interfere with business." Ironically, they could have mixed business and pleasure any time they liked. No one ever dropped in at their office. They didn't even need an office in order to conduct their business, nor did they need to live the area for that matter. But Rockwell had insisted it was essential they become part of the community here and placing headquarters here was an important step in building trust, both with the locals and with people whom he hoped to bring over to their cause.

"Come on back whenever you're ready. I made coffee."

"I've trained you well." Lilith grabbed her tablet and

briefcase and followed him.

Rockwell's office was simply furnished, with a desk, a work table, and a pair of comfortable chairs. His collection of framed motivational posters would have put Barney Stinson to shame.

INNOVATION- Seeing what everyone has seen and thinking what nobody has thought.

COMMUNICATION- The art of communication is the language of leadership.

PERSPECTIVE- Distance has the same effect on the mind as on the eye.

There were more. She could probably recite them all from memory, not that she wanted to. She thought, or at least she hoped, that Rockwell displayed them ironically. Or, maybe he believed the sort of power broker whose money or influence they craved would appreciate the simple aphorisms. Not wanting to know the answer, she had never asked. She had, however, added another poster of her own choosing to the collection a few weeks back. It depicted a pair of figure skaters crashing to the ice, with the caption: *TEAMWORK- Ensuring that your hard work can always be ruined by someone else's incompetence.*

Rockwell had never said a word about it. Nor had he taken it down. God, the man was an enigma.

"Monday report," he said, rubbing his hands together.

Lilith opened her tablet and consulted her meeting notes.

"Nothing new on water rights. Water is gold and the powers that be are going to sell as much of it as they can to the highest bidder."

"San Diego," Rockwell mumbled.

"We're actually seeing growth on the real estate front. More than I expected. Congratulations on that." One of Rockwell's initiatives to spur growth in the area had been a program to provide affordable housing for struggling working-class people—those whom the government did not deem impoverished, but were being left behind economically. A second was to accept deposits on future luxury lots. The latter was doing surprisingly well. "The downside is, we're getting pinged for our alleged lack of diversity, and I have to say the numbers are on their side. I'd like to evaluate the vetting process, see what's going on."

"I'll take care of it," Rockwell said. "That's a simple problem to correct. In the meantime, let it be known we're reviewing our policies. Also emphasize the diversity of Bombay Beach, and that we're excited to be part of expanding that community. Let's also announce that we'll be giving away a home to one of the families that currently live there."

"The margins are thin on the affordable housing side," she said doubtfully.

"We don't have to build it any time soon. We'll drag it out, make a big deal of it. When the time comes, if things are tight, we can move money around."

Lilith's throat clenched; her heart raced. She took a breath and calmed herself. "Orry, I'd really like to be more hands-on with the real estate in general." She could tell long before she finished what his answer would be. His eyes narrowed slightly, but that was enough of a tell.

"There's no need to duplicate efforts, nor for you to take time getting up to speed in an area that doesn't require your oversight."

She understood his logic, but the rebuke stung. The housing projects were his babies and he was protective of them.

"Fair enough. So, who is showing interest in the luxury lots? I didn't expect it to happen so fast!"

"A mishmash of people. No one you would have heard of. I can send you a list if you want it."

"That would be terrific."

"How about the race? Did we get any nibbles from the attendees?"

Lilith shrugged. "Lots of tweets. And of course, you've got the Saroyans."

Rockwell buried his face in his hands. "That poor

guy. He's allegedly an adult. I mean, raw water? It's like my speech bounced off him."

"His sister is not completely hopeless." Lilith had never dreamed she would have something positive to say about either of the Saroyans, but she always acknowledged a woman's strengths as a matter of principle. She could tell that Spenser, like herself, was a sharp analytical thinker. The fact that they shared this trait was a source of ambivalent feelings. The girl had potential, but at the end of the day she was still a social media personality.

"What about the others in your group? Dakota kept me so occupied I didn't get to chat with them. Any potential there?"

"Jashawn Powell works for NutriMax and they're already on board with us. The other two are Grizzly's friends, Maddock and Bonebrake. The ex-military fellows who were there to make sure the course wasn't too difficult for us common folk."

Rockwell nodded. "Yeah, they seem like decent guys. See what you can learn about their time in the service. If there are no skeletons in their closets, it wouldn't hurt to have the endorsement of a couple of veterans."

"Will do."

"All right. Anything specific that needs my immediate attention?"

Lilith scanned her notes one more time and then shook her head. "Other than the housing demographics issue? No. Looks like you get to play Choose Your own Adventure today." She stood, stretched, and yawned.

"I guess I kept you up too late," Rockwell said. "Sorry about that."

"I don't mind." Her eyes fell on a map of the Salton area. Bright red lines and dashes cut across the surface. "What is that?"

"The latest fault line map." Rockwell sat down at his desk then turned the map around. "Geologists think this area could be rife for California's next big earthquake."

His finger traced the series of red lines that ran along the eastern shore of the Salton Sea and up into Coachella Valley and beyond. "They found what they call a 'highly faulted volume of rock' that is nearly four kilometers wide in places."

Lilith knew the San Andreas Fault extended all the way down through Salton, but she'd never thought of this as earthquake country. The thought made her feel slightly ill. "Can you imagine a major earthquake striking Coachella or Palm Springs?"

Rockwell turned and gazed out the window.

"It would change everything, wouldn't it?"

CHAPTER 7

"That's where we spotted Shipman." Maddock pointed in the direction of the pathway that ran down the slope and vanished among the boulders and low growth clinging to the parched hills up ahead. The limited research they'd done on the Lost Arch Gold Mine hadn't uncovered anything beyond the well-known version of the legend, and certainly nothing that connected it to the area around the Salton Sea. He, Bones, and Spenser decided to explore the area where they'd last spotted Shipman to see if they found anything interesting. Dakota had opted to remain at the ranch to rest up from the previous day's ordeal. Maddock would have preferred only Bones as company, but if he had to deal with one of the brother-sister team, Spenser was by far the more palatable choice.

"Lead the way," Spenser said.

The footing was uncertain, the way steep, and they skidded in a cloud of dust down to a level spot.

"Falling!" Spenser called. Maddock turned around just in time for her to crash into him. He caught her around the waist and for a moment was hyper aware of her body pressed against his. "Thanks for the catch," she said breathlessly as she clung to him, showing no sign of letting go.

"No problem." He released his grip on her and quickly stepped back.

"This seemed like a much longer trek last time," she said. "It hasn't even been an hour since we set out."

"That's because we were following the racecourse yesterday," Bones said. "Today we took a more direct route."

Spenser nodded, looked around. "Well, what's the plan? Just follow the path and see where it takes us?" she asked brightly

"That's the general shape of it," Maddock said. "Let's have Bones take the lead. He's got sharp eyes and might spot something you and I overlook."

"Translation—the white guy thinks that just because I'm Native American that means I'm an expert tracker," Bones said as he moved past them and took the point.

"No, I think you're an expert tracker because you *are* one."

"I know," Bones said. "I just like hearing you admit it."

The way grew rough and the pathway faded into nothing, but Bones was more than up to the task of tracking Shipman. He picked out the occasional partial footprint, scuff mark, or broken branch. Soon they were inching along a narrow ledge twenty feet above a pile of jagged rocks. They moved slowly, their bodies pressed against stone warmed by the intense sun.

"This would make a great shot!" Spenser said. "Grizzly could climb around this and if the camera angle is just right, it will look like he could fall to his death."

"The drop is far enough that we should probably focus on the task at hand at the moment," Maddock said.

"I'm fine. Don't worry about me."

They reached the other side to find themselves looking up at a high rocky face. There was no obvious way up or around it.

"You're certain he came this way?" Maddock asked.

"Yep. At least, somebody came here recently."

"He must have climbed to the top." Before anyone could stop her, Spenser began scaling the rock face.

"Dude, you should really plan out your path before you free climb," Bones warned.

"Who says I didn't? I've been climbing for years." They couldn't deny the young woman climbed well. Already she was halfway up, moving with confidence. The feat was particularly impressive since, at just a shade over five feet tall, she didn't have long legs or a wide wingspan, which meant that many footholds and handholds were beyond her reach.

Maddock and Bones took a bit more time to choose their own routes to the top. When free climbing, it was important to plan ahead and pick out handholds and footholds all the way to the top. Otherwise, a climber might end up stuck, able to go neither go up nor down. They were about to begin when Spenser called down them.

"Um, guys? I think I'm sort of stuck." Sure enough, Spenser had run out of handholds about six feet from the top. "I can hold on, but I don't think I can climb back down."

"We'll be right there," Maddock said.

Bones scrambled up the rock, headed up to the ledge, while Maddock began climbing in the direction of the stranded young woman. By the time he reached her side, she was breathing heavily, and her body was slicked with sweat—an unusual sight in this arid climate.

"I'm hanging in there. Literally." She forced a smile.

"You'll be fine," he assured her.

He was wrong. At that moment, Spenser let out a cry as one of her feet slipped and she began to fall.

Maddock moved with lightning-fast reflexes and a touch of recklessness. He jammed his right hand into a crack in the rock and made a fist. At the same time, he caught Spenser by the belt and arrested her fall.

"Did anybody bring a clean pair of underwear?" she joked when she was once again on firm footing.

"Sorry, don't wear any," Bones called out from up above. He didn't see anything promising.

Maddock scanned the cliff face directly above them, looking for a way up.

"When you were planning out your route, what was it you saw up here that made you think you could make it all the way to the top?"

"I didn't look very carefully before I started," she admitted, her cheeks going pink. "I wanted you guys to see that I really am a good climber. Joke's on me, huh?"

"Every climber runs into trouble from time to time.

You're skilled, though."

"Thanks. Not really in the mood to accept an undeserved compliment, but your efforts are noted and appreciated."

"Okay, chick," Bones called. "Time to give you the belt."

He hung down over the ledge as far as he dared and dropped the looped end of his belt down. Spenser grabbed on with one hand. While Bones and Maddock helped her along, she climbed the last several feet to the top. When she was safe, Maddock joined them at the top.

"I was first to the top, as usual," Bones said.

"Whatever." Maddock looked around. Before them, loose boulders were piled against the mountainside. They were large, all at least four feet across.

"They look like a giant's toy blocks," Spenser observed. She took out her phone and began snapping photographs. "Nice view from up here."

"Would Shipman really climb up here just for the view?" Bones asked.

Maddock shook his head. There had to be more here. He inspected the rock pile.

"There's something odd about this formation. It's not like a natural rockfall. It really does look like someone loosely stacked them."

"Who could do that?" Spenser asked.

"Oh, I'm sure it's just an odd natural formation, but my point is, there are wide spaces between some of these boulders, some large enough for a person to climb through."

"I think you're right. Hang back for a second and let me take a look." Bones took a few minutes to give the ground in front of the rockfall a close inspection. Finally, he beckoned them over. "Look in there." He pointed into a tight passageway. "Someone's been here and tried to obscure their tracks, but they left a partial handprint."

Maddock saw it, noticed the direction in which the fingers pointed. "It looks like whoever left the print was on the way in, not out."

Bones shrugged. "Could be. Or they've already been in and out and just happened to miss that print. Either way, we're not turning around, are we?"

"Of course not." Maddock got down on all fours and crawled into the dimly lit crevice between two massive boulders. It was a snug fit for him, and Bones would find it a very tight squeeze, but they could make it. He squeezed through a series of tight turns, all the while smiling at Bones' grunts and complaints. They hit a couple of dead ends along the way and were forced to turn back.

"Is treasure hunting always like this?" Spenser asked. "Crawling around in the dirt."

"Not always," Bones said. "Sometimes it's really boring. Like when Maddock makes you work a grid 'just to be thorough' even though we know exactly where a shipwreck is."

"You guys have found sunken ships?"

"One or two," Maddock said.

They finally emerged in an open space large enough for them to stand. Lances of sunlight pierced the dust cloud they'd stirred up and illuminated the bizarre sight that stood before them.

A heavy iron door was set in the mountainside. Its surface was pitted with rust, but it remained sturdy, its heavy hinges set deep in the stone. It stood ajar, and Maddock could see that it unlocked only from the outside.

"It looks medieval," Bones observed. "Why would you set an iron door in the side of a mountain like this?"

"It could have been a secure area where miners stored their explosives," Maddock offered. "Although I've never seen one this heavy duty."

"This would be a strange place to store explosives." Spenser asked. "Scale the cliff and then crawl through that maze while shoving a crate of dynamite in front of you?"

"Point taken," Maddock said. "Simply getting this door up here would have taken at least a couple of very strong people. Maybe the answer lies on the other side of the door?" He and Bones took out their Maglites and were surprised when Spenser did the same.

"What?" She frowned at their twin stares. "I always carry one when I'm hiking. You never know what kind of hole you might climb into."

"How do you know so much about Maddock's love life?" Bones said.

Spenser winced but smiled. Maddock ignored him. He approached the door slowly, shone his light inside.

Beyond the door lay a small, soot-blackened cave. A trickle of water ran down the wall to pool in a small depression in the rock. To the right, bits of straw and scraps of fabric lay flattened to the floor like a worn-out scrap of carpet.

"What the hell is that?" Bones directed the beam of his light to a chain and leg iron anchored to the stone floor.

They moved inside. Spenser could stand up straight, but Bones and Maddock had to hunch.

"You did say it looked Medieval," Maddock said to Bones.

"I think I know what this place is." Spenser's voice came in a whisper. "We all thought it was just a campfire tale."

"We're all ears," Bones said. Spenser let out a sigh and sat down on the dusty cave floor. Maddock and Bones followed suit. "If anybody makes a crack about me sitting Indian style," Bones warned.

"The story goes like this," Spenser began. "Back in the 1800s, a miner's wife gave birth to a badly deformed baby. He grew into a huge, hideously deformed thing that was more monster than man. His family kept him hidden, but eventually he became so violent and erratic that they had to take steps. Not having the heart to kill him, they instead locked him up in a mountain cave with a door that bolted from the outside. He had a supply of water, and his father would bring him food. One day the father arrived at the cave to find the door open and his son gone.

"He searched far and wide but couldn't find him. The family believed their son had fled out into the desert and died. But then the rumors began. People reported seeing a monster lurking around the desert at night. Thefts were reported, mostly food. As the rumors swirled, and a few eyewitnesses claimed to have gotten a look at the man they called the Mojave Monster, the father could no longer deny that his son was still alive. He set out in search of his son, but before he could find him, the killings began. Ranchers were found beaten and strangled to death. And then a child was kidnapped. The ranchers teamed up to go after the monster."

"So, what happened?" Bones asked.

"It depends on which version of the story. In some versions, the monster murders the child and is killed, either by the mob or by his own father. In others, he's brought back here and chained to the wall for the rest of his life."

They fell silent for a moment, contemplating the tale.

"That's grim," Bones said. "So, assuming that's what this place is, what would Shipman or anyone else want with it?"

Maddock didn't have an answer. While Spenser took out her phone and began snapping photos and making notes for Grizzly, he began a thorough inspection of the small prison.

It didn't take long to find what he was looking for. Spenser sat on a three-foot-wide slab of stone pressed against the far wall. Unlike all the other stone surfaces, it was free of soot.

"Could you stand up for a second?" he asked.

Bones read his mind. As soon as the young woman had stepped out of the way, he leaned down and shoved the slab aside to reveal an opening.

"There's a tunnel back here," he said, shining his light through. "Man-made. Can't tell where it leads."

"Can you squeeze through?" Maddock asked.

Bones smirked. "I can get through fine. It's your swollen head I'm worried about."

The opening proved to be little more than a hole in a thick rock wall that opened into a passageway that wound away into the darkness.

"Holy crap," Bones said. "This is a natural formation. There's no telling how far back it might go or how many caverns and corridors these mountains might hide."

"Spoken like a true treasure hunter," Maddock said.

Spenser couldn't contain her excitement. "You guys, Grizzly is going to freak when he finds out about this. It literally makes no difference if he finds any treasure. This is going to make for amazing television."

"If I were you, I'd report everything directly to Riv and let her decide what Grizzly needs to know and what he doesn't," Maddock said.

She nodded and pushed a stray lock of golden blonde hair out of her face. "I'm going to go back outside and take some video as if we're just discovering the dungeon room, or whatever the hell we're calling it. I think Grizzly will like that." She turned and climbed back out.

"I saw you checking her out," Bones said.

"No, I wasn't."

"Why not? She's cute, smart, likes to climb, doesn't mind getting dirty. And she's into you. What the hell is wrong with you, anyway?"

Maddock was spared the need to reply when Spenser called out to them.

"Guys?" She sounded confused and maybe a bit frightened. "I think somebody locked us in."

CHAPTER 8

Spenser was right. The iron door was sealed shut. They tried brute force, but it was more than their match. Try as they might, they could not get it to budge.

"No point calling for help," Bones said. "The only person within earshot is probably the same person who locked us in here."

Maddock nodded. "Must have been hiding in the rocks eavesdropping on us. Locked us in once we moved beyond the dungeon."

"But why?" Spenser asked, trying in vain to call 911.

"It's got to be Shipman," Bones said. "We know his secret now. He couldn't let us report back to Grizzly, so he locked us in."

"To die?" Rather than fearful, Spenser sounded affronted. "What could he be hiding up here that is worth killing us over?"

"I'd like to know the answer to that question myself," Maddock said. "And since we're not getting out this way." He rapped on the iron door.

Bones grinned. "Maddock, I like your thinking."

They returned to the natural cavern and began to explore. They periodically marked the walls to track their passage. Spenser did her best to sketch out a map of the passageways, but it was a challenging task. Some of the tunnels corkscrewed downward, others crisscrossed. It was confounding.

"One thing's for sure," Maddock said. "It would be very easy to hide something in here and it would never be discovered. Unless a person knows exactly where they're going, they could wander around in here forever."

An uncomfortable silence ensued. They'd been exploring the network of passageways for quite some time and hadn't seen any hint of a way out. None of them voiced their concerns, though. There was nothing to do except keep searching, so why bother talking about it? They continued on in silence.

"Do you think it was Shipman who made the tunnel from the dungeon room to these passageways?" Bones asked, probably to distract an increasingly nervous-looking Spenser.

"Maybe. The digging didn't exactly look fresh, but it could have been cut in the years since he moved here."

"Do you think he believes the Arch Gold Mine is in here somewhere?" Spenser asked.

Maddock shrugged. "If that's the case, then he's working from information that's completely different from the legend. But it certainly could be. Often, the most commonly accepted version of a legend is the one that proves inaccurate."

"Really? Like what?"

"Yeah, like what, Maddock?" Bones deadpanned.

The two of them could have provided countless examples from their own experiences, but many were classified and others so unbelievable as to make the two men seem unhinged, should they ever recount them.

Spenser's eyes brightened. "Do you mean like how everyone thinks Moses crossed the Red Sea, but now scholars think it was the Sea of Reeds."

Maddock was impressed. Even Bones nodded in approval.

They came to a fork in the passageway. Maddock shone his light down each in turn. Something about the way to the left caught his eye. The tiniest glint of yellow. A closer investigation revealed a gold necklace wedged into a tiny crack in the rock.

"How did you even see that?" Bones asked.

"In that tiny crack in this dark tunnel?" Maddock shrugged. "I just happened to be standing in the perfect spot with my flashlight held at just the right angle. Dumb luck." He took out his Recon knife, carefully fished the necklace from the crack, and held it up on the tip of his knife. A golden unicorn pendant dangled from the fine gold chain.

"That's gorgeous," Spenser said. "Might even be hand-crafted. I'll bet whoever lost it would love to have it back."

"We'll turn it in at lost-and-found on our way out," Maddock said. He pocketed the necklace. "I think we should try this passage. The necklace at least proves someone came this way."

Bones nodded. "Which hopefully means there's a way out somewhere up ahead."

"What are we waiting for? I want to be home in time for dinner." Buoyed by this sliver of hope, Spenser bounded down the passageway.

And then Maddock saw it.

"Spenser! Stop!" He sprang forward and gave her a shove just as light flashed and a deafening boom filled the air. They hit the ground hard and she let out a grunt of pain. "Are you all right?"

"No."

Maddock's heart lurched. He pushed himself up to his knees and shone his light down. He saw blood.

Bones appeared at his side. "Is she shot?"

"No, but he busted my damn lip. Why did you tackle me?"

"The passage was booby trapped. It's just a cheap trip wire and a pistol, but it would have done a number on you."

Spenser's eyes were like saucers. "You can't be serious."

"Look for yourself." Bones shone his light on a hastily rigged trip wire running up a series of pulleys to trigger a .22 revolver.

"How did I not see that? I deserve a bloody lip."

Relieved, Maddock helped her to her feet and wiped the blood away. "It's not too bad. Don't women pay a lot of money to get puffy lips?"

She grinned, touched her split lip. "Yes, but the puffiness is typically a little more evenly distributed."

Bones hastily disarmed the trap and pocketed the

revolver before they continued. They proceeded with caution, watching and listening.

Maddock thought the booby trap was odd. It hadn't been very well hidden, which said it was either the work of an amateur, or it was intended to nab only the unwariest of passersby. But why was it here? What lay down this passageway that needed guarding with a deadly weapon? And had the sound of the trap discharging warned someone up ahead?

Finally, Bones broke the silence. "Can you smell it?" he whispered.

Maddock inhaled slowly, shook his head.

"I smell sage. I think we're close to a way out."

"Watch out for more booby traps," Spenser cautioned.

They came to another fork. The way to the right seemed to be a continuation of the main passage, while the tunnel that angled off to the left quickly shrank to a hands and knees affair. But it was this tunnel Bones insisted they follow.

"This is where the smell is coming from. And the air is drier this way."

"As much as I hate to admit it, he's almost always right about these things," Maddock said to a doubtful-looking Spenser.

Fifteen minutes later and Maddock was having his share of doubts. The passageway twisted and turned, and they found themselves inching forward on their bellies.

"Almost there," Bones said.

"We're not going to get stuck, are we?" Spenser asked.

"Anywhere Bones can fit, you and I can fit too," he assured her. Privately, he hoped Bones was right, because he didn't relish the idea of scooting backward for however long it would take to get to a place where the tunnel was wide enough for them to turn around. The mere thought of it made him want to lie down and take a nap.

"And score!" Bones proclaimed.

There was low grunt, the clack and clatter of moving rock, and then…

"Sunlight!" Spenser breathed.

"The nose always knows," Bones said.

Minutes later, they were standing in daylight, breathing the warm afternoon air. Maddock stretched and took a few deep breaths.

"I can't believe we squeezed our way out of that tiny crack," Spenser said, looking down at the opening from which they'd climbed.

"Whoever set that booby trap, I don't think this is the way they've been coming in and out. I think we just got very lucky that Bones found it." Maddock turned and looked down the narrow slot canyon in which they'd emerged. The way was choked with fallen rocks and razor-sharp yucca. "I wouldn't be surprised if this way into the caverns has gone undiscovered until today."

Bones took a bow. "It's what I do. Now, how do we find our way back to the ranch?"

"Or at least to a spot with coverage," Spenser said, gazing sadly at her cell phone.

They took a minute to pile a few rocks in front of the small entrance before making their way. They clambered over tall boulders and loose piles of rock, enduring a few cuts and scrapes, but after their crawl through the darkness, Maddock was happy to put up with it. They followed its path until it emptied into a tiny canyon dense with juniper and manzanita.

"East is that way." Bones pointed to the left.

"But how do we know that's the direction we want to go?" Spenser asked. "We wound around in those passageways forever."

"The entrance to the dungeon is east of the ranch house, so I'm going with our only piece of data. Worst case scenario, we miss the ranch but eventually we get to the sea."

"We can climb out over there." Maddock pointed to a series of chimneys, ledges, and cracks that ran up the canyon's eastern rim. He turned to Spenser. "Don't worry. If it's too much, one of us will stay behind with you."

"I wasn't worried. At least let me try before you start planning around my imminent failure."

"That's Maddock for you. Always the worst-case scenario," Bones said as they headed east.

"We need to prepare for every possible disaster," Maddock said. "You just never know."

Spencer let out a giggle.

"What's funny?" Bones asked. "That's actually how he thinks. I don't know why he isn't selling insurance or bomb shelters."

"Someone needs to be in charge of risk management," she said.

"Whatever. Who wants to climb this thing first?" They had arrived at the canyon wall. The first climb was an ascent up a narrow chimney.

Spenser went first. Bones boosted her up as high as he was able, and then, bracing her hands and feet against either side, she worked her way up inch by inch. Finally, she reached the first ledge and vanished from sight.

"You want a boost, too?" Bones asked.

Maddock didn't get the chance to retort. At that moment, a voice rang out from behind them.

"Hands in the air, or you die!"

CHAPTER 9

"Turn around slowly." It was a man's voice, youthful, anxious. Maddock didn't like that. Nervous people were prone to accidents or rash decisions.

"Take it easy," he said. "We're just lost and trying to find our way back out."

He and Bones turned around slowly, hands in the air. He couldn't help but frown when he saw the man who held them at gunpoint.

He was a young man, late twenties perhaps, of mixed Anglo and Latin American descent. Clean shaven, hair neatly trimmed, eyes hidden behind mirrored sunglasses, he was clad in a black tie, crisp, white shirt, a cheap black suit sprinkled with trail dust and cactus spines, and black hiking boots.

"You almost got the costume right," Bones said, eyes flitting to the man's feet.

"What are you doing here?" the man asked.

"Like I said, we got lost."

"Where did you come in from?" The man looked around, his pistol moving to and fro as his head turned. Maddock inched closer. "There's only one way in and I know you didn't come that way."

"We came down a narrow slot canyon to the west," Maddock said truthfully. "We came down a hill and that's where we ended up."

"You ain't supposed to be here. This is," the man swallowed hard, "a classified project."

He wasn't a very good liar. The guy might be trying to dress the part of a government agent, but nothing about him or his bearing suggested he was anything of the sort. Still, whatever he really was up to, it must be serious business.

"We didn't mean to intrude," Maddock said. "We're just lost hikers trying to get the hell out of here, which we'll do right now." He made to turn, but the man waved his pistol. "No, man. You can't just go like that. We've got to…" He paused, glanced up and to his right, eyes narrowed. "We've got to debrief you. You're coming with me."

So that was it. The man wouldn't be content to simply let them walk away. Maddock knew what to do. Hands still raised, he nodded.

"No problem. We'll answer any questions you have." Maddock began to walk slowly forward in the direction their captor indicated. "We'll just need to see your credentials."

The man's eyes narrowed. "Credentials?"

"Your badge and ID. I'm sure it's there in the breast pocket of your jacket."

Reflexively, the man looked down at his jacket for a split second.

It was the opening Maddock needed. He sprang forward, seized the man's gun hand in both of his and forced him backward. They tumbled to the ground, the pistol firing wildly. Its sharp report set his ears ringing. He heard the ping of the bullet whizzing from stone to stone, caught the acrid smell of gunpowder, felt the impact of their bodies hitting the ground.

With his free hand, the man punched Maddock in the jaw, but at close quarters the blow did no damage. Maddock lifted his head and brought it smashing down on the fallen man's nose. He felt the satisfying crack of his forehead finding its target, heard a pained grunt, felt the pistol slip from the man's grasp.

"Got it." Bones wrenched the pistol free. He held the .22 he'd freed from the booby trap in his other hand, and he now trained both on the fallen man.

"What's your name?"

The young man scowled. "Reggie."

"All right, Reggie. You've got one chance to tell us the quickest way to get back to civilization. If you don't tell me, you get a bullet in the eye. If you tell me, and I find out you lied, I promise I'll hunt you down, take you out, and then leave your body smeared in peanut butter for the coyotes to eat." The man winced. In this part of the world, that was a common technique used by criminals to dispose of a body.

"You were headed in the right direction," he said. "Climb out, head east. There's a dude named Shipman who lives there."

"You know him?" Maddock asked.

Reggie made a noncommittal wag of his head. "I've seen him."

Maddock stood, helped Reggie to his feet, and searched him. The man carried no identification, only two spare magazines for his pistol, a pocketknife, and a bottle of water clipped to his belt. Maddock relieved him of all three.

"Hey, man. You can't do that," Reggie said.

"One more word and I take your boots, too," Maddock warned.

"If we're taking his boots, let's tie him up with the laces so he can't follow us," Bones suggested.

"No, please. You can go. Just don't come back."

"That was several more words," Maddock said. It was cruel to take Reggie's boots, but Maddock, not willing to execute him, was already taking a risk by leaving him alive. If he was careful, the man should be able to make it back to wherever he came from without his feet suffering any permanent damage. "Now, get the hell out of here. If Bones sees any part of your body other than your back, he opens fire. You got it?"

The man nodded. Maddock seized him by the shoulders, spun him about, and gave him a shove. The man began to run as fast as his stocking feet would allow on the uneven ground.

"Faster!" Bones fired a shot from the .22 pistol. "That got him moving."

"It also probably caught the attention of any of his friends who might be in earshot."

"Uh oh," Bones said. "Maybe we should get out of here."

He handed the .22 to Maddock and pocketed Reggie's .38 revolver.

Maddock clambered up the chimney and onto the first ledge. Spenser was nowhere to be seen. He hoped that meant she had heard the confrontation and had the good sense to keep moving. He scaled a sheer wall to another ledge, then clambered up a rockfall to another sheer face.

"Somebody's coming," Bones warned from just behind him.

Seconds later, Maddock heard voices in the distance, angry shouts. He was suddenly keenly aware of how exposed they were on this open slab of rock.

"Not much further," Spenser's voice called from somewhere up above.

"Get behind cover! Now!" Maddock shouted.

The pop of small arms fire rang out and slugs peppered the rock all around him. Maddock scrambled over the ledge, a bullet buzzing past his cheek. He reached down and helped Bones up and over. Bones came up with pistol in hand, but Maddock warned him away.

"They won't climb up after us. They'd be sitting ducks."

"Well, let's make them think we plan on staying here and making this a shooting gallery." He took aim and squeezed off a single shot. Down below, a man went down, cursing and pressing his hand to his thigh.

"I think you winged him," Maddock said. "And I know there's no point in asking if you meant to do that."

"Of course I did," Bones said with a grin.

"Sure, you did. Now, let's get out of here. I think the local police will be interested in our story."

CHAPTER 10

The Salton Sea Police Department was headquartered in a small adobe-style building a short drive from Grizzly's ranch. It was clean and neat on the inside, if a bit confining. Maddock carried a drawstring bag containing the items they'd taken from Reggie. They'd left Spenser behind at the ranch. Considering the physical and mental strain of the day, she was bearing up well, but had opted to soak in a bathtub rather than visiting the police station.

The front desk was being minded by an officer Franzen. She was of average height with long, dark hair which she wore in a bun. She greeted them with a weariness bordering on indifference, and her demeanor didn't change when Maddock told her he'd like to report a crime.

"Grab a clipboard and pen and fill out the complaint form." Her blue eyes never leaving her paperwork, she waved them in the direction of a table and chairs that stood in front of the picture window.

Bones took a step toward the desk, but Maddock shook his head. Depending on his mood, Bones would either flirt or argue with the officer, and Maddock could tell neither would go over well. No point in getting on the wrong side of local law enforcement if it could be avoided.

"There's coffee in the break room," Franzen said.

While Maddock began filling in the complaint form, Bones went for coffee. He returned a minute later with three cups.

"Looked like you needed a refill and I saw that you take it black," he said.

"Thanks," Franzen said, still not looking up.

Bones rolled his eyes, sat down at the table, and began to crack his knuckles—all of them at once, and then one at a time until Maddock told him to stop. Two seconds later, Franzen cracked her own knuckles. Bones and Maddock exchanged a puzzled glance. Franzen didn't look up but Maddock thought he saw the hint of a smile.

When Maddock completed the form and handed it over, Franzen accepted it without looking at it, then set it to the side while she continued her paperwork. When she completed the form she was filling in, she signed with sharp jerks of her hand, the ball point pen digging into the paper.

"Bad day?" Maddock asked.

"No more than any other day," she said, finally meeting his eye. "We're a small department, so during business hours, the officers take turns playing receptionist." She glanced at the time on her computer screen. "But it's almost quitting time and my paperwork is finished. Except, of course, for processing your report. Let's see what we have." She picked up the clipboard and began to read. "I'm sorry to say we almost certainly won't recover your property. The only pawn shops are…" She froze in mid-sentence.

"It's not a property crime," Maddock said.

Franzen slowly raised her head and glowered at them. "Is this a joke?"

"Absolutely not," Bones said. "And we've got the proof."

Maddock handed over the pistol, knife, magazines, and water bottle they'd taken off Reggie.

"You brought a concealed weapon in here?" Franzen sprang to her feet, upending her chair and knocking her coffee to the floor. Maddock was amused to see she was wearing a battered pair of red cowboy boots. "Dammit!"

Maddock was losing patience. "Officer, I get that you're bored out of your skull sitting at that desk, but on the scale of bad days, I really think ours trumps yours. Respectfully," he added.

Franzen clenched her fists, took a deep breath, and

blinked twice. "Fair enough," she said, relaxing a little. "But the first thing out of your mouth when you arrived should have been that you had a weapon in the bag."

"Understood," Maddock said.

"Let's start over." Franzen held out a hand and they shook. "I'm Janet Franzen but friends call me Turtle."

"I'm Maddock, this is Uriah, but everyone calls him Bones."

Franzen shook hands with Bones. "I definitely prefer Bones to Uriah. Fewer syllables."

"Me too," Bones said.

After the spilled coffee was cleaned up, they sat down around the front table and recounted the incident. Maddock and Bones described their journey through the caverns. Franzen's brow furrowed deeply when they mentioned the booby trap. Once they'd finally answered all her questions, she went into a back room and returned with a topographical map and a mechanical pencil.

"Can you show me where this happened?"

Maddock made a small circle at the spot where they'd climbed out of the canyon and drew a small arrow to show the direction in which Reggie had run.

"Probably drug related," Franzen said.

"A drug deal out in the desert?" Bones asked.

She shook her head. "Not an individual transaction. We're probably talking about drugs being trafficked up from Mexico. We're far enough from the border that they feel safe lying low here. And as you observed, this area is filled with canyons and caverns that make perfect hideouts. A lot of places can't be spotted from the air. It's a losing battle for us, I'm afraid."

Maddock nodded. "We understand. Just wanted to turn in these items. Maybe they'll be helpful."

"Maybe," Franzen said, doubtfully. "The gun's probably stolen, but maybe we can get some prints off of it or the water bottle." Her expression grew serious. "Even if we find and arrest this guy, the two of you would be asked to testify. If he's affiliated with a major drug gang, that could be dangerous."

"That doesn't frighten us," Bones said.

Franzen took a long look at each man in turn, as if truly seeing them for the first time. "No, I imagine it doesn't."

They thanked her for her time and stood to leave when Maddock remembered something.

"Oh! One more thing." He reached into his pocket and took out a folded tissue. "When we were wandering through the caverns, we found this necklace. I know it's a long shot, but we thought we should turn it in. The charm is finely crafted. Maybe someone's missing it?" He unfolded the tissue to reveal the thin gold chain and unicorn charm.

Franzen snatched the tissue-wrapped necklace from Maddock's hands and gaped at it. She recovered herself almost immediately.

"That was rude of me. Sorry, it's just been quite a day. Thanks for turning this in. If we meet again, I promise I won't be quite so... abrupt."

"That was weird," Bones said when they were back inside the car.

"No kidding. It was obvious that necklace meant something to her. Like she'd seen it before."

"You think she's hiding something?" Bones asked.

"Hiding something or looking for something."

CHAPTER 11

Dining at Lord Fletcher's was like entering a time capsule. The iconic Rancho Mirage dining spot, which had long been a celebrity favorite, was decorated in the style of a cozy English pub, and was heavy with dark wood and gentle lighting. The original owner, an Englishman by birth, sought to capture the warmth of the dining room of an English inn, and Maddock thought the man had succeeded, from the architecture to the decor. A cheery fire burned in the fireplace. Horse brass, brass plaques used to decorate the harnesses of shire and parade horses, hung from posts. Copper pots hung from ceiling beams and historical artwork adorned the walls.

"This place is fantastic," Maddock said. Grizzly and Riv had insisted on bringing them here, calling it essential Palm Springs nostalgia. Bones had begged off at the last minute with an upset stomach but had taken the liberty of lining up Spenser to take his place. Now, Grizzly kept calling it a "double date."

"Palm Springs nostalgia at its finest," Riv said.

"True. You can't have an authentic desert experience without it," Grizzly said. "This was a favorite haunt of Frank Sinatra's for thirty years. Lots of other celebrities, too. That's Frank's favorite table right there." He pointed to a table above which hung a portrait of the famed crooner.

"Frank gave them that portrait," Spenser added.

"What is up with those things?" Maddock asked, pointing to the row of ceramic mugs that lined the mantle above the fireplace.

"Those are Toby mugs," Spenser said, "or Toby jugs. They come in two forms: a tipsy looking seated person, or just the head of a recognizable person. They sometimes play games of 'Who's mug is on that Toby mug?' here."

They sat in the Shakespearean room, which boasted a beautiful stained-glass window along with fine china and two-hundred-year-old prints of scenes from Shakespeare's plays.

While they waited for their drinks, Spenser explained that, prior to opening the restaurant, the original owner had spent six months traveling the English countryside procuring the furnishings and decorations. Since then, everything had remained the same.

"Walk in here in 1966 and it would look just the same," Spenser said. "We could be sitting here fifty years ago, and Bob Hope might walk in, or Steve McQueen, Lucille Ball, or even Sinatra."

"I can almost believe that any minute, Old Blue Eyes is going to walk through that door and order a brandy ice," Grizzly said.

"Bones is going to regret missing out on this," Maddock said.

They all ordered the "King's Cut" of Lord Fletcher's famous prime rib. Maddock had expressed surprise at Spenser's order.

"I thought you were a vegetarian."

"Why would you think that?" She closed her menu and handed it back to the server without taking her eyes off Maddock. Her cheeks turned a delicate shade of pink.

"Sorry, I thought I remembered you saying that."

"I didn't."

She proceeded to fill Grizzly and Riv in on the details of the day's events. She didn't sound or appear upset, but every time Maddock tried to interject, she raised her voice and kept talking. He gave up after three tries.

"This iron door," Riv said, "is it on our property?" She took out her phone, called up a satellite image of the ranch, and zoomed in. "Can you show me where it is?"

With Grizzly's help, they traced the racecourse until they reached the spot where they'd had the encounter with Shipman. At this point, Spenser finally relented and let Maddock mark the remainder of the route and pinpoint the spot where the rockfall hid the secret door.

Grizzly smiled and banged his fist on the table. "That's totally on our land! And you say there's a dungeon there?" His smile stretched from ear to ear as Spenser showed him the photos of the rock pile, door, and dungeon area. "The viewers are going to love this. If we weave in the story of the Mojave Monster, we can make an entire episode just out of this."

"I'm taking notes," Riv said as she worked at her tablet, "so we can circle back to this when it fits our calendar."

Grizzly nodded and beckoned for Spenser to continue the story. His head bobbed like a cork on choppy water as he drank in the details.

"These caverns have got to hide the secret to the lost mine!" he proclaimed.

"Bones and I discussed that earlier," Maddock said. "If it's true, then we have to throw out the old legend and start over from scratch."

"What if there really is a mine underneath an arch somewhere in the area?" Spenser began, "and one of the passageways leads to it?"

"I love that idea," Grizzly said. "Write that down, Riv."

"Way ahead of you, as always," she said with a touch of affection.

"With that as our premise, we can explore the entire cavern system, map it out. There's so much potential there."

Their meals arrived and they continued their conversation around bites of tender prime rib, Yorkshire pudding, and creamed spinach.

They went on to describe the booby trap, the encounter with Reggie, and their narrow escape. The news gave Riv concern, but Grizzly only laughed. "That's just another day at the office for Maddock. The man is bulletproof."

Maddock grinned. "Hardly. And I've got the scars to prove it."

Spenser cast him a sideways glance. "It's not the years, it's the mileage."

"Back to the subject at hand," Riv said. "I can't believe I'm saying this, but there's a great deal of potential here. Is there anything else you found? Unusual? Interesting?"

Spenser frowned. "There was the necklace." She described the discovery.

"Probably just lost by some random hiker," Grizzly said.

"Maybe," Riv said, "but we might be able to get an episode out of it." She frowned and tapped her pursed lips with her stylus. "About ten years ago, a local woman named Megan Keane disappeared. She was a few years ahead of me in school, but I remember it well. Her body was never found but her car was discovered abandoned in the desert not far from the spot where you three found your way out of the caverns."

"That's an awfully thin connection," Grizzly said.

"Of course it is. We'd have to be careful how we presented it, but what if she was searching for the lost mine and Shipman killed her?"

"I think we should slow down." Maddock held up his hands. "Shipman has gone from annoying neighbor to murderer awfully fast, don't you think?"

"He locked us in the caverns to die," Spenser said. "It had to be him. Why else would he have been guarding that path during the race?"

"I'm not saying it wasn't him," Maddock admitted. "I'm only pointing out that we literally have no evidence against him. We can't even prove it was he who locked us in."

"More layers to the mystery," Grizzly said. "I love everything about it. We need to start digging for local legends that could tie into these caverns. Let's set the Arch Mine aside and broaden our search. Any mystery will do as long as there's a plausible connection."

"Define plausible," Spenser said.

"Any connection will do, no matter how thin." He thought for a moment. "I think we should look into the case of the missing girl, too. Just in case there's something there."

"Tread carefully," Riv cautioned. "Her parents still live in the area."

"It occurs to me that Striker is a significant figure in all this," Maddock said. "He's the one who initially bought this land because he believed something valuable was hidden here. He was the first to report men in black in the area, and then decades later we encounter someone dressed the same way."

Grizzly nodded. "He's also the initial source of the ghost and UFO legends on the ranch."

Maddock took a bite of prime rib and chewed slowly, turned the situation over in his mind. "There's something odd about Striker's behavior."

"Something? As in singular?" Riv asked.

"I mean aside from the obvious. If he thought the Arch Gold Mine was somewhere in the area, why let that slip? And why go around telling wild stories that only serve to draw attention to you? If he believed there was gold on his property, wouldn't he go about his business as quietly as possible?"

"Maybe he was crazy," Spenser said.

"Maybe, but we also know he was a successful author and screenwriter—a professional storyteller. What if the Striker the locals thought they knew was just a character of Striker's own creation? A mask he wore to hide some deeper secret?"

An uncomfortable silence fell over the group.

"What kind of secret?" Spenser asked.

"That," Maddock said, "is something I think we need to investigate."

CHAPTER 12

Evening shadows hung low over the valley. The last rays of the setting sun painted the mountains in shades of purple. The desert heat was fast giving way to a cool night. Terry Gold paused to scan the horizon.

"Over there," he pointed. "That's where we'll set up camp."

The spot he'd chosen was no better or worse than the ground upon which they currently stood, but his crew didn't know that, and neither would the viewers who would someday watch this. He was, in fact, an experienced outdoorsman. When not touring, he spent most of his free time hunting, fishing, camping, and even dabbling in a little treasure hunting. It was the treasure hunting that had led to this contest.

He'd been thrilled when his friend had come across tantalizing clues that pointed to the Lost Arch Gold Mine being real. What was more, the clues pointed to its location being in a very different place than where the legends said it was.

It was then, during an intense bout of gold fever, that inspiration had struck. A treasure hunting contest between himself and his longtime rival, Steven Segar. It was an opportunity to expose Segar for a phony, as well as guaranteed income whether they found treasure or not.

"I'm going to go find dinner," he said to no one in particular.

"We've got hot dogs in case you don't kill anything," a young man with shockingly red hair called out to him. Roddy Green was an up and coming actor. He was there to draw in younger viewers.

"Like that would ever happen," Gold said. "And you don't kill your prey, you take it."

"I'm sure that's a comfort to the dead animals."

Muttering a curse under his breath, Gold hefted his rifle and strode out into the dying light.

Up ahead, he spotted a flicker of movement, and something large and furry sprang out from behind a cactus and dashed away. Jackrabbit. A big one, too. And where there was one, there might be more.

"Hold up! I'm coming with you." Roddy came trotting up behind him, carrying a single-shot, bolt-action .22 rifle. It was the only weapon Terry trusted the young man to carry. Because, although Roddy had starred in war and action flicks, he was utterly clueless about weapons.

Gold gritted his teeth. He had hoped the young man would remain behind, along with the camera crew. Watching the actor pitch a tent made for hilarious television. Then again, this was day three of the contest and the joke was growing stale.

"Ace and Platt told me to bring the crew and join you," Roddy said, glancing back at Ray and Becka, the brother-sister duo who handled sound and audio. It was a small team, mobile, and more important, inexpensive.

"I'll have a talk to them when we get back," Gold said. Ace was his best friend, and Platt his son, and both had a mean-spirited sense of humor.

"I thought you had a problem with hunting."

"No, I was just roasting you. So, what are we hunting for?" Roddy asked.

"Peace and quiet."

"I understand," Roddy said. That was apparently a lie, because he went on. "Where do you think Segar is right now?"

"Hampton Inn. I hear they have free breakfast."

Roddy laughed, then turned and gave the camera a thumbs-up. "That's my partner."

Somewhere out of sight, but very close by, a coyote let out a yip. Seconds later, its pack had joined in. To the untrained ear, the high-pitched yelps and yowls sounded unearthly, but they brought a smile to Gold's face.

"Run wild and free, my brothers," he whispered.

"Aren't they dangerous?" Roddy asked.

"Sure, if you're a domestic house cat. But you're not a pussy cat, are you, Roddy?"

Roddy forced a laugh. "Well, I'm no Terry Gold, but hopefully I haven't slowed you down too badly."

Gold reached out and put his arm around the young actor. "Roddy, my friend, it would be impossible for you to slow me down." He paused. "Because I will leave your ass behind in a heartbeat."

Roddy gaped, blinked twice, then guffawed. "You are a trip." He looked around. "We need to do our end of the day talking head. How about over by that boulder pile?"

"Works for me."

When they were positioned satisfactorily, the cameras rolled, and Gold leaped into character.

"All right, all right brothers," he began, leering at the camera, "we've just wrapped up another day of exploration out here in the Mojave Desert. And we are closing in. I can feel it. Terry can smell gold!"

"It's been another amazing day." Roddy paused, frowned.

"What's wrong?" asked Bert, the cameraman.

Gold heard it, too. Something behind them, moving closer in the darkness. He held up a finger to his lips then turned in the direction of the sound. Roddy raised his rifle, too, but Terry grabbed the barrel and pushed it down.

"Nobody does anything unless I say so," Gold whispered. He'd been waiting for just such an opportunity. He looked back at the camera and spoke in a low voice. "When people think of hairy ape men, they think of Bigfoot roaming the rainforests of the Pacific Northwest, or Jason Momoa." *That ought to get us some social media buzz when this comes out.* "But the Mojave has legends of its own. It's had different names over the years: Hairy Man, Sand Man, Yucca man. But there have been reports of these creatures since Native American times." He glanced at Roddy, who nodded.

"In fact, you can find countless newspaper accounts going back to the 1800s. And they paint frightening tales of terror. Let's hope that's not what we're facing right now."

On cue, Gold waved him to silence. They made a show of listening.

The sound came again. Closer this time. Gold turned to the camera and winked. Cool on the outside, but on the inside, he wasn't quite sure what to think. Whatever was out there was no rabbit or coyote, as he'd assumed. It was large. Gold scanned the twilight-shaded hill behind the boulder pile. It was nearly full dark now. The sound came again, but nothing appeared to move.

"It sounds large," Roddy whispered to the camera.

Gold nodded. "And I can't see it, which means it knows how to move around out here without being spotted." His heart raced. What was out there?

And then a dark figure rose atop the boulder pile. Roddy let out a yelp and pointed.

For an instant, Gold was a true believer. And then his eyes adjusted, and he saw it was a woman with long, dark hair and red cowboy boots.

"That was risky," Gold called up to her. "We're armed and my partner here is a nervous Nelly."

"Bigger risk to you," the woman grunted as she clambered down the boulders, "seeing how I'm a police officer." The woman slid down to the ground, paused to dust herself off, then flashed a badge.

"Janet Franzen."

"Terry Gold." He was pleased to see that, though a few decades his junior, Franzen reacted to the name.

"My mom has some of your records," she said.

"Not all of them?" Terry made a sad face for the camera.

"No. She says you went too commercial."

Roddy buried a laugh beneath a stage cough and turned away from the camera.

"May I ask what you gentlemen are doing out here?" Franzen asked.

"That depends. Are you asking in your official capacity, or as a fellow hiker out here enjoying this beautiful place we call America, the land of freedom?" He gave the camera a double thumbs-up.

"I'm asking in whatever capacity will get an honest answer."

Gold nodded. "We're filming a television show. A treasure hunt."

"And you need weapons for that?" Franzen folded her arms and frowned at his rifle.

"Sister, you never know when you might be called upon to take up arms and defend this great nation of ours!" Franzen tilted her head a fraction. Gold could tell no amount of his shtick would charm here. "That was for the benefit of the camera. Seriously, the weapons are props. His isn't even loaded."

Roddy did a double take, then took out his phone, turned on the flashlight, and shone it down the barrel of his rifle. Franzen stared at him for a full three seconds before shaking her head and murmuring, "Darwin."

"My weapons are loaded," Gold continued, "but I'm properly trained and permitted." The words were bitter on his tongue. He hated having to justify exercising his own rights.

"This is private property. Do you have permission of the owner to film here?"

"My representative took care of everything well in advance," he said, inventing on the spot.

Franzen looked them over but appeared satisfied.

"If I can ask you, officer," Gold said, once again looking at the camera. "Have you heard of the Lost Arch Gold Mine?"

Franzen flinched as if Gold had slapped her.

"Never heard of it." She turned and stalked off into the night. "I advise you to steer clear of this area," she called back to them. "We've had reports of armed drug dealers in the area."

Gold waited until he could no longer hear her footsteps then turned to the camera

"And that, brothers and sisters, is what we call a flimsy cover story."

CHAPTER 13

It was going to be a scorcher. The morning sun beat down on the parched earth. Grizzly's Jeep Wrangler bounded along the rough dirt road, sending a cloud of dust up in its wake. Up ahead, low mountains ringed a flat plateau where a lake had once stood. Nestled against a rocky hill stood their destination.

"I can't believe Riv let you off your leash," Bones said.

Grizzly smiled. "I pointed out to her that, when it comes to the adventure race show, there's not really much for me to do outside of hosting. I asked which of her responsibilities she'd like me to take over since I had so much free time. It didn't take her long to decide I should work on developing new projects."

"You're a devious man when you want to be," Bones said.

Giant Rock was a massive, free-standing boulder located in a dry lakebed in the town of Landers, just north of Joshua Tree National Park. They parked nearby and hiked in. Bones marveled at the sight as he and Grizzly slowly approached. A lone figure stood in front of it, lending perspective. Bones shook his head. The thing had to be at least seven stories high. The exterior was muddy gray in color, weathered, and marred in spots by graffiti.

"This thing covers over six thousand square feet," Grizzly said. "It's either the largest free-standing boulder in North America or in the world, depending on who's doing the measuring."

"It's impressive," Bones agreed. A section of boulder had sheared away, but even this broken piece was a good twenty feet tall at its higher end.

Where the section had fallen away, it exposed smooth, white granite streaked with desert varnish. "I hate to see the way it's been mistreated, though," he said, looking at the many names carved or spray painted on the surface.

"I'm sure the local natives feel the same way," Grizzly said. "This site is sacred to them." He glanced up. "That must be the guy we're meeting. The biographer."

Up ahead, the person who had been standing beside Giant Rock turned and waved. Bones did a double-take when he saw the man's face.

"No freaking way," he said. "Nigel Gambles."

Nigel Gambles was a slim man with short hair and an easy smile. An Englishman by birth, he now resided in Florida. An author and an expert in the field of cryptozoology, he and Bones had met on a previous occasion, while Bones was searching for the Florida Skunk Ape.

"Bones Bonebrake! I always hoped our paths would cross again, but I expected it would happen closer to home."

They shook hands, then Bones introduced Grizzly.

"I was pleased, and more than a bit flattered to receive your call," Gambles said.

"We appreciate your time," Grizzly said. "How is it that you two already know one another?"

"We met through Joanna Slater. You might know her; she is also a television presenter in your field," Gambles explained.

Grizzly's face went blank. "We know one another."

"So, you're the guy who's writing a biography of Kirk Striker," Bones said to Gambles, steering the conversation away from the subject of Slater, for whom Grizzly could never quite manage to conceal his envy.

"That's correct. I've written non-fiction, but never a biography. And Striker is a fascinating subject. I've been living in Salton for over a year. I purchased one of Rockwell's lots. If you can ignore the foul-smelling air, it makes for a nice little second home. I've also uncovered plenty of mysteries and legends for future projects. The

Mojave is a fascinating and mysterious place."

"You've certainly chosen an unusual place for us to meet," Bones said as they began a circuit of the giant stone.

"I chose this place not only because it's interesting, but because you wanted to try and understand Striker's eccentricities. And I believe that begins with his father." Gambles paused, looked out at the parched horizon. "Kirk Striker was born Jacob Critzer."

"Sounds German," Bones said.

"He was the son of Frank Critzer, a German immigrant. A man who came to be known as the Cave Man of Giant Rock."

"You have my full attention," Bones said. Knowing Gambles' fascination with the odd and unexplained, he had no doubt this story was going to be right up his alley. Grizzly was also listening with rapt attention.

"Frank Critzer was by all accounts a brilliant but highly eccentric man. A restless type who moved around a lot, he came to this area in the 1930s and was immediately drawn to a place the Native Americans called Great Stone." Gambles inclined his head toward Giant Rock. "I don't know when, exactly, he and his family parted ways, but it's certain that by the time he arrived here, his son, the man we know as Kirk Striker, was no longer in his life. Critzer literally made a home here in a cave he tunneled out underneath the rock."

"Really?" Bones asked. "Can we see it?"

"Afraid not. It was eventually filled in. Photographs have survived, though. It was a simple, one-room apartment with carpet and standard furnishings. But it wasn't the cave home that made Critzer notorious."

"What was it, then?" Grizzly asked.

"First of all, he was a German, which didn't win him any popularity contests. He was also a short-wave radio enthusiast, even constructed a tall antenna in the rocks. That, plus sighting of strange crafts in the skies around Giant Rock, sparked rumors that he was a Nazi agent.

"He was a cantankerous fellow, always armed, chased away anyone who came too close to his home."

"That's rich, considering he was squatting on someone else's sacred site," Bones said.

Gambles and Grizzly nodded in unison.

On the far side of the rock stood a trio of boulders. On their own, any of the three would have impressed, but their appearance was almost apologetic standing in the shadow of giant rock. Gambles wandered toward the smallest stone, his eyes cloudy.

"This place has an odd effect on people. It draws them like a magnet. The Hopi tell tales of journeys made to this place to worship. Shamans returned here again and again to draw spiritual power on behalf of their people. Some even say this stone is the beating heart of Mother Earth. New Age spiritualists claim this is a site of powerful magnetic vortices. It's also a UFO hotspot. I think Critzer was sucked in just like so many people before him. Over time, he became more reclusive and paranoid. In addition to the UFO sightings, he claimed to be developing advanced technologies and synthetic materials, which he claimed the government wanted to steal from him. He said he was frequently shadowed by men in black."

"Sounds like Striker," Bones observed.

Gambles nodded. "In Critzer's case, it became a self-fulfilling prophecy. He was suspected of stealing large quantities of gasoline and dynamite from railroad depots and mines in the area. Locals also blamed him for several disappearances in the area, though nothing was ever proven. Finally, he came to the attention of the FBI. It culminated in July 1942 when Critzer died during a raid on his home. Depending on which version you believe, Critzer either blew himself up or was inadvertently killed when a tear gas grenade was dropped through a ventilation shaft and ignited an open case of dynamite."

Bones contemplated the story in silence for a few moments. Either version was plausible.

"So, Critzer's story has ended. Where does Striker's begin?"

"Striker was desperate to distance himself from Critzer, due to his reputation and his German ancestry. He changed his name, moved to Hollywood, and pounded out a living writing pulp adventure novels. He admitted to drawing inspiration from tales his father told him as a young boy. He moved at the fringes of Hollywood circles, trying desperately to make it as a screenwriter. All the while he lived in fear."

"Afraid his father's reputation would catch up with him?" Bones asked.

"Not only that, but he learned that some form of madness ran in the male side of his family. He never interacted with his father, but he kept tabs on him from a distance. And the more bizarre Critzer became, the more convinced Striker became that he would suffer the same fate."

"And then his dad goes and blows himself up," Bones said.

"I think that was the nudge that really pushed Striker over the edge. To his peers, he seemed his normal self. He was churning out novels and screenplays, rubbing elbows with the rich and famous. But he was leading a double life. He began making treks out into the desert, first here, and then other places, wherever the spirits guided him."

"Was he searching for the Arch Gold Mine?" Bones asked.

"It's possible, but according to my research, his interests were broader than that. He was interested in pre-Columbian contact, legends related to Spanish explorers, Native American tales of mystery and treasure. The sorts of things he would write about in his screenplays or his adventure novels."

"Is it possible that's all it was?" Grizzly asked. "Just research?"

"Maybe. In any case he stopped writing almost immediately after he'd finally achieved his dream of having one of his screenplays produced for the big screen. In 1949 he dropped everything and moved out to his so-called UFO Ranch. Which you now own."

"Do you think that move was somehow connected to his father?" Bones asked. "Maybe Critzer had found clues to a treasure. He was a miner, after all. That might have been what the stolen dynamite was for."

"It's not impossible," Gambles said. "But although I believe Striker's reason for leaving Hollywood was linked to his father, I don't think it had anything to do with treasure hunting."

"Why do you think he moved here?" Grizzly asked.

No one else was about, but still Gambles paused, looked around, then lowered his voice.

"I believe Kirk Striker was the Black Dahlia killer."

CHAPTER 14

The following morning, Maddock and Spenser paid a visit to the parents of the missing girl. Spenser was still friendly, but her previous warmth was absent. She focused on navigating and had little else to say.

Hank and Nancy Keane lived in a modest house that was part of Rockwell's new development. The exterior was brightly painted. The inside was a different story. The curtains were drawn, the living room lit by a pair of table lamps with low wattage bulbs that emitted a sickly yellow light.

There was no need to come up with a way of broaching the subject of their missing daughter. Framed photos of Megan Keane hung from every wall and stood on virtually every level surface. A bookcase in the corner of the room held trophies, mementos, a graduation portrait, and a stuffed unicorn. Maddock's heart leapt at the sight of the toy. Spenser saw it too and shrugged.

"A lot of girls like unicorns," she said quietly as the Keanes headed to the kitchen for coffee and cookies.

They spent a few minutes in polite conversation, first explaining in broad strokes the premise of Grizzly's investigative show, and then sharing a bit about themselves.

Hank was a retired police officer and a veteran himself, of the Marine Corps variety. He and Maddock light-heartedly agreed to avoid any Navy versus Marine discussions. Nancy was a retired psychotherapist. Her face was drawn, her brown hair streaked with silver. She sat wringing her hands as they spoke.

"We don't talk about Megan very often," she said as Maddock brought the conversation around to their intended topic. "It's too painful."

"But we hope that a television show might help turn up some new clues. Maybe jog someone's memory,"

Hank said.

"What was Megan like?" Spenser asked.

"She had an inquisitive mind," Hank said. "She loved puzzles, mysteries, anything that required logic and reasoning."

"We expected her to go into law enforcement as a detective," Nancy said. "I discouraged her because I thought it was too dangerous." She let out a tiny sob.

"What career did she choose?" Maddock asked.

"Journalism. She earned her degree from San Diego State and was working as a freelancer, mostly writing about places of local interest."

Maddock perked up at that. "Do you know what she was working on before she went missing?"

"The police examined her laptop. They didn't find anything they thought was pertinent, but we'll be happy to give you printouts of what she was working on."

"That would be very helpful," Maddock said.

"Do you know if she had any interest in the Arch Gold Mine?" Spenser asked.

Hank and Nancy looked at one another then shook their heads.

"Doesn't ring a bell," Hank said.

At Maddock's request they described Megan's movements on the last day they'd seen her. She'd left early, saying she was going to do some research for a new article. They didn't worry about her until night fell and they hadn't heard from her and were unable to reach her. They notified the police and waited.

"And we're still waiting," Nancy said. "We've done what we can, of course. Followed up on the places she was researching for her articles, talked with her friends, made public pleas. Nothing."

"They did find her vehicle, right?" Maddock asked.

"Yes. Out in the desert. No tracks, no clues, no evidence left behind," Hank said.

"Could she have been investigating something out in the desert?" Maddock asked.

"Not as far as we know. Of course, I don't believe

she parked the car there. The steering wheel, ignition, and door handles had been wiped clean of fingerprints. Hell, even the handle that adjusts the seat had been cleaned."

Maddock nodded sympathetically. It seemed clear what the young woman's fate had been.

"Did your daughter know Bryce Shipman?" Spenser asked.

Nancy flinched. Hank sat up straighter.

"She knew who he was, had probably spoken to him on occasion, same as any local. But the police investigated thoroughly and could find nothing that connected him to Megan."

"Except that her car was found close to his house."

"Close is a relative term," Hank said. "It was still a long hike through some rough terrain."

Nancy let out an angry breath. "Shipman murdered our daughter."

"You don't know that," Hank said gently.

"I know him." She threw a challenging look at her husband. "That's enough."

"What can you tell us about him?" Spenser asked gently.

"Nancy," Hank warned.

"What are they going to do? Take my license? I'm retired." She turned back to Spenser. "Shipman booked a counseling session with me. Oh, he didn't call it counseling, said he was conducting research for a novel, but it was clearly a therapy session wrapped in a flimsy cover story."

"What kinds of things did he talk about?" Maddock asked.

"He wanted to talk about murder. Specifically, its impact on the children of murderers. I'm a child and family therapist, and he thought I might be able to offer some insight on whether or not those sorts of criminal tendencies tended to be passed along to future generations."

"Nature versus nurture?" Maddock asked.

"Exactly, but he was mostly interested in whether or not there was a genetic component. Did serial killers tend to beget serial killers? Could tendencies toward violence be inherited? What forms of mental illness were hereditary?"

"In fairness, all of that does sound like the sort of research a murder mystery writer might conduct," Spenser said.

"I was there. I saw it in his eyes. The intensity. The need to know. This subject was very personal to him. And he never married, even though he had plenty of prospects, especially after he hit the bestseller lists."

"So, you think Shipman is a murderer and was worried about passing his traits along to any children he might have?" Spenser asked.

"Or maybe he's the offspring of a murderer and was dealing with murderous impulses," Nancy said. "He fought it for as long as he could but eventually…"

"I want to emphasize this is all conjecture," Hank said.

"Please, he was always quizzing you about police procedure."

"He's an author. He wanted his books to be as accurate as possible."

"Or maybe he wanted to know how to get away with murder," Nancy replied.

Maddock looked at Spenser, who nodded back. It was time. He paused, wondering if he was about to turn the grieving parents' lives upside down.

"There's a reason we are researching Megan's story as part of the television show." He went on to describe the series of caverns they'd discovered, and the necklace they'd found.

Spenser took out her phone and called up one of the photographs she'd taken. She held it up for them to see.

"Is there any chance this belonged to your daughter?"

Nancy let out a wail and buried her face in her

hands. Hank looked poleaxed. He reached out a trembling hand and took the phone from Spenser. He and his wife gazed at it for a full minute before he nodded.

"Yes. That's Megan's necklace. How can I find these caverns?"

"You don't want to go there right now," Maddock said. "We've turned the necklace over to the police and I'm sure they're going to investigate."

"Not likely," Hank said, "but I'll pay them a visit."

"It's so strange," Nancy said. Tears streamed down her face as she gazed at the image. "It's like the years never passed, and I'm grieving her loss all over again."

"We're truly sorry for the pain we've caused you," Maddock said. "I've lost a lot of people I loved, but never had to wonder about what happened to them. I figured if I were in your position, I'd want all the information I could get."

"You did the right thing," Hank said, handing back the phone. "We appreciate you coming to see us."

After assuring the Keanes that they would keep them apprised of any new discoveries, he and Spenser bade them goodbye.

"Well," Spenser said as they squeezed into her Smart car, "Shipman is not looking very good, is he?"

"I don't know," Maddock said.

"Are you kidding me?" She tossed back her golden locks and turned a puzzled frown his way. "He literally tried to kill us by locking us in the dungeon room, or have you forgotten that?"

"Assuming it was him, which we don't know for certain, that doesn't mean he killed Megan Keane a decade ago. He might just be an overzealous treasure hunter. Gold fever makes a person do strange things. For all we know, he did it on an impulse, came back to let us out, and we were already gone."

"Bones is right," she said as they turned onto the main road that ran along the seashore. "You can be a real Pollyanna sometimes."

"I'm just saying I wouldn't want to be convicted on so little evidence and I don't think you would either."

They lapsed into silence. Spenser turned on the radio just as Chris Cornell belted out the first lines of *Burden in My Hand*.

Follow me into the desert, as thirsty as you are.

Spenser grinned. "That's a fitting soundtrack for the day we had."

"How's that?" Maddock asked.

"Seriously? It's about a man who murders a woman and leaves her body in the desert."

Maddock hadn't ever paid much attention to the lyrics. "So, it's sort of a *Cocaine Blues* for a younger generation."

Spenser rolled her eyes.

"Now what did I say?"

"The song is almost as old as I am. It's not like you're fifty."

Maddock smiled, a small, sad thing. "I've seen a lot, been through a lot. I'm old on the inside."

"I'm going to make it my business to bring out the young man that's trapped inside you."

Maddock wasn't sure

CHAPTER 15

The UFO ranch was a ghost town when Orry Rockwell pulled into the parking area. There were no vehicles to be seen, no one milling about. The silence was eerie after the bustle of the race just a few days before. He parked his Subaru in the only available shady spot, on the far side of a storage building, and headed to the ranch house. He knocked but no one answered. Damn. The one time he actually wanted to talk to Grizzly and the man was nowhere to be found. He was probably out on the racecourse somewhere, fine-tuning one of the obstacles.

Sighing, he took out a folded map of the ranch—a leftover from the race. He scanned it, took a few seconds to get his bearings, then set out across the dirt parking lot. A sudden gust of wind, hot and dusty, swept in, sending tumbleweeds rolling across his path. The sight brought back childhood memories. He smiled and shook his head. Of all the things to get nostalgic about.

He followed a steep path that wound into the hills that surrounded the ranch. The footing was iffy and the going slow. Good thing he'd come dressed for a hike, including proper footwear. When he crested the first hill he paused, took out a pair of mini-binoculars, and scanned the horizon. Still no sign of them. Of course, he could only see a couple of obstacles from here. He'd have to keep moving.

Twenty minutes and a few tall hills later and he still hadn't spotted anyone. He checked his map again, then gave the binoculars another try. This time he spotted something. A hunched figure moving along a rocky trail.

"Who are you and why are you sneaking?" Rockwell whispered aloud. He tucked away his binoculars and set off at a quick jog. He was a triathlete, an adventure racer, and experienced outdoorsman. He was confident he'd could catch up with this fellow in no time without giving himself away.

The way grew steeper and the path narrower until it vanished completely. But by this time, he had caught up with his quarry.

It was Bryce Shipman!

The man was decked out in khakis and a brown cap, and wore an olive-green backpack, perfect for blending in against the backdrop of the parched landscape. He no longer skulked but moved with a confident stride.

Rockwell wasn't remotely frightened of Shipman, but something told him to remain out of sight. The man was up to something, and Rockwell wanted to know what it was. Like a cougar stalking its prey, he trailed Shipman, slipping easily behind boulders, juniper, and even the occasional cactus. The man never noticed. It was too easy.

Finally, Shipman came to a halt at a steep rock face. He stopped to take a drink of water and don a pair of gloves before beginning the climb. He moved with a grace and agility Rockwell had not expected. A minute later, he was out of sight.

Rockwell waited two minutes before following. It was a gamble. He didn't know what waited at the top of the wall. Shipman might be right there waiting for him. But he couldn't risk losing his quarry.

He scrambled up the cliff quickly and quietly, paused at the top, just out of sight, to listen.

All was quiet.

Heart in his throat, he put a hand over the top of the ledge and pulled himself up. His subconscious conjured images of Shipman standing above him, some sort of weapon raised. But would Shipman really do something like that? Rockwell wasn't sure. Perhaps it had been a bad idea to put himself in such a vulnerable position.

All of this flashed through his mind in the time it took for him to pull himself up and peer over the ledge.

Shipman wasn't there. He let out a relieved breath and climbed up onto the ledge.

Before him stood a huge rock pile, the boulders loosely stacked, forming narrow passageways throughout.

"He must have gone in there."

Rockwell crept over to the closest passageway, knelt, and peered inside. He could only see a few feet in before the passageway took a sharp right. It would be like a maze in there, and no telling what or who he'd run into. Perhaps it was juvenile of him, but the idea excited him. He fished out his pocketknife and opened the largest blade. It wasn't much, but at close quarters it might make a difference should he run into something nasty. Heart racing, he got down and crawled into the darkness.

As he worked his way deeper into the warren of passageways, he began to feel foolish. There were plenty of reasons Shipman might be poking around here that didn't involve anything sinister. Sure, he'd been sneaking around, but maybe he simply didn't want to be spotted trespassing on Grizzly's property—property that had, until recently, belonged to Shipman.

Orry, you're going to feel like an idiot if you come out on the other side to find Shipman worshiping at a magnetic vortex.

The thought had scarcely passed his mind when he heard a squeak and a metallic clang, followed closely by a muttered curse.

"What could that possibly be?"

Rockwell followed the sound, squeezing himself through narrow crevasses, banging his head on low rocks, and several times being forced to double back. When he finally came out on the other side, Shipman was nowhere to be seen, but there was little doubt as to where he had gone.

Set in the stone was a bizarre-looking iron door. Rockwell couldn't help but make a closer inspection. Its hard surface was pitted, its edges roughly hewn. He assumed it would be locked, but when he tried it, it swung back an inch.

He froze, remembering the squeak it had made. No sense sounding the alarm. Bit by bit he nudged it open until he could peer inside. A sliver of sunlight shone a narrow beam across a small, dungeon-like room. On the opposite side was a small tunnel. Where it led, who could say.

Rockwell slowly closed the door, took a few steps back, and mopped his brow. He stared at the door, shook his head.

"This," he said to himself, "can only be a bad thing."

He only wished he knew what to do about it.

CHAPTER 16

The Joshua Tree Saloon was a short drive from Giant Rock. Billed as the Gateway to Joshua Tree National Park, the iconic restaurant was a tourist-friendly joint with an Old West aesthetic. The exterior looked like a set out of an old television western. Before they stepped inside, they were greeted by upbeat music and the savory aroma of grilled meat.

"Nice choice," Bones said. It was a typical bar environment, with lots of worn wood, from the floors to the furnishings to the beams supporting the ceiling. "If I'm going to listen to a long story, it's always better to do it over a beer.

They took seats at the bar and Grizzly sprang for a round of Hangar 24 Betty, a California-brewed IPA. The label featured an old-school prop plane. Its nose art depicted a classic Hollywood-era blonde bombshell in a blue dress and red heels.

"She's a real Betty," Grizzly said, admiring his bottle.

Bones ordered a Mineshaft Burger, medium rare, but only after registering his complaint that the All-American Beef Dip was served on a *French* roll. The bartender, a purple-haired Latina, was not amused.

"She's going to spit on your burger," Grizzly whispered as she put in their order.

"Nah, she laughed," Bones said.

"I think that was a wince." Grizzly took a drink, frowned. "Remind me again what you have against the French?"

"Screw the French."

Gambles raised his bottle. "I concur," the Englishman said.

"You guys are hopeless," Grizzly said. "Jean-Claude Van Damme is French, and he's awesome."

"He's not French," Gambles said. "He's from Belgium."

"That's right," Bones said. "The muscles from Brussels."

Grizzly stared at Bones for a full three seconds. "You're serious? I thought that was… never mind."

"No, you have to tell us," Bones said.

Grizzly hung his head. "I thought it was because Brussel sprouts were a big part of his training diet. It's how he got pumped up." He tapped his bicep.

Bones and Gambles exchanged a pitying smile.

"Don't worry," Bones said. "Your secret is safe with us."

Their meals arrived, and as they dug into the juicy burgers, the conversation returned to Kirk Striker and the bombshell Gambles had dropped.

"The Black Dahlia killer?" Bones asked. "That's difficult to believe."

The Black Dahlia was the name that had been given posthumously to Elizabeth Short, an aspiring actress who was found murdered in Los Angeles in 1947. Due to the graphic nature of the crime, the case had quickly gained notoriety.

The ensuing police investigation was exhaustive. Over one hundred fifty suspects were identified, but no one was ever arrested. Elizabeth Short, whose face had been mutilated and her torso cut in half, quickly became the subject of all sorts of lurid gossip. It was from one such story that the Black Dahlia moniker had sprung. Over time, the unsolved mystery grew to legend status, and the Black Dahlia became a part of the cultural lexicon.

"Why hard to believe?" Gambles asked. "Someone has to be the killer. Why not Striker?"

"I think the better question would be, why Striker?"

"Please understand I don't make this accusation recklessly. I've done a great deal of research on this."

"We're all ears," Grizzly said.

"The police didn't believe the so-called Black Dahlia

was the victim of a serial killer because no other victims turned up in the same condition as that poor girl. I asked myself, what if there were other victims killed with a similar MO, but the bodies were never found? So, I started digging through missing persons reports and I came up with several young women who were either new to Hollywood, or on their way to Hollywood but never arrived."

"What makes you think there's any connection to Striker?" Bones asked.

"First of all, the time frame fits. Second, all the missing girls were aspiring actresses, and of those who never reached Hollywood, all were last seen east of here. Striker was well known for romancing naive young girls with Hollywood dreams. He was a successful author and always hanging around with Hollywood types. They all assumed he was a mover and shaker in the industry."

Bones chewed his burger, nodded to show he was listening.

"I can't link all of them to Striker, but I've made a few connections." He took out his phone and called up a set of notes. "The first was a young woman named Marian Gray. Early twenties, wavy dark hair, even looked a little bit like Elizabeth Short. She disappeared in July 1942. A week after the death of Striker's father. She was last seen in the Salton area."

"I like it so far," Grizzly said.

Bones was unmoved, but he knew Grizzly was approaching the story from a television standpoint. In the sorts of mystery and conspiracy shows he produced, what Bones saw as a flimsy set of coincidences might seem like interesting connections in the minds of viewers.

"Six months later, five years before the Black Dahlia murder, a young actress named Jane Strine disappeared without a trace. Her family back east was concerned, but when the police investigated, her friends agreed that she ran away with a rich guy she met in a club. One of the friends who repeated that story to the police was Kirk

Striker."

"Okay, I'll give you that one," Bones said. "It's a connection, but it's tenuous."

"May I beg you for a modicum of faith and a measure of patience?" Gambles asked.

"Sorry. I'll shut up and listen."

"The victims follow a pattern of every six months. Not to the day, but close. Victim number three is another missing actress. I found a photograph of her at a party, laughing with Kirk Striker. His arm is around her in a possessive way."

"Score another one," Grizzly said.

"I could find no connections between Striker and the next two missing girls, save that the timing is right, and they fit the profile."

"I don't get it," Grizzly said. "Why didn't the police recognize this pattern?"

"You have to consider the times. Before cell phones and the Internet, it wasn't unusual to go long stretches without speaking to someone who lived in another part of the country. And in the case of a young person with an independent spirit and a sense of adventure, you might go years without hearing from them, and you might not consider that unusual."

Bones understood the logic. These days, packing up and moving to Hollywood was a cliché. Back in the 1940s, it was different, especially for young women who were confined to very specific social roles. He imagined a lot of the parents were so ashamed that they might not have wanted to hear from their daughters again.

"Most of the time, if an aspiring actor or actress disappeared, the general assumption was he or she had given up the Hollywood dream and gone back home. And you didn't have social media to check in on old acquaintances."

"That makes sense," Grizzly said. "Have you discussed television rights with anyone?"

"Let him finish," Bones said.

Gambles grinned. "I won't list every person I've

identified, but one of the more interesting cases is not a missing person, but an actual murder victim. Well, I say she was murdered. She was found in the wilderness in the Joshua Tree area. Scavengers had gotten to her body by the time it was found, but she'd been cut in half at the waist, just like the Black Dahlia. Of course, this was a few years before the Black Dahlia murder, so there was nothing to make a connection to, and the local police treated it as a terrible accident. The official report is that she suffered a fall from a great distance, and the animals did the rest."

"But you don't think so?" Grizzly asked.

"She was last seen in Flagstaff, hitchhiking to LA. As far as anyone knows, she never arrived. I doubt she took a side trip into the desert to do a little climbing. But here's what makes it so interesting. One of the reasons police were so quick to close the case was the persistent rumor going around that the victim was killed by a Desert Reaper."

"What the hell is that?" Bones asked.

"It's a cryptid. It's sort of like a velociraptor, but it has chameleon-like skin and it has a sickle-like claw on each hand."

Bones and Grizzly exchanged frowns.

"Never heard of it," Grizzly said.

"Neither have I," Bones said.

"That's because it only exists in one place—in Kirk Striker's debut adventure novel. Which very few people read."

"Whoa!" Bones said. "So, you think Striker killed her, did his usual number on her, and when the body was found, he put out that story as a cover?"

Gambles shrugged. "It makes a certain, twisted sense." He glanced at his notes again. "And then, six months before the Black Dahlia murder, the body of a young waitress was found caught up in fishing nets. She had been cut in two. The authorities assumed her body had been cut in half posthumously, perhaps caught up in 'anchor lines or some other sort of rope' was their speculation. Their words, not mine."

"And the connection to Striker?" Bones asked.

"According to her coworkers, her best customer was a flashy guy who was always boasting about his industry connections and promised to get her a job when his adventure movie began production. Those are the connections I was able to make." Gambles put his phone away.

"Here is my theory. I think Striker did suffer from the madness that plagued so many men in his family. His father's death triggered something in his mind, and he began his ritual of taking a victim once every six months, for reasons I haven't puzzled out. Most of the time, he managed to make the victims disappear permanently. That is easily done in this part of the world. But as his madness grew, he got careless. When Elizabeth Short's body was found, the media firestorm put the pressure on him. He tried to stop, but he couldn't."

"He took a big risk staying in Hollywood after that," Bones observed.

"I think he knew he was getting close to the film deal he'd been working so hard for. He tried to make it work, tried to battle the darker part of his nature. He held on until his movie was finally made. And then, unable to take the pressure, he fled to the desert, leaving his old life behind. Mostly."

"Did the killings continue?" Bones asked.

"I believe they did. I've found no other crimes I can connect him with, even tangentially, but there are plenty of disappearances that match the profile. They are few and far between, though. Always in January. I think he battled against the darker aspects of his nature until the very end."

Bones ordered another round of drinks and they sat discussing Gambles' theory. Bones found it persuasive but couldn't see how it connected to what was happening on the ranch today.

"Do you think Striker was any kind of treasure hunter, or was it all just a cover for his true identity?"

"Oh, he was a treasure hunter. Always out in the hills, always collecting stories. Looking at old books and newspapers. It was in his blood. That's probably why he wrote adventure novels."

"That's unsettling," Grizzly said. "To think that a fellow adventurer could harbor such a dark side."

"Believe me, I've met a few." Bones turned back to Gambles. "Can you give us any idea what he was looking for out there? Any clue at all?"

Gambles considered the question for a long time. "I'll go back and review my research, see if anything catches my attention that seemed unimportant before. I remember thinking he was putting heavy emphasis on Spanish gold and treasure fleets. Of course, that's not surprising in this part of the world."

Bones took another drink and tried to view the mystery from an entirely different point of view. He put the treasure aside in his mind and tried to imagine the ranch from inside the mind of a compulsive murderer.

"The dungeon!" he said. "What if it had nothing to do with the so-called Mojave Monster? Maybe Striker built it for his own reasons." He hastily described the little cave he and Maddock had discovered.

Gambles perked up right away. "I would love to see it."

"We can arrange that," Grizzly said.

"Hold on," Bones said. "Do you know anything about Bryce Shipman?" he asked.

"Not really. I interviewed him briefly when I first started my research, but he didn't know much about Striker, aside from his novels."

"That's not true," Grizzly said quickly. "He's fascinated by Striker. Just ask around."

Gambles nodded, scratched his chin thoughtfully. "I wonder why he lied to me."

"I just think it's interesting that he shows up, buys Striker's land, learns all he can about him, follows his career path, and now he's out wandering the same hills Striker did."

"When you put it like that," Gambles said, "that certainly casts things in a darker light."

CHAPTER 17

The folds of the cliff sheltered a shallow cave. The walls were soot-stained from centuries of campfires, miners and Native American hunters, probably. Steven Segar made a show of examining every inch, although he could tell right away that it was a dead end.

"No garbage, no graffiti," he said for the benefit of the camera. "I think it's safe to say this place has gone untouched by modern man."

"Do you think this might have been a stop on the way to the gold mine?" Yoshi, his cameraman, prompted. Without a script, Segar had struggled to keep up the kind of narrative expected in this sort of show. There was no time to stop and write everything out for him, so the crew had taken to nudging him in the right direction from time to time.

"Absolutely." He began inventing wildly. "This is the sort of place a miner always looked for. It's high up on the mountainside, safe from predators. It's also the kind of place that could hide a secret passageway. Perhaps an entrance to a lost mine."

He began a circuit of the rock shelter, scrutinizing every inch, pressing on every bumpy surface until his hands were blackened with soot. Then he scanned every inch of the floor, pacing back and forth, covering every inch like a treasure-hunting ship working a grid out on the sea.

"What are you looking for?" Yoshi asked. "Anything specific?"

"A secret door, a symbol that might be a clue, a trapdoor hidden in the floor."

"How would you locate something like that?"

"If I fall through the floor, I'll know I've found it."

There was no trapdoor, and Yoshi finally stopped filming. "Mister Segar, we've got to give them something better than this. We haven't turned up a single clue."

Segar understood. The reality of treasure hunting wasn't as exciting as viewers might like. He looked around, searching for inspiration.

"Give me five minutes."

He moved to the deepest part of the rock shelter, took out his knife, and gouged a rough map into the wall. Mounds to represent hills, a jagged peak that probably matched no mountain in the area, and an arch with an X marking the spot. Next, he rubbed some ash and dirt into the grooves. Finally satisfied, he washed his hands, smoothed his hair, and called to Yoshi.

"I found something. Let's take it from the top."

He cleared his throat, found his mark, and waited for Yoshi to give the word.

"In 1848, while searching for water, Jim Fish and his partner, Crocker, took shelter in a place very much like this one. Let's take a look."

He repeated his examination of the cave, this time doing a better job of making it interesting. He talked about hidden clues and secret passageways. And then he reached the back of the overhang.

He let out a gasp, clutched his chest, then dropped down to his knees.

"According to the story of a priest who gave Fish his last rites, the miner carved a map on the rock wall, but he was never able to find the rock shelter again." It was all nonsense, but Segar had written a few screenplays that he someday hoped to produce and had even penned a novel that was an Amazon bestseller in Native American Action Thrillers, or something like that. "That might seem hard to believe, but look at this."

He moved aside so the camera could zoom in. He drew his Bowie knife and used it to point to the lines on the map.

"This is clearly an arch." He tapped the image with the tip of his knife. "And X marks the spot. The question is, how do we get there from here? There's no compass rose, so we can't orient ourselves in the traditional way.

This means we'll have to find one of the spots on this map." He pretended to consider the conundrum. "This hill," he tapped a low mound with a few oddly shaped boulders at its base, "looks like a turtle to me. The hill is the shell, these boulders are the head and legs, and this jagged mark is the tail." He turned and gave the camera his most thoughtful look. "Legend has always placed the Arch Gold Mine in the Turtle Mountain area. That's not especially close by, which is why we are among the first to ever seek it in this part of the Mojave. Perhaps this rock is the reason the treasure became associated with that place."

He stood, walked slowly back out into the sunlight, and stood on the ledge, staring out at the hills. "I find that meditation helps me focus." He sat cross-legged, closed his eyes, and took a few cleansing breaths.

"Do you want us to film you meditating?" Yoshi asked.

Segar opened one eye. "I'm not actually going to meditate. Just stop talking and let me work."

"Yes, sir."

Segar practiced meditation on a daily basis. He'd invented his own technique: an amalgam of the practices of his Native American ancestors and the various martial arts disciplines he'd studied. For the sake of the camera, he opted for the stereotypical "Ohhm!" After a few repetitions he opened his eyes and stood. The studio would edit the footage to make it look like he'd spent time in reflection.

"As I look out on this forbidding landscape, I can't help but wonder how Fish and Crocker felt, standing in this very spot, knowing they had to cross all of this or perish. And knowing that they were leaving behind the treasure of a lifetime."

"That was perfect," Yoshi said. "Now, there's one more thing I'd like to do before we leave here."

Just then, Segar heard a shuffling sound behind him. He turned around and saw a man in a black suit and mirrored sunglasses appear from the rocks. He strode toward them, a pistol in his hand.

His heart leapt! His crew had hired an extra to play a man in black. What a brilliant idea.

"Hands in the air!" the man ordered.

Segar knew this was the time he should utter a memorable line, something wise but also badass. They should have forewarned him so he could plan something suitable for the occasion, but he supposed that would have impacted the authenticity of the moment. That was fine. They wanted to see the real Steve Segar in action and that's exactly what they would get.

As a lifelong practitioner of martial arts, he was trained to remain calm in any situation, especially one that wasn't real.

"You are making a big mistake, friend." He began to walk calmly toward the armed man. "I know everyone sees me as a sex symbol, but I'm so much more. I'm a writer, an actor, a martial artist, a spiritualist, but most of all, I'm a warrior."

"What the hell are you talking about?" The man leveled his pistol at Segar's head.

"I'm going to help you find the right path. And you can take that to the bank; the blood bank!"

"Listen fat man…"

He should have pulled the punch so it just missed. The camera couldn't tell the difference. But he was not about to let a disrespectful little punk ad-lib like that. His fist caught the man full on the jaw and he went down in a heap.

"Never go off script with me."

In a flash, two of his team had the fellow pinned to the ground. Segar calmly picked up the fallen pistol and tucked it into his belt.

"The safety," Yoshi whispered. "You might want to check it before you lose a little something down there."

Segar laughed. "Like you guys would have given him a real gun."

"What are you talking about?"

A cold flash turned Segar's skin to ice. He felt a

fluttering in his pelvic region and prayed his bladder wouldn't release. It had been real? All of it?

"What should we do with him, sir?" one of the crew asked.

Segar thought fast. He couldn't kill the guy, nor could they afford to stop filming while they hauled him out and dealt with law enforcement.

"Let him go," Segar said.

They did as they were told, and the bewildered man climbed slowly to his feet and dusted himself off.

"We don't want any trouble, friend, but if you bother us again, we'll be forced to take steps."

"You got me on camera? What the hell is this?"

"This is your chance to turn your life around. I advise you take it." He spun the young man around and gave him a shove. The fellow hurried away, muttering something about "losing another one."

"Shouldn't we have at least asked him what he was doing wandering around out here armed and dressed like that?" Darren, one of his crew mates, asked.

That probably would have been the wiser course, but it was too late now.

"I gave him a clean slate. The past doesn't matter."

Segar grinned. The gravity of the situation was finally dawning on him. He'd taken down an armed enemy with one punch. On camera, and not in a movie. It was for real. He really was a warrior.

"Somebody's coming," Darren warned.

Everyone took cover while Segar took out a pair of binoculars and zoomed in on the group that was making its way along an arroyo far below them. He recognized the leader's angular face, lean build, long stringy hair, and trademark cowboy hat.

"It's Terry!" he said.

"Should we hide until he's gone?" Darren asked.

"No. Let him see us but pretend we don't see him."

Segar stood and scanned the horizon with the binoculars. One by one the others stood and pretended to be in the middle of filming a scene.

"They saw us," Darren whispered. "They just ducked down out of sight. Wait, I see a flash of light. Somebody's got binoculars on us."

Segar grinned. "Perfect!" He tucked his own binoculars away and turned to the camera. "I think we've learned all we can from this place. Let's resume our search before any more trouble finds us."

"Before we go, do you have any thoughts on what just happened?" Yoshi asked him. "That was a dangerous situation we were in and you dispatched the guy like it was nothing."

Segar cupped his chin and nodded thoughtfully. When he spoke again it was in the husky voice he used when imparting wisdom on screen.

"Hurting people is easy. It's healing them that makes a man a hero."

CHAPTER 18

Maddock rose early the following morning and went out for a jog in the cool dawn air. He and Bones had compared notes and felt they were no closer to whatever treasure, if any, Striker had been searching for. Both felt that the Arch Gold Mine just didn't fit, although neither was willing to dismiss the possibility out of hand. They also agreed that the parallels between Shipman and Striker merited further investigation.

He followed the racecourse, bypassing the obstacles and following the winding trail through the hills. It didn't take long for him to regret that decision. Later today, he and Bones would be guiding Gambles to the iron door and possibly explore the caverns. No sense in wearing himself out.

He came to a halt at the top of a steep defile that sliced down the cliff like an aqueduct. In a rainstorm, it would be the last place he'd want to be. Right now, it looked like the quickest way down.

Bracing his hands against the sides, he worked his way down, stepping, slipping, and skidding in fits and starts. As the sun began to rise and the morning mist cleared, he realized the way down was a lot further and the way more precarious than he'd initially believed. His footing became less sure and he struggled to control his descent.

A loud crack like a cue ball striking a billiard rang out in the quiet morning somewhere above him. Maddock stole a glance over his shoulder, nearly tumbling face first in the process.

"You have got to be kidding me." A beach ball-sized boulder was tumbling down the crevasse right on his tail. It thundered down the hill, eating up the space between them at a rapid clip.

He assessed the situation in an instant. There was

no way he could arrest his slide enough to climb out of the way. And there was no chance of the boulder missing him in this narrow space. He would have to make a run for it.

Letting out a "Hooyah!" he launched himself down the hill, the crevice boxing him in like a bobsled in its track. He felt weightless as he half ran, half plummeted down the hill. Each step felt like flying.

As steep as this incline is, even if I can remain on my feet until I hit the bottom, I'll probably land flat on my face, he thought.

Behind him the sound of the pursuing boulder grew louder. It was gaining on him. Up ahead, the steep incline gradually sloped outward and the walls of the crevice grew shorter. If he could only make it a little farther.

Thud! Crack!

He wasn't going to outrun it. It was time to try something stupid. He focused on the sound as it grew louder.

Three... two... one...

He sprang into the air, arms and legs wind-milling as he flew. The boulder passed beneath him, but not before it clipped his heel. He came down awkwardly, his ankle twisted beneath him, and he stumbled forward. He managed to tuck his shoulder and roll.

Again and again the hard stone battered his body, scoured his flesh, as he rolled forward. He tumbled to a halt and opened one eye.

Another boulder was bearing down on him.

Every muscle screaming in protest, he lurched to his feet and, calling upon resources he didn't know he still had at his disposal, he leapt out of the crevice. He came down on his injured ankle, which gave way, sending him sliding down the hill. The dry, crumbling earth made for a soft descent, but the California barrel cactus that arrested his fall more than made up for it.

Maddock gritted his teeth and let out a grunt of pain as what felt like a thousand pinpricks burned into his thighs and backside. But there was no time to worry about that right now.

He flipped over onto his stomach, scooted back behind the cactus, and scanned the slopes above him. One boulder he could accept as an accident, even if it looked like it had been hand-selected for a game of human tenpins. But a second boulder? He shook his head. Someone had tried to kill him.

He watched the slope for a full five minutes before he was satisfied that his would-be assailant had fled. Once he was back on his feet, he took a moment to assess the damage.

Twisted ankle, chipped tooth, busted nose and lip, more abrasions than he could count, a possible broken rib, and one ruined Captain America t-shirt.

"Dammit. When Bones finds out I fell down the hill and got an ass full of cactus." Visions of Bones gleefully firing off texts to the rest of the crew. "What the hell? I'd do the same to him."

With a sinking feeling of resignation, he limped back to the ranch. He'd hoped to make a quiet entrance, but it was not to be. Gambles was sitting on the front porch with Riv and Dakota. The three of them were alarmed by his appearance but he assured them it wasn't as bad as it looked. They reluctantly took his word for it, as well as his assurance that he'd merely taken a spill while climbing.

That hurdle cleared, he slipped inside, only to find Grizzly and Bones sipping coffee at the bar that ran between the living room and kitchen.

"What the hell happened to you?" Bones asked.

Maddock motioned for his friend to keep his voice down, stole a glance out at the porch.

"I don't want to cause an alarm, but somebody just tried to kill me." He recounted the tale as quickly and superficially as he could. Fortunately, Bones didn't press for details beyond what Maddock told him.

"You're right. There's no way that second boulder could have been dislodged accidentally."

"You think it was Shipman?" Grizzly asked.

"As usual, I have no evidence against him but he's our only suspect."

"Maybe it was one of those dudes who took a shot at us the other day," Bones said. "Maybe they were poking around here and recognized you."

Maddock made a non-committal bob of his head. "I really think it was Shipman. He saw me poking around near the iron door and decided to play a little human ten pins."

"Do we call the police?" Grizzly asked with a touch of reluctance.

"Let's do some scouting around first and see what we can find out. If there's no proof Shipman, or anyone else, did it, what's the point? But I do think we should make sure the ranch is safe before we take Gambles or anyone else out into the hills."

Maddock wanted to be part of the group that went out scouting for the assailant but was forced to admit he was in no condition to hike or climb. In the end, it was agreed that Bones and Riv would take on the task.

A few minutes later, Lilith and Rockwell arrived. They had heard about the dungeon room and wanted permission to pay it a visit. When they heard about the attack on Maddock, Rockwell offered to help with the scouting and Riv gladly accepted.

While the trio prepared to leave, Maddock made the long, slow trek up to the second floor where the guest bedrooms were located. He showered and dressed, then texted Bones to come up for a quick word.

"I've got kind of an embarrassing problem," he said when the door opened and his friend's puzzled face peeked inside.

"I know," Bones said. "You wear those tight shorts and you don't have much business going up front. In fairness, my sister says you have a nice butt."

"Says or said?" Maddock had been engaged to Angel Bonebrake, but she had broken it off.

"Both, but that's not important. What's your

problem?"

"I'm in what you might call a sticky situation. I slid into a cactus and I can't reach a few of the spines."

Bones stared blankly at him. "You realize this is going to involve tweezers and up close and personal inspection?"

"I'm already having second thoughts. Forget it."

"No, it's all right. I've got you covered, man." Bones turned and shouted down to the people gathered in the living room. "Yo, Spenser! Maddock needs your help with something!"

Maddock blinked. "What the hell did you just do?"

Bones grinned. "I've always got your back, but never your backside."

CHAPTER 19

It was well past noon when Bones and Grizzly led a group that included Gambles, Rockwell, Lilith, and Dakota out to the dungeon room. The search of the ranch had proved fruitless. Bones had located the spot where Maddock was attacked, but the area had been so heavily trod by racers and crew that tracking anyone was impossible. On the plus side, he was satisfied that the culprit had bugged out. Still, he and a few others were now armed.

"How much further?" Dakota asked.

"We're getting there," Bones said, too busy keeping his eyes peeled for danger to really listen to the young man. Dakota had joined them as a substitute for his sister, who had begged off for unspecified reasons. Not that anyone doubted what she was up to. Bones grinned at the thought.

"What are you smiling about?" Grizzly asked.

"I just love it when a plan comes together."

Grizzly's brow knitted, but before he could respond, a voice called out from behind them.

Everyone was on high alert, and the newcomer's sudden appearance took them by surprise. Only Bones and Rockwell didn't jump like startled house cats.

"Who is that?" Lilith asked, squinting her eyes against the bright midday sun.

"It's that police officer," Bones said. Even at a distance, the red boots were hard to miss. "What's her name? Franzen."

They waited while the officer caught up, which she did quickly, and was barely breathing heavy when she reached their group.

"Sorry to slow you down," she said. "I needed to speak with you. It's important."

"Maddock's back at the ranch," Dakota said. "He's

the one who got attacked."

Franzen's eyebrows shot up. "Attacked?"

Bones took up the explanation, describing the incident as if it could have been intentional or an accident. "I looked for footprints, but no joy."

To his relief, Franzen considered for a few seconds, then nodded. "I'll check in with Maddock on the way out, see if there's anything he wants us to do." Then she turned to Grizzly. "I understand you are headed to the so-called dungeon room. I want to see it, and the caverns beyond."

"Do you have a warrant?" Dakota chimed in.

Grizzly waved him to silence. "You're welcome to come along," he said to Franzen.

Franzen cocked her head. "Come along? I don't want anybody in there with me. I'm securing this area until further notice."

"For that, you *will* need a warrant," Grizzly said. "I'm happy to work with you, but I won't be bullied." He folded his arms and met her with a challenging stare.

Bones was impressed, but he also sensed trouble coming — the kind that could only interfere with each party's aims.

"I don't see any reason we can't accommodate each other," Bones said. "It's not an easy climb, so it could take a while for everyone to make the last climb up the boulder pile. How about Officer Franzen and I go up first and she gives the place the once-over while everyone else takes their time climbing up safely."

"I can live with that," Franzen began, "on the condition that, if I find something, no one goes in until I can obtain a warrant and get a team out here."

Grizzly's doubtful expression melted into something like resignation. "All right, that's fair enough. If you find something, you have my word I'll shut this place down while you go through proper channels."

"Deal. And you can call me Janet or Turtle."

Bones didn't know how Janet had gotten her nickname, but it had nothing to do with being slow. She was an able hiker and skilled climber, who navigated the rock face almost as quickly as he.

"If my arms and legs were as long as yours, I'd have reached the top first," she panted as Bones offered a hand and hauled her up and over the ledge.

"You sound like Maddock. Always an excuse for his shortcomings."

"Not an excuse, a reason." Franzen dusted herself off then stood and looked around. "Show me the way to this cave."

"First we'll have to do some crawling. Just follow me."

Bones didn't remember the exact path he'd taken to get to the iron door. There had been a few twists and turns involved, and he'd left the cave by another route. Still, he was confident he could find the way with ease.

Which is why, fifteen minutes later he let out a stream of curses when he ran into another dead end.

"Are you messing with me, Bonebrake?" Janet asked from behind him. "Take me on a wild goose chase while the others sneak away? I swear if you're playing me for a fool…"

"I'm not!" Bones snapped. "I don't freaking know what's going on. We should have gotten through already."

"I've got half a mind to arrest you."

"I'm telling you something weird is going on here."

"I'm taking the lead," Janet said. "It's your turn to breathe my trail dust for a while." Soon it was her turn to swear as she inadvertently guided them out of the boulder pile and onto the ledge, where the rest of their group was waiting for them.

"Back already?" Grizzly asked. "That didn't take long."

"I can't find it," Bones said. "Every passageway I've tried has been blocked off."

"I still think I'm being played, here," Janet said.

"This is the spot," Bones said. "I just can't figure it out." He took several steps back and stood staring at the boulder pile.

And then it hit him. When he'd been here before, the boulder pile had been pyramidal in shape. But now, it was more of a flattened-out dome, as if the inside had collapsed.

"Holy freaking crap."

"What is it?" Grizzly asked.

"Do you smell something?"

Grizzly inhaled deeply, but Janet already had an answer.

"An acrid, scorched smell," she said. "I'm surprised you didn't smell it earlier. It's stronger in the passageways."

"I did smell it, but I thought it was connected to the race. There's smoke and explosions involved with some of the challenges. I should have known better. I was so focused on trying to find our way through that I didn't see the obvious."

"Unbelievable," Grizzly said, catching on immediately.

"But surely someone would have heard," Rockwell said.

"It would depend on what time it happened," Grizzly said. "There were a few hours yesterday when everyone was off-site doing one thing or another."

"Wait, are you saying somebody blasted it?" Dakota said.

"That's what it looks like to me," Bones said. "They collapsed the boulder pile on top of it. It would take years to clear it all away."

"That literally blows," the young man said. "Now we'll never find out what's in the caverns."

Bones was surprised and impressed that Spenser hadn't told her brother about the exit they had discovered after being locked in the cave. From their downcast expressions, neither Lilith nor Rockwell had heard the full story, either.

"I didn't think to mention it before since everyone was focused on the attack on Maddock," Rockwell said.

"But I dropped by the ranch yesterday. Must have been while you were all out. Anyway, I saw Shipman up in the hills."

"Big surprise," Grizzly said. "I don't suppose he was carrying explosives, was he?"

"He was wearing a backpack."

Grizzly heaved a tired sigh. "I vote we head back to the ranch. I could use a drink."

Bones turned to his friend and smiled. "You read my mind."

CHAPTER 20

Maddock and Bones spent the afternoon drinking beer and speculating about Shipman and apparent destruction of the dungeon cave. Although the situation had grown dangerous, neither man was deterred. Not only were they eager to solve the mystery, and maybe find some treasure, they felt an obligation to their friends, old and new, to stick around and see things through. No way were they leaving while Grizzly and his team might be in danger.

It was now apparent that the network of underground passageways held the key to unlocking the mystery of the UFO ranch. Thankfully, that proved to be the main topic of conversation. His tumble down the hill, which Spenser had likened to Indiana Jones' legendary race with a giant boulder, was largely forgotten.

"We'll have to go back in," Grizzly said. "There's no other choice."

"That presents a problem," Spenser said. "We can get back inside the caverns easily enough. Well, not easily, but we can do it. But that place is a literal maze, and that's not even taking into consideration the fact that it's pitch black in there. And it's dangerous."

"The challenge is what makes it fun." Bones turned to Maddock. "When do you think you'll be back on your feet?"

"I'll be good to go tomorrow." Spenser rolled her eyes and Bones smirked. "I'm not saying I'll be a hundred percent, but I'll be up and moving." Privately he thought he'd be lucky to be at fifty percent. Every inch of his body felt like it had been beaten with a sledgehammer. His ankle still pained him, though it supported his weight.

"As frustrating as it is, the fact that someone wanted

to hide that door so badly that they blasted it shut will be a great selling point for the show," Grizzly said.

"Someone? You mean Shipman?" Spenser asked.

No one replied. They still had no hard evidence against the man, but neither did they feel obligated to voice his presumption of innocence whenever the name came up.

"How do you plan on getting back into the passageways?" Rockwell asked. "Are you going to try and dig through?"

"Something like that," Grizzly said.

As the day wore on, their numbers shrank. Lilith had work to do and caught a ride with Gambles. Riv had errands to run. Maddock did not miss the knowing glance she shot at Grizzly when she told him. Dakota also said his goodbyes. He claimed he had appointments in Los Angeles at the end of the week and said he needed to get home and prepare for them.

"The only business he has to attend to is buying a clean pair of jockeys," Spenser said. "He is frightened to death. Thinks one of us is going to get killed."

"You're not worried?" Maddock asked.

She shrugged. "Are you planning on letting something happen to me?"

"When did that become my responsibility?" Maddock said, laughing.

"Ever since I spent a quarter of an hour plucking tiny, almost invisible needles, out of your butt."

Bones put down his beer. "Fifteen minutes? That was a ten-minute job at most. What were you doing the rest of the time?" He propped his elbow on the table, cupped his chin, and pretended to think. "What could Maddock do twice, and very badly, in five minutes?"

Rockwell headed home around sundown. Maddock found him a friendly enough sort, but there was something about the man that made him not quite fit in. He drank a beer but didn't seem to enjoy it. He listened to their conversations but didn't really participate, except to ask the occasional question. Maddock wasn't the only one who held this opinion.

"You know what that guy reminds me of?" Grizzly asked after Rockwell had driven away. "An anthropologist trying to immerse himself into a new culture."

"He is kind of tightly wound, isn't he?" Maddock agreed.

"The three of us have been through some stuff together." Bones made a circular motion with his beer bottle, a gesture that took in Maddock, Grizzly, and himself. "Maybe he feels like an outsider."

"Spenser just met us, and she didn't act all awkward," Maddock said.

"That's because I've seen your butt," she deadpanned.

Bones laughed and raised his bottle. "You are fitting right in." He flitted his eyes in Maddock's direction. It was scarcely a glance, but the pair were like brothers, and Maddock recognized it as a look of challenge.

Riv chose that moment to return, providing a welcome distraction. She moved stiffly, her jaw set, eyes hard. In her left hand she held a manila envelope pinched between her thumb and forefinger as if she despised its touch. They fell silent as she locked the door behind her and joined them in the living area.

"Read that. I'm going to make a pitcher of margaritas. And I'm not sharing."

"That bad?" Like a man petting a stranger's dog, Grizzly reached out with a nervous hand, picked up the envelope, and slid the contents out. Inside was a stack of papers. Grizzly riffled through it, but Maddock could tell that the top few sheets were a printout of an email chain. The others appeared to be scans of documents, articles, and photographs.

Grizzly began to read. After a few seconds he let out a gasp. "Is this legit?" he called to Riv.

"The documentation is all there," she said over the clack of ice being poured into a blender.

"Would somebody like to clue us in?" Bones asked.

Grizzly glanced back down at the papers and gave his head a shake.

"According to this, our friend Bryce Shipman is the son of Kirk Striker."

The walls of the slot canyon seemed to close in around her. Franzen closed her eyes, took a few breaths, and exhaled. As she forced the air out of her lungs, she squeezed her body forward.

Almost. If I could just...

She pushed harder. And then nothing. She'd pushed it too far and now she was stuck.

Panic welled up inside her. Her heart raced, her breath came in gasps. But each intake of breath was agony, forcing her rib cage to push against the cold stone that confined her.

She tried to throw her weight back. She didn't budge. Again. Nothing.

"Got to get out." Her words were little more than mere breath. She started to twist and thrash about until a mournful, ghostly wail froze her in her tracks. It took a moment to realize the sound came from her own lips. A sudden wave of anger burned away the fear.

What is wrong with me? This is not my first rodeo. Why am I losing it?

But she knew the answer. Maddock and Bonebrake had turned her life upside down with that necklace. Megan's necklace. She knew to whom it belonged even if no one else in the department believed her. And ever since then, she'd been behaving recklessly. And now, here she was, wedged in a slot canyon, no partner, no way of calling for help. It was a fine predicament but freaking out was not the solution.

Up ahead, something crept out into a sliver of moonlight. It inched toward her on eight hairy legs.

A tarantula!

The venomous, desert-dwelling arachnids were nocturnal hunters, creeping out of their burrows at night in search of insects, other spiders, and even small lizards. They relied on their extreme sensitivity to vibrations to help them track their prey, and right now, this spider with a leg span the size of a dinner plate, was locked in on her. It cast a long, sinister shadow in the moonlight.

Franzen gathered her wits about her and focused. She imagined her body soft, like a sponge, pictured a force inside of her, like a black hole, drawing all her mass inward. Little by little, she let the vision envelop her. She could almost feel her body getting smaller. Her panic subsided. Now she created the mental image of an inexorable force pushing her backward. Bit by bit she allowed herself to move back until, with a painful grunt, she tore free of the narrow space. She left a bit of skin behind, too.

"Mom's always saying I need to exfoliate," she mumbled, gingerly touching her scraped cheek. "Well, I guess that's a dead end."

The tarantula was still creeping in her direction and she spared a moment to kneel and give the creature a closer inspection. She'd never understood the aversion some people had to these fascinating creatures. She found them beautiful in their own way. "You wouldn't happen to know where that stupid cave entrance is, would you?" The spider didn't reply.

She took out her flashlight and a topographical map and tried to determine her location. What if Maddock had misled her about the location of the entrance to the caverns? She'd run background checks on him and Bonebrake. She'd learned precious little, save that both were decorated veterans and treasure hunters. Bonebrake also dabbled in cryptozoology and conspiracy theories. If the men were searching for treasure, they could very well have sent her off in the wrong direction.

"There's probably no man in black, either."

Something caught her eye. A shadow, a shade darker than the night sky, crossed the corner of her vision. She reached for her revolver, but she was too slow.

Something struck her on the forehead. She saw stars and stumbled backward, tripping on a rock and falling hard to the ground. The air left her lungs in a rush, and she found herself pinned between two boulders, her weapon stuck beneath her body and the ground. She struggled to catch her breath. Pain seared her skull and her eyes watered, turning the night sky into a kaleidoscope of stars. She felt blood running down her face.

She heard the crunch of booted feet on the hard earth, coming closer.

Franzen thrashed and jerked, trying to free herself, reach her sidearm.

The footsteps came closer. Her lungs now burned for oxygen. Panic rose anew. She had to get out of here. She kicked and thrashed. Invisible bands constricted her chest.

Finally, she managed to suck in a ragged breath. With a monumental effort, she levered herself up. She could almost reach her weapon.

And then a shadow blotted out the moonlight.

She had only a moment to raise her hands in a half-hearted defense before something heavy struck her on the head and the world went black.

CHAPTER 21

"**Let me get** this straight," Maddock said. "There's been at least two attempted murders here, and our prime suspect is the son of the man who just might be the Black Dahlia killer?"

"That sums it up nicely." Riv took a sip of her margarita and waited for his next question.

"Where did all this come from?" Maddock pointed to the stack of papers. There was a lot of information there.

Riv set her drink down on the coffee table, leaned forward, folded her hands. "A few weeks back, I hired someone to investigate Shipman."

"What prompted that?" Maddock asked.

"He hadn't done anything terrible, if that's what you mean. It was the same stuff as before the race—always snooping around the sets, showing up in places he wasn't supposed to be, the pervy stares. I just had a feeling, so I hired someone to dig into his past. With the show about to launch, I figured if we've got a dangerous neighbor, we ought to know about it."

"The fact that Striker had a son seems to be new information," Maddock said. "I don't think Gambles is aware of it."

Riv took the papers from Grizzly and slowly began shuffling through them.

"Here's what we know and what we believe," Riv said. "Bryce Shipman was the son of an aspiring actress. Being a young, unmarried mother in 1959, the pregnancy ended her Hollywood dreams."

Spenser muttered a curse that expressed just what she thought of that sort of misogyny.

"No father is listed on Shipman's birth certificate," Riv continued, "but when Shipman turned twenty-one, he received a substantial inheritance: this ranch, a vintage Jaguar XK120, and a whole lot of money."

"From Kirk Striker?" Maddock asked.

"From Jacob Critzer." Riv held up a copy of the will. "Apparently, Striker kept his wealth under his birth name. That was a major breakthrough. We discovered that, in 1969, Critzer, aka Striker, wrote a check in the amount of ten thousand dollars to Shipman's mother."

"Unpaid child support?" Bones asked. "Why wait so long?"

"Maybe he didn't know about the child at first," Spenser offered. "Even if Shipman's mother didn't know Striker was a murderer, she might have got a glimpse of his dark side and decided to ghost him."

"Ten years later, he somehow learns about the child and makes a conciliatory gesture," Maddock said, thinking as he spoke.

Riv nodded. "We haven't found records of any further payments. Doesn't mean they didn't happen, but my hunch is Shipman's mother was desperate enough to accept the first check, but not so desperate that she was willing to allow Striker into her son's life. Striker died two years later, in 1971."

Bones nodded. "So, he backed off and left everything to the son he would never know."

"Ten years later and fresh out of university, Shipman claimed his inheritance and moved into Striker's house," Riv said.

"He had a house?" Grizzly asked.

"Oh, didn't I mention? It appears Striker led a double life after moving to the UFO ranch. Shipman's house, the one just a few miles away, was built in secret, or as secretly as he could manage, by Jacob Critzer. It's a weird-looking place, too. He went with a castle motif, out here in the middle of the Mojave. Weirdo."

"Striker was known to disappear for days, even weeks at a time," Grizzly said. "Everyone just assumed he was out prospecting, but maybe he was up to something else."

"Sounds like he was chilling out at his casa," Bones

said.

"I think it goes deeper than that," Maddock said. Pieces were falling into place. "To the public, he's crazy Kirk Striker, the writer who took his subject matter a bit too seriously and ended up going off the deep end. They see him as the scruffy, crazy guy who wanders the desert searching for lost treasure and running from men in black."

"Never suspecting that when the urge strikes him," Spenser said, catching on, "he takes on a new identity. He goes to his house, his *real* house, cleans up, cuts his hair, puts on his fancy clothes, and drives his flashy imported sports car over to Palm Springs or maybe LA. Even if one of the locals spotted him, they wouldn't associate him with the mad prospector."

"This was the middle of nowhere, so he wasn't likely to be spotted coming and going, especially if he did it in the middle of the night," Maddock said.

"Ironic, isn't it?" Bones said. "Striker changed his name to escape the reputation of his crazy father, but he ended up using that same name to continue his serial killing."

"Assuming Gambles is correct in that theory," Maddock said. He thought Gambles had it right, but he refused to convict Striker without evidence.

"The parallels between the lives of Shipman and Striker are…" Riv paused.

"Striking?" Grizzly offered.

Riv pretended she hadn't heard. "If we're correct about this, both had criminally insane fathers from whom they were estranged, but about whom they were desperate for information. Both interested in treasure hunting and conspiracy theories. Both loved to explore this patch of land."

"Same land, same house, same car, same career," Bones said absently.

Spenser let out a tiny gasp. "Remember what Megan Keane's mother said? Shipman wanted to know whether or not the children of murderers tended to be murderers themselves."

"He wasn't asking for the sake of his future children," Maddock said. "He was asking for himself!"

A dark silence fell over the group. For a few minutes, no one seemed to know what to say, and the room was filled by the clinking of bottles and glasses, the crackle of the fire, and Bones' slow, deep breaths as he teetered on the verge of sleep.

Spenser leaned in close, rested her chin on Maddock's shoulder. "He's a very relaxed person, isn't he?" she whispered in his ear.

"Not relaxed; just oblivious," Maddock said.

Bones didn't open his eyes. "Screw you, Maddock."

"You'll have to take a number," Spenser said to Bones. She shifted a little and rested her head against Maddock's shoulder. Unfortunately, that shoulder was still badly bruised. Hot pain shot through him and he flinched.

Spenser sat bolt upright, her cheeks crimson. "Sorry."

"No, it's fine," Maddock said. "Just bruised."

"Oh, okay." The air between them grew frosty and she wouldn't meet his eye. She folded her arms, sat back, and let out a sigh. "You know what's bothering me?"

"The fact that Maddock's awkward charm wears off after a couple of days?" Bones asked.

Riv hid her face behind her hand but didn't manage to hide the grin.

"The caverns. What has Shipman been doing in there? Why does he want so desperately to keep us out?"

"Maybe that's where he hides the bodies," Bones said.

"That would explain why we found Megan Keane's necklace in the caverns," Maddock said.

"So, the treasure was just a myth all along?" Grizzly stared down at his beer. His face suddenly brightened. "But the viewers don't need to know that. Just the rumor of treasure will buy us a few seasons."

"What happens when you're wandering the caverns

searching for treasure and instead come across a body? Or several bodies?" Bones asked.

Grizzly smiled. "Our ratings double. Ratings gold is almost as valuable as the real thing."

"I don't think we should dismiss the treasure angle altogether," Maddock said. "Just because Striker might have been a killer doesn't mean he wasn't also a serious treasure hunter, and Gambles did say that Striker had particular interest in lost Spanish treasures."

Spenser tapped a finger against her pursed lips, deep in thought. "If Megan wandered into the caverns, Shipman might have killed her to protect the secret of the treasure."

"I hate to even bring this up," Riv said. "It feels distasteful to even mention it, but the first episode of the new series starts very soon. We need to be able to guarantee the safety of our cast and crew. I can put procedures in place, maybe hire a couple more security guards, but it would be nice if our friendly neighborhood serial killer, if that's what he is, is no longer a threat. If, Goddess forbid, he harmed one of our contestants, and we already knew about him…" She didn't have to finish her thought.

"I suppose we can't assassinate him," Bones said. "I guess we should take this to Franzen. Gambles can talk with her, too. Give her the full picture."

"I agree that she should be kept in the loop, but what can we actually prove right now?" Maddock asked. "A kooky treasure hunter left all his worldly possessions to his son, who understandably kept his parentage a secret so people wouldn't think he, too, was a nut job."

"But the murders," Spenser said.

"We have no hard evidence. Lots of intriguing correlations, but that's not enough. Don't misunderstand. I think our theory is correct, but right now a theory is all we have."

Bones rubbed his hands together. "So, let's get some evidence."

"Shipman is the key to everything," Maddock said.

"I say we take a break from the treasure hunt and instead focus on trying to find out what he's been up to out in the desert."

"Works for me. Grizzly and Riv can focus on their show. The three of us will zero in on Shipman. Let the caverns wait until you're not so banged up."

As everyone headed off to bed, Bones stood and announced that he and Maddock would sleep downstairs. No one felt as if they were in immediate danger, but with the new revelations about Shipman, it seemed like a good idea.

"You should really sleep in a bed," Spenser said to Maddock. "You're really banged up."

"I'll take a short watch and then go to bed," Maddock said.

When the others had left, he turned to Bones. "Are you thinking what I'm thinking?"

Bones took a long look, assessing his condition. "Do you really think you're up to it?"

"No, but I'm going anyway."

CHAPTER 22

Maddock didn't bother to hide his limp as he and Bones climbed through the foothills in the direction of Bryce Shipman's home. He was in bad shape, but Bones trusted him to judge whether or not he could handle what they were about to attempt and be honest about it. Right now, Maddock knew he was up to the hike, but anything more strenuous might be beyond him.

They came to a steep slope and Maddock accepted a hand up from his friend, letting out a grunt when hot pain shot along his arm. Right now, there was no part of him that didn't hurt. Bones cast an appraising glance at him.

"What's your plan?" Maddock asked by way of redirecting Bones' thoughts.

"The plan is to wing it. Sneak over to Shipman's house, see what we can see. Go from there."

"Just like that?"

Bones flashed a wolfish grin. "It's always worked for me in the past."

Maddock was mentally listing the many times winging it had gone wrong when Bones halted.

"Someone's coming."

An instant later, Maddock heard it, too. Footsteps coming toward them. They ducked beneath a juniper and waited. A few seconds later, Shipman appeared out of the darkness. Anger flared inside of Maddock. His first impulse was to grab the man and extract a few answers from him by any means necessary. But the flare of rage was quickly doused by common sense. They were likely to learn more by following the man and seeing what he was up to than by beating a confession out of him.

Shipman stopped a few feet away from the juniper and looked around. He craned his neck, listened, then headed off at a fast walk. But he wasn't going toward either his home or the ranch. Instead, he headed out into the hills, moving in the general direction of the spot where Maddock and Bones had made their escape from the man in the black suit and his companions.

"I'll follow him," Bones said quietly. "You scope out the house."

Maddock nodded. He was in no condition to stalk anyone. As Bones melted into the darkness, he lurched to his feet. He managed to do it without any sort of groan or grunt, which he claimed as a small victory. Even better, he managed to jog all the way to Shipman's house. The trek had left him feeling like Daniel Boone running the Shawnee gauntlet, but he was still on his feet.

Shipman's house sat all alone, hidden by the hills that hemmed it in on all sides. This was the first time Maddock had laid eyes on it, and he was surprised by what he saw.

As Riv had said, the house was constructed in the motif of a Medieval castle, boxy with gray stone walls, tall, narrow windows, and a third-floor garret at the top. Maddock made a quick inspection of the grounds. There wasn't much to see. Like most people in this region, Shipman didn't bother with landscaping, but left the desert to its own devices. Other than a paved driveway, the land around his house remained untouched. As he took in the surroundings, a gust of desert wind whipped up, sending a tumbleweed bounding across their path.

"Tumbleweeds and a castle," Maddock said to himself. "One of these things is not like the others."

He saw no sign of security cameras, unsurprising considering the remote location, so he felt safe making a closer inspection. He circled the house, peering through the windows, and seeing nothing of interest.

What did you expect? he thought. *You'd peer through a window and see a signed confession lying on the kitchen table?*

He let out a tired sigh. He was going to have to do this Bones-style.

He wasn't as skilled a burglar as his friend, but he'd picked up a few things over the years. He discovered that the first-floor doors and windows were alarmed. Of course, it couldn't be that easy. Depending on the type of system, Bones might be able to disarm it, but that wasn't within Maddock's skill set. He was banking his hopes on theory that, out here in the middle of nowhere, Shipman wouldn't bother with alarms above the first floor.

The faux-castle walls provided ample handholds and toeholds and he made a quick, painful climb to the nearest second-story window. It opened into what looked like a guest bedroom, and as he had suspected, it was not alarmed. He eased the window open and rolled inside. He hit the floor with an awkward thud, sending fresh waves of agony running through him.

He lay there for a few seconds but had to accept that the pain wasn't going away any time soon. He got up, muscles complaining, and began his inspection of the house. He started on the first floor, where he found Shipman's office. Not sure what he was looking for, he riffled through the papers, flipped through the mail, then scanned the shelves for anything that stood out. Nothing. A search of the second floor proved equally fruitless.

The third floor consisted of a small garret with a sloped ceiling. A shaft of moonlight shone in through an oculus set high in one wall. The room was unfurnished, save for two suits of armor flanking a single bookcase. The books were cheap paperbacks—airport thrillers, mostly. Dan Brown and John Grisham were well represented. Maddock frowned. Why keep your pleasure reads in such an out of the way place, with nowhere to sit? Was he that embarrassed by his own taste in fiction? No, that didn't make sense.

And then he realized what was wrong. The room was too small. He pictured the exterior of the house. The top floor, though smaller than the levels below, was larger than this.

"Which means you must be hiding a secret door,"

he said as he took hold of the bookcase and gave it a firm tug. It swiveled open on silent hinges, revealing another, slightly larger room. Maddock stepped inside and closed the door behind him. He took out his Maglite and flicked it on. What he saw shocked him.

"Holy crap."

The room was a shrine to Kirk Striker, the Black Dahlia killer.

Framed photographs of Striker lined the top shelves of a quartet of bookcases, standing alongside framed newspaper clippings of Elizabeth Short, the so-called Black Dahlia. Maddock had seen photographs of the young woman many times. Her porcelain China doll looks, fair skin, and dark hair were familiar sights to him. In the case of a notorious crime such as this one, it was easy to think of those involved in the abstract. The killers and their victims almost seemed like fictional characters. No, Maddock truly appreciated that Elizabeth Short was more than the pop culture phenomenon that was the Black Dahlia. She had been an actual flesh-and-blood person.

There were others memorialized here. More victims, Maddock assumed. The lower shelves sagged with the weight of psychiatric textbooks, books on genetics, and a variety of books relating to serial killers in general and the Black Dahlia killer in particular. The desk in the center was heaped with file folders stuffed with papers. Maddock flipped through them. Most covered similar themes to the books on the shelves, but a few stood out.

One folder contained copies of receipts from a pawn shop in Hollywood. Another folder was stuffed with copies of articles and handwritten notes related to lost treasures. He tucked both folders inside his jacket and replaced them with a couple from the stack of crime folders so that their absence wouldn't be noted upon first glance. A stack of books adorned one corner of the desk. Maddock couldn't take them all so he settled for taking a snapshot so he would at least have the titles to refer back to.

One thin volume had no printing on the spine or the cover. Maddock immediately recognized it for what it was—an old journal. Its leather cover was cracked and worn, the pages yellow. He opened it and his eyebrows shot up.

"You are coming with me," he said, tucking it in with the folders.

A wave of fatigue washed over him, and he became even more keenly aware of the pain that pulsed through his body. He sensed he should get a move on. He spared a few moments to take several photographs. Something in the far corner of the room caught his eye. It was a small table topped with a half-melted votive candle and a photograph of Megan Keane. She was an attractive young woman with long, sandy blonde hair and a friendly smile. Anger boiled inside him.

"Shipman, you sick freak," Maddock said, snapping another photo. "Is this your version of a trophy, or is this a guilt thing?"

He froze. He heard the sound of someone moving quietly up the stairs. How had he not heard Shipman come home? And where the hell was Bones? Why hadn't he warned Maddock that Shipman was headed home?

Bones probably figured you'd be gone by now. You wasted too much time.

He looked around but he already knew there was no way out except down the stairs. He ducked down behind the closest bookshelf, his knees protesting. He'd just have to wait until Shipman went to bed and then sneak out.

But the footsteps kept coming. The man moved quietly. Maddock could barely hear the soft footfalls. His mind raced. If Shipman was trying to sneak up the stair that meant he suspected someone was there. Maddock drew his Recon knife. If Shipman were unarmed, Maddock was confident that, even in his diminished state, he could easily subdue him. But if the man was armed, things could get dicey. Hopefully it wouldn't come to that.

The door opened an inch.

"Maddock? You up here?"

"Bones." Relief flooded through him. He sheathed his knife and clicked on his Maglite. A moment later Bones did the same. "What the hell are you doing sneaking in here like that? Where's Shipman?"

There was a slight hesitation before Bones spoke. "I lost him."

"You couldn't track a middle-aged writer?"

"His narrow ass can slip through places that are a tight squeeze for me."

"It's the cheeseburgers," Maddock said.

"Screw you. Anyway, he gained too much ground on me and it was too dark to track him, especially with so much rocky terrain that doesn't take footprints. It's cool. We can go back in daylight and pick up his trail." Bones shone his light around the room, taking it all in. And then his eyes went wide as he finally noticed what was inside the room. "What the hell is all this?"

Maddock gave him a quick rundown of the observations he'd observed and the items he'd taken. "I have a feeling we'll find something important in here." He patted his chest where he'd stuffed the items.

"This will not remain secret for long," Bones said. "The police will be all over this, probably the Feds, too. If there's something to be found we'd better find it now."

No sooner had Bones spoken than he held up a hand for silence. He cocked his head to the side, listened intently.

"Too late. Somebody's unlocking a door downstairs," he whispered. "I think we should get the hell out of here."

"There's no way out up here. Come on." They hurried down to the second floor. Rather, Bones hurried, Maddock hobbled. Just as they reached the second floor landing, they heard Shipman mount the stairs. He gave Bones a rough shove through the nearest doorway.

It was the wrong room. This wasn't the spare bedroom through which he'd entered the house earlier, but one given over to storage. Boxes of books were stacked floor to ceiling on three sides. There was probably a window in the far wall, but there was no way to get to it quickly and quietly. Especially not with Shipman practically on top of them. He and Bones pressed themselves against the wall on either side of the door.

The footsteps came closer.

Maddock's heart raced, all the pain of his injuries forgotten. He remembered his tumble down the hill and suddenly his fingers itched to be around Shipman's throat. *I kind of hope you find us,* he thought. *Try and kill us. Give us a reason.*

But Shipman didn't find them. He continued on up the stairs to his secret room on the third floor. They waited until they heard him close the door, then slipped down to the first floor and out the back door.

"That was close," Bones said when they were well away. "A part of me wonders if we should have grabbed him right then and gotten some answers out of him."

"We can't break into somebody's house, steal from him, apply enhanced interrogation techniques, and expect to get away with it. At least, that's what I keep reminding myself."

Bones shook his head.

"You know something, Maddock? Sometimes you're no fun at all."

CHAPTER 23

After a quick shower, Maddock made a call to Franzen, who had left them both her work and cell phone numbers. He was taking a calculated risk, given that he and Bones had just broken into Shipman's home and stolen the man's property, but the garret with its eerie shrine to Megan Keane, was too important to keep secret. He didn't feel he had the full measure of Franzen just yet, but his instinct told him she was someone he could reason with. And it was obvious she took the missing girl's case personally and was driven to solve it. He was confident she'd find a way to get a warrant without blowback to him and Bones.

Franzen didn't answer. He left his name and number, then collapsed onto the bed and turned out the lights, but sleep eluded him. His body felt like a giant toothache. Everything throbbed all the way to the bone. He changed positions, tried calming techniques, but nothing worked. The lure of the journal lurked in the back of his mind. What might he find there?

After twenty minutes he gave up. Already bemoaning tomorrow, he turned on the light and sat up. The journal lay on his bedside table. He picked it up and ran his fingertips across the cover, felt the years held in its dry, cracked leather. He opened the cover to reveal the name written in elegant hand on the first yellowed page.

Kirk Striker

The gravity of the moment hit him hard. He held in his hands the personal journal of the Black Dahlia killer. How had he even considered trying to sleep?

There was a soft knock and then his door opened a few inches.

"I saw your light was on and wondered if you're okay," Spenser said as she stepped in and closed the door behind her.

"As good as can be expected."

"What are you reading?" She hopped onto the bed and scooted in close.

"Just some light reading. Kirk Striker's journal."

"Shut up!" She slapped him on his bruised shoulder. "Sorry," she said absently, her eyes locked on the journal. "It's legit?"

"I think so."

"Where did you get it?"

"Bones and I broke into Shipman's house and stole it." He quickly recounted the details of their impromptu investigation of Shipman. Spenser's eyes grew wider as he described the odd garret at the top of the house.

"What are we going to do?" she whispered. "The police need to know, don't they?"

"I left a message for Franzen. I figure we'll tell her what we know and see how she wants to handle it. I think what we found is important enough that she won't get in a twist over a little breaking and entering."

"And burglary." Spenser tapped the book with a red lacquered fingernail.

Maddock frowned. "I don't think I'm going to tell her about the journal just yet. I know we haven't found a shred of evidence to support any lost treasure theories, but I still believe there's something out there. Shipman wasn't just researching Striker; he was studying lost treasure. And I think this journal is the key."

Spenser nodded. "As soon as the existence of this journal becomes public knowledge, you'll lose it." She began counting on her fingers. "Local police, the FBI, criminal profilers, movie producers…" She froze, as if mesmerized by some invisible sight. "Oh my God," she whispered.

Maddock waited but she didn't finish the thought. "Are you going to let me in on your epiphany?"

"You don't need to find buried treasure. You could sell this for an insane amount of money."

Maddock shook his head. "I really don't think so."

She made a pouting face. "I wouldn't do it either. But I'm not wrong. If this is authentic, it's worth a ton. But, since we won't be listing it on eBay any time soon, I say we get started reading." She rested her head against his shoulder and settled in.

Maddock turned to the first entry. It was written in code.

Neatly aligned rows and columns of numbers and letters covered the first page. And the second. And the third.

Spenser let out a rueful laugh. "Here I was thinking this would be easy. When will I learn?"

"You know, I say that all the time."

He continued thumbing through the journal. The code switched to something like hieroglyphs with numbers and letters mixed in. Here and there was an entry in what appeared to be written in Morse code.

They continued paging through. It was all the same—lots of strange-looking codes and symbols. The few Morse code entries were cryptic. The last was particularly odd. Maddock decoded it.

"Cluster guardian," he read aloud.

"What is that? Some mythical creature that guards the treasure?"

Maddock slowly closed the journal, turned to stare at her.

"Sorry, did I say something wrong?" Spenser tilted her head, touched his arm.

"No. It's just that my mind went to that same exact place. Great minds, I suppose."

"Let's test that theory." She took the journal from him, set it aside then leaned in close. "Look me in the eye and tell me what I'm thinking."

"That it's going to take a lot of work to decipher the journal," he said.

"Nope, too obvious. That's strike one."

"You're wondering if he's already deciphered the journal and has beaten us to the punch."

She shook her head. Once again, a stray lock of hair

fell across her face. It was almost as if she did it on purpose. Maddock liked it. "Also readily apparent. Strike two."

"Don't let Bones hear you say 'readily apparent.' He claims I'm the only human being under the age of seventy to use that phrase."

"Quit stalling. You've got one more guess." She was so close he could feel her breath against his lips.

"What happens if I get to strike three?"

"You don't make it to first base, so you definitely won't score."

Even Maddock could recognize an invitation when he heard it. He leaned in and planted a soft kiss on her lips, which she returned with more intensity. She let out a soft whimper. And then she pulled away.

"Hold on. That was cheating. You can't steal first base."

"I think I just did."

"Fine. Here's what I'm thinking," she said, sitting up straight. "Bones wasn't there for very long before Shipman came home, was he?" When Maddock shook his head, she went on. "So, unless Shipman was just out wandering aimlessly, wherever he was going couldn't have been far from where Bones left him, and he couldn't have stayed there very long. If he left tracks, you guys could follow his trail and find out where he was going."

Now it was Maddock's turn to sit up, sending bolts of pain up his spine. "That makes sense," he grunted.

"Yes, it does. Didn't we just discover that you and I think alike?"

"I thought we played that game and I struck out."

"No. You definitely got on base." Spenser reached across him and turned out the light.

CHAPTER 24

The sun hung high in the sky when Maddock woke the following morning. He sat up, every joint in his body protesting like a rusty hinge. On the positive side of the ledger, his pain level had gone from stabbing to throbbing and now stood at dull ache. He could live with that. He stretched gingerly, yawned, and sorted through his sleep-clouded memories of the night before. He and Spenser had read through the journal and then…

"Spenser. The journal."

Both were gone.

Heart racing, he hopped out of bed and hurriedly dressed. It wasn't that long ago he'd lost a priceless artifact to a woman he trusted, in circumstances very much like this. He remembered how Spenser had speculated about its value.

"She wouldn't do that, would she?" Not sure he wanted to know the answer, he made his way to the living area.

Spenser and Riv sat hunched over their laptops, the journal open in between them. Bones sat with his feet propped up on the coffee table, a big mug of coffee in his hands. He flashed a knowing smile when his eyes fell on Maddock.

"Morning," he greeted Maddock with exaggerated warmth. "Sleep well?"

"I'll say," Spenser said, not looking up from her laptop. "Starting about ten seconds after we finished discussing the journal. And he snores."

Bones' smile melted. "So, when you said 'not much' happened," he said to the young woman, "that's exactly what you meant."

"A woman can crash in a guy's room and not hook up," Riv said to Bones. "It's perfectly normal among mature adults."

"And Maddock proves that time and again." Bones returned his attention to his coffee, an injured expression painting his face.

Spenser paused from her work long enough to greet Maddock, while Riv merely grunted, never taking her eyes from her work.

"You're not working on the show?" Maddock asked.

"Are you kidding?" Riv said. "This is way too juicy to pass up, and it's not the sort of thing Grizzly could help with. So, today I'm experimenting with this thing called 'delegating.' I've heard of it but never tried it. Grizzly's taking care of the show while Spenser and I work on this."

Maddock poured a cup of coffee and joined them at the table. "How's the project coming?"

"Very little," Spenser said. "Nothing we've tried has worked. Every once in a while it spits out a word, but that's probably a coincidence."

"There's one page that we could tell right away was different," Riv said. "It turned out to be a simple substitution cipher, so we got a few words and phrases out of it. Looks like research notes."

"We've got a friend who is pretty good at these things," Maddock said.

"If you're talking about Jimmy," Bones said, "I already called him. He's on vacation with his new girlfriend and said he didn't have time to fool with it." Jimmy Letson was a fellow Navy vet, a journalist, and an accomplished hacker. His computer skills had assisted Maddock and Bones on many occasions. "I sent the first four pages to him anyway."

"Have you heard back from him?"

Bones nodded. "He said it looked to him like it wasn't any code at all, just a bunch of random stuff. He also said that I should jump up my own ass, or something like that."

Maddock chuckled. He knew Jimmy. The man wouldn't be able to resist the lure of an uncracked code that might lead to a lost treasure. In fact, he was probably already at work on it.

"The bits you did manage to decipher, what did they say?"

Riv consulted her legal pad.

"Lake Cahuilla ebb and flow. Map the shoreline. Stages."

Maddock took a sip of coffee and turned the words over in his mind. Lake Cahuilla was a prehistoric lake that once covered portions of southern California and northern Mexico. It occupied an area of nearly six thousand square miles and encompassed the Salton area as well as the fertile regions of the Coachella and Imperial Valleys. Fed primarily by the Colorado River, the lake formed, disappeared, and reformed many times over the centuries, before disappearing for good sometime after 1580. The Salton Sea now stood in Cahuilla's lower basin.

"Any idea what to make of that?" Maddock asked.

"If the treasure predates the last known incarnation of the lake, it could mean we shouldn't bother looking in the area covered by the lake," Spenser suggested.

"Oops. You made a mistake in your Morse code decryption," Riv said. "You thought it was 'cluster guardian' but this word is not 'cluster;' it's 'Clusker' with a k. Could that be somebody's name?"

And then Maddock knew why the phrase had rung a bell the night before.

"It is a name. Charley Clusker."

"Was he a guardian of some sort?" Spenser asked.

"The Guardian was a newspaper." He took another swig of coffee and tried not to smile triumphantly.

"I'll save you all some time," Bones said. "Maddock will sit there with a smug look on his face until somebody asks him to tell them the story."

"Screw you, Bones." Maddock drained his cup and went for a refill. "Charley Clusker was a prospector who came west to California during the Gold Rush. When he passed through this area, he met some Cahuilla tribesmen who told him the story of a great stretch of water that once covered the land. According to legend, one day a giant white bird died and eventually turned into a tree. Clusker didn't think much about the story until years later, when he saw an article in the San Bernadino Guardian about a party of travelers who came across an old sailing ship half-buried in the desert sands."

Bones was nodding. Spenser listened in rapt attention. Riv was typing furiously on her keyboard.

"Clusker thought back to the Cahuilla legend and it occurred to him that the white bird that turned into a tree could have been a sailing ship that had run aground. The white bird represents the sails, but as they grew tattered and the winds stripped them away, the masts that remained looked like trees."

"I remember this story," Bones said. "Clusker got in late on the Gold Rush and didn't strike it rich, so he was determined to be the first to find the ship and recover any cargo that might be on it."

"Hold on," Spenser said. "How does a ship like that end up in Lake Cahuilla in the first place?"

Maddock explained that Lake Cahuilla had drained into the Gulf of California, and it was believed that in years of extreme flooding, a large ship could have easily navigated its way well up into the Salton Sink area. "The water level can rise and fall rapidly, which would make it easy for a ship to run aground."

"What kind of ship might it have been?" she asked.

"Depends on which legend or account you believe. The more far-fetched tales say it's a Phoenician vessel, a Viking longboat, or a pirate ship."

"I heard it's a graveyard for ships from the Bermuda Triangle," Bones added.

"I think that's the Gobi Desert," Maddock said. "If the ship existed it would most likely be Spanish in origin." He took another sip of coffee. "Clusker gathered a team and set off in search of the ship. The wreck was about seventy miles from San Bernadino in the middle of a remote part of the desert."

Riv nodded. "Seventy miles through the desert on foot or horseback would be dangerous even today. Back then that was a daunting journey."

Maddock nodded. "The terrain itself is rough. Mountains, valleys, cliffs, rockfalls, pits, caverns, arroyos, wide open stretches under the burning sun. You've got to deal with the heat and the lack of water. Then there are the natural perils: poisonous snakes and spiders, wolves, coyotes. And then you've got the human factor. Outlaw gangs, some American, others coming up from Mexico, and of course, not all Native Americans are friendly to trespassers on their land."

"But the thing that could really get you is a simple accident," Bones said. "A broken leg or even a sprained ankle could mean death out here."

Maddock nodded. "So, Clusker and his team set out in the fall of 1870, and it's not long before they find themselves in the middle of nowhere. They navigated by dead reckoning, which is a highly subjective process involving estimates based on known distances and travel times. It's an unreliable method in the best of situations, but it's even more difficult in the desert. Distances are difficult to estimate. A mountain that looks like it's three miles away is in fact, thirty, or vice-versa. It's slow going for Clusker and his team. They finally get within ten miles of their destination when Clusker's horse walks into quicksand."

Spenser gasped and covered her mouth.

"The horse was okay," Maddock assured her, "but it was the final straw for Clusker's team, and he was forced to return to San Bernadino with them."

"Was that the end of it?" Spenser asked.

"He made another attempt. This time he went alone, following a new route that he hoped would keep him out of quicksand. Problem was, this route proved to be so slow-going that he ran out of food and water. But just as he was about to turn back, he found seashells."

"Which meant he was somewhere along the old

shoreline," Riv said.

"Exactly. This convinced him that he was close to finding the ship, so instead of turning back, he kept moving forward, searching for food and water as he went. Finally, he came to a cliff overlooking the desert. He scanned the area with his telescope and spotted what appeared to be an old sailing ship far in the distance. He didn't believe it at first, but every time he looked, it was there. But without supplies, and in his weakened condition, there was no way he would survive a journey to the ship and back. In fact, he barely lived through the return journey to San Bernadino. But he never gave up on the lost ship of the Mojave, as it came to be called.

"Back then the competition between newspapers was cutthroat, and a story like Clusker's was bound to sell papers. He sold his story to the highest bidder, which ended up being one of the San Bernadino Guardian's biggest competitors. The story was picked up back east and Clusker became a minor celebrity. The editor of the Guardian, I don't remember his name…"

"Josh Talbott," Riv prompted, her eyes locked on her laptop screen.

"Thanks. Talbott made a deal with Clusker. The Guardian would finance his next excursion in exchange for exclusive rights to the story. Clusker agreed, and Talbott joined him on the next excursion. This time he had plenty of supplies and a support team. Once again, he tried to approach from a different angle. Because he was navigating by landmarks, this made it even more challenging."

"Because a landmark can take on a quite different appearance when viewed from a different angle," Spenser said.

"Also, the desert landscape can change rapidly. Flash flooding can cause erosion and collapses, sand drifts can cover or uncover large objects. Long story short, Clusker never found his way back to the spot where he claimed to have seen it. Talbott eventually concluded that Clusker was a con man who was using the newspaper to improve his celebrity status and to finance his prospecting."

"And no one ever found the ship?" Spenser asked.

Maddock shook his head. "As I said earlier, if it even existed."

"There have been plenty of sightings," Riv said. "Starting in the late 1800s all the way up to the mid-1900s. And those are just the ones I've found. And there's even a pictograph in a canyon near the southwest shore of the Salton Sea showing what many believe to be a Spanish sailing ship."

"I wouldn't believe it were possible if I hadn't seen for myself just how desolate the land in this area is," Maddock said.

"And it's possible that the ship has been intermittently covered and uncovered by shifting sands," Bones offered. "Which would explain why people sometimes see it but others don't."

"According to the party who first reported finding it, only about a third of the ship was visible above the sand," Riv said. "But what they could see was in pretty good condition."

"Do you think it's possible?" Spenser asked hopefully.

"Hell yes!" Bones said.

"It's possible," Maddock admitted. "But we should probably decode the journal before we jump to any conclusions. But it's our first lead. We might as well follow up on it."

CHAPTER 25

It was early afternoon when Maddock and Bones set out beneath the scorching sun. Spenser and Riv had remained at the ranch, working on decrypting the journal and digging into the legend of the lost desert ship. Riv was ecstatic with the new developments and was convinced she could have networks bidding on a new series tomorrow if she wanted. Meanwhile, he and Bones would attempt to follow Shipman's trail from the night before.

They followed a path that wound through parched hills and down into a rock-strewn valley. Maddock was still suffering the ill-effects of the previous day's accident and sleep deprivation, but now that they finally had a clue related to lost treasure, he was eager to continue the search. They soon came to the spot where Bones had abandoned his pursuit of Shipman.

"The desert opens up out there," Bones said. "We should hydrate before setting out."

"Assuming you can find his tracks," Maddock said.

"Oh, ye of little faith." Bones unhooked his water bottle from his belt and took a drink. "Sundown can't come soon enough. It is freaking hot out here." He cast a baleful glance up at the sun's blazing orb.

"It's going to be a while." Maddock took a swig of water. "But it should start cooling off soon."

"Not soon enough." Bones said. "Did you ever hear from Franzen?"

Maddock shook his head. "I tried her cell phone again, but it went directly to voice mail. Then I called the station and the officer I spoke with said she wasn't working today."

"You appear skeptical."

"Maybe I'm overly suspicious, but there was something in his voice. I think something's up." He turned and gazed back in the direction of Shipman's house as if he could see through the arid landscape. "I hope the girls are all right."

"They're fine. Grizzly's got security there at the ranch house."

Maddock nodded. "And Riv can handle herself."

"Spenser might surprise you, too," Bones added.

"Did Shipman leave any tracks?" Maddock asked, abruptly changing the subject.

"I'm not seeing any, but I know the general direction he went. We can start there."

"Can't wait." They took out bandannas and tied them on, do-rag style, before setting out again.

Although he was accustomed to working long hours beneath the blazing sun, the desert was a different animal from the sea. The dry air sponged the moisture from a person's skin. You never even got the chance to sweat before it evaporated, leaving the skin dry and salty. Dehydration was a constant threat, so water was a must. It was an environment that was not meant for humans.

They soon picked up Shipman's trail, with Maddock being the first to spot a freshly dislodged stone and a scuff mark on the ground. Bones insisted he'd seen it first but had allowed Maddock to find it as a gesture of goodwill.

"I figured it was obvious enough that a white guy could find it," he explained.

Maddock was about to offer a rejoinder when a flicker of movement caught his eye—a figure slipping behind a boulder.

"I think someone's following us."

"Not many places to hide out here," Bones said.

"Let's keep going. Maybe we can find a place to duck out of sight."

They continued in the direction they had been heading but could not find any more signs of Shipman having come this way. Wherever possible they moved behind cover, boulders, rock piles, juniper, or cactus, and tried to espy the person who was shadowing them, but never spotted anyone. After several failed attempts, Maddock began to wonder if he'd imagined it, or merely misidentified what he'd seen. The desert played tricks on the eyes, messing with apparent size and distance.

The heat began to take its toll. The exposed skin on his arms and legs began to prickle beneath the hot sun. His battered body was beginning to tire. He might have to turn back soon or risk not making it back.

"What do you think?" he asked Bones when next they stopped for water.

Bones looked out at the vast bowl that swept out before them. The hot desert air shimmered, giving the distant hills a surreal quality, as if they were floating.

"I think we're headed in the wrong direction," he said. "Even if he knows a shortcut, I don't think Shipman could have gone this far and still gotten back to his house so quickly."

"Agreed."

From where they stood, the ground sloped gently downward. Maddock knelt and brushed at the sand. It was soft and loose. He scooped up a handful and let it spill between his fingers until only a bleached seashell remained.

"Bones, look at this." He held it up. "This place was underwater at some point in the past."

Bones knelt and sifted through the sand. "Lots of shells and they've been here a long time."

"If there really is a lost ship, we're headed in the right direction," Maddock said.

Bones looked around. "It's hard to believe. This place is so wide open," he made a sweeping gesture that took in the wide expanse of desert, "you'd think any ship that was lost out here would have been found by now."

"Not if it's been covered up by the desert."

"That's true. As far as we know, Striker never found it, and neither has Shipman. Which suggests it's buried," Bones said, his lips curling in a smile. "And finding undiscovered treasure is what we do."

He clapped Maddock on his bruised shoulder,

sending sharp knives of pain shooting down his arms.

"Yeah," Maddock grunted. "Which means there's a whole lot of ground to cover. This could take a long time."

"Better than someone beating us to the punch."

Maddock stood, folded his arms. "I think we should try and chart the old shoreline. Then we can identify the most likely places to search, and we can formulate a plan."

"That sounds like a great plan," Bones said.

"Really?" Maddock was surprised his friend didn't argue.

"But we can't start on that until we get back to the ranch, so for now, I say we wing this mother."

With that, Bones stood and set off down the sandy slope. Grumbling, Maddock followed behind.

They hadn't taken fifty steps when something pinged off a boulder ten yards in front of them. The distant report of a gunshot rang out.

Instinctively, they dove behind the questionable shelter of a juniper. They lay silent, listening. They heard nothing—no voices, no footsteps, and most important, no more gunshots.

"Who do you think it is?" Bones asked.

"Shipman or one of the jokers who shot at us the other day would be my best guesses."

"Not the person who was following us?" Bones asked.

"Why wait all this time and take a shot at us from a distance?"

Bones slowly turned his head and fixed Maddock with a speculative look. "Maybe we're getting too close to something."

Another shot rang out, but they couldn't hear where the bullet struck.

"I'd really like to get behind more cover," Maddock said.

"Follow me." Bones hit the dirt and belly-crawled down the slope. Maddock followed along. The hot sand burned beneath his palms, and twice he ran afoul of a yucca and was rewarded with a jab that burned like a bee sting. Another shot rang out, closer this time. "We run on three," Bones said. "Three... two... one... go!"

"That wasn't on three," Maddock said as he followed his friend in a dead sprint.

They dodged around the graying remnants of tree branches, half buried in the sand, and kept running. Up ahead, the bleached skeletal remains of some large animal lay stark white against the unrelenting brown and yellow. Before Maddock could identify the creature, a bullet smacked into it, shattering two ribs.

"Almost there," Bones said.

Up ahead lay a sunken area the size of a swimming pool. They dashed forward as another shot boomed in the distance, then skidded down the slope and into the soft sand at the bottom.

"No one will see us here," Maddock said. "Unless they stumble upon us, in which case we're trapped, and they've got the high ground."

"Always looking on the bright side." Bones drew his pistol. "I'll climb up to the edge and take a look around." He made to turn, then halted. He looked down at his feet and frowned. "I think we've got a problem here."

"What's that?" Maddock's hand went to his own pistol. He scanned the rim of the bowl-shaped depression. Was someone coming?

"Well," Bones said, "we've just confirmed one part of Charley Clusker's story."

Maddock turned and looked at his friend. Bones was still staring down.

"Which part is that?" Maddock asked.

Bones slowly raised his head to meet Maddock's eye.

"The part about quicksand."

CHAPTER 26

"**This is impossible**." Spenser flung the journal to the side and rested her face in her hands. She'd spent hours poring over the damn thing and it had been one giant fail.

"Hey, now," Riv said. "That thing's an antique."

"A worthless antique."

"Well, that Jimmy dude did say it was crap. Looks like it was just another Striker smokescreen."

"Yes, but Jimmy only analyzed the first four pages. I was sure there would be something buried deeper in the text." She trembled with suppressed anger and frustration.

"It's okay," Riv said. "These legends and clues almost never turn out to be true."

"But the dungeon room is real. And the caverns!"

"Exactly! We've already got fantastic material to work with. The journal is great! We'll make deciphering it a minor story line, stretch it out. And we've deciphered the random bits of Morse code. That will be enough to keep viewers on the tips of their toes." She reached out and took Spenser's hand. "You're doing great! Grizzly and I think you're a natural. Go easy on yourself."

Spenser wasn't in the mood to be placated.

"I want it to be real. I need it to be real." She clenched her fists. It was the only way to stop her from grabbing something and flinging it. She hadn't made a scene like that since she was a teenager, but right now she couldn't think of anything more satisfying than smashing something. Maybe a couple of wine glasses.

Riv's eyes were rimmed with concern. "Why is this such a big deal?"

"He thinks I'm Willie. I need to show him I'm Marion."

Riv's face screwed up in a puzzled frown. "Oh,

Indiana Jones." She thought for second and then her features softened. "Oh," she said again.

"It's nothing. Just a stupid joke between me and a guy who thinks I'm a walking SoCal cliché." Spenser couldn't meet her friend's eye.

"I'm sure he doesn't think that," Riv said. "You know, I've got a different problem. My man got Indy's reckless courage and Willie's critical thinking skills. It's not a good combination but I love him in spite of it."

Spenser patted Riv on the arm, stood, and turned away. It took a lot to make her cry, and she was right on the edge. Lying open at her feet, the journal swam in and out of her vision as she blinked back unshed tears.

And then she saw it.

She blinked twice and wiped her eyes just to make sure it wasn't her imagination.

"Riv, would you look at this?" Her heart was in her throat. She almost didn't dare hope.

"I'm looking."

"No, stand beside me and look at the journal. It might help if you squinted a little bit."

Riv did as instructed. She squeezed her eyes almost closed and looked at the journal. They popped open immediately.

"There sure are a lot of capital Xs. They're big, too."

"And dark," Spenser added. "He was bearing down on that paper like he was mad at it."

"So, what does it mean?"

"Give me a second."

Heart racing, she hurried to her room and returned with the note pad she'd taken down into the caverns.

"I did my best to map the passages as we went through them. I went back and tried to piece everything together. Obviously, it's not perfect, but I think I did a fair job. Anyway, take a look at this." She pointed to a spot on her map where three looping passageways formed a clover. "This is one spot I'm absolutely certain I got right, because we looped around three times. Drove Bones crazy. Compare it to the journal."

A broad grin spread across Riv's face. "It's a perfect match!"

She picked up the journal and the two women went back to the beginning and started over. The first nine pages still seemed to be useless, and they had already deciphered page ten, but the rest of the journal was something different. It was a map.

They quickly sketched it out. It twisted and turned in a chain of dark, blocky Xs across twenty pages. Along the way, side passages branched off, many running off the edge of the page. They quickly identified patterns in Striker's code that showed which was the correct passageway to follow. After an hour of work, they had a map. But where did it lead?

"Here's the thing," Riv said. "As far as we know, Striker never found the treasure. Which means this could be useless."

Spenser considered this. "Could be. Or maybe he did discover the treasure, but decided he wanted to keep it for himself. It wasn't like he needed the money."

"You could be right," Riv said. "If he's everything we think he is, I could see him taking pleasure in that." She looked at Spenser. "I just wished we knew for sure."

Spenser saw mischief sparkling in the woman's eyes.

"You know," she said, looking down at the map they had made. "This clover-shaped chamber is right by the hidden entrance Bones and Maddock found. It's not much farther from there to the end of the map." She forced a fake sigh. "I just wish I knew when the guys were coming back. I mean, I've done plenty of caving but I guess you need a Y chromosome if there's treasure involved." In truth, she'd been caving once with her Girl Scout troop as a kid, and had toured Carlsbad Caverns a couple of times, but she wasn't about to admit that.

Riv cupped her chin, thinking hard. "I did promise Grizzly that the two of us wouldn't go anywhere. I think he's worried Shipman is going to go all Jason Voorhees on us."

A knock at the door made Spenser nearly jump out of her skin. Through the window they saw Orry Rockwell standing on the porch.

Spenser looked at Riv and smiled. "You did promise that 'the two of us' wouldn't go anywhere, right?"

Eagerness burned in Riv's eyes. "That is exactly what I promised."

The late afternoon sun baked the ground upon which Terry Gold and his team stood. He raised his binoculars and scanned the horizon, his eyes on the distant peaks. They stood hazy gray on the horizon like the humps of a sea monster. Nothing he saw looked anything like a turtle.

"What do you see?" Roddy asked, tugging at his elbow.

"Don't touch me, son." Terry bared his teeth in something just short of a smile as Roddy backed away.

"We're looking for anything that might resemble the image of the turtle mound we found carved on the cave wall," Roddy said to the camera.

"And we're keeping an eye out for our buddy, Segar," Gold added. There had been no sign of their competition since spotting them on the ridge near the cave.

"Somebody's coming this way. West northwest." Platt, short for Platinum, was Terry's twenty-five-year-old son. He was a virtual clone of his father, both in physical appearance, tall and lean, and in personality, intense and enthusiastic. Some would say overbearing, but Gold wasn't one of those people. "Doesn't look like Segar."

"Can I see those?" Roddy reached for Platt's binoculars but was ignored.

Gold swung around and zoomed in on the spot his son had identified. Two men, Latino if he didn't miss his guess, stood on a ridge line in the distance. Gold frowned.

"They're wearing suits. Black suits out here in the middle of the desert. What the hell is that about?"

Roddy immediately jumped in front of the camera.

"Legends of men in black are part and parcel of the lore of this part of the country. Remote, isolated stretches of desert make the perfect setting for things like secret laboratories or even alien bases."

As Gold watched the men, one of them took out his own binoculars and raised them to his eyes.

"Everybody down!" Gold said.

Everyone obeyed except Roddy, who turned slowly about, a puzzled look on his face.

"On the ground!" Ace, Gold's best friend, snarled through gritted teeth. He grabbed the actor by the belt and hauled him roughly to the ground. It was a good thing, too, because a moment later, a bullet whizzed through the air so close Gold could hear it.

"Oh my God! Did somebody just shoot at us?" Roddy asked, too shocked to be frightened. "That's crazy."

Gold let out a little whoop.

"Looks like we've got us a fight on our hands, boys!"

"Why a fight?" Roddy asked. "Let's just get the hell out of here!"

"You take a shot at Terry Gold, Terry Gold takes a shot at you. And he keeps shooting until he's put one between your eyes." The truth was, Gold had never shot at a man in his life, but he was fed up with the false accusations of draft-dodging. He was going to prove to everyone, here and now, that he was a true warrior. When it came down to it, shooting a man was the same at least in principle, as shooting a deer. And he was death on deer. "Keep the camera rolling," he ordered.

He sighted the ridge through his scope. The men had hunkered down behind cover, same as Terry and his team. It was a hell of a long shot, farther than he could hope to hit his target, but he'd give them something to think about.

"Son, you got eyes on them?"

"Yes sir," Platt replied.

"Tell me where the bullet hits." Patiently, he squeezed off a shot. The report of the rifle, the familiar buck, were better than a kiss.

"You almost got one, Pops! You hit right between them."

"So, you just shoot a foot to the left and it's all good?" Roddy asked.

Gold shook his head. "Best to remain silent and be thought a fool," he said softly.

"Man on the left is taking aim," Platt warned.

Terry fired.

"I don't know if you got him, but he hit the deck hard."

"This could go on all day," Ace said. "Think we should go after them?"

"What the hell are you saying?" Roddy said. "It's not a war."

Ace grabbed him by the collar and gave him a shake, an odd sight since both were lying on their bellies. "This is war at its most basic. Mano a mano, with only the rifles God gave us."

"We've got two men approaching from the east," Platt said. "They're trying to flank us." He dropped his binoculars, took aim, and fired. "Missed. They're gone now."

"Were they wearing black suits?" Gold asked.

"Looked like they were dressed for hiking. A weird-looking pair. A blond dude and a big Indian. The feather kind, not the dot."

"Give Roddy your binoculars and have him keep an eye out for them. I'm not convinced those guys are on the same team as these jokers." He squeezed off another shot for emphasis.

"Three separate parties out here in the middle of nowhere?" Roddy asked. "And none of them is Segar's crew? What are the odds of that?"

Gold was struck by a sudden thought.

"If we're finally getting close to the treasure, I'd say the odds are pretty good."

CHAPTER 27

Steven Segar sat cross-legged atop a boulder, gazing at the sun as it sank beneath the hills. Sunset was his favorite time of day. The open vistas and low horizons made it a sight to behold. Gold turned to orange, which yielded to scarlet, then purple. It was the perfect time to reflect on his day and prepare for the next.

There had been no sign of Gold and his crew. Clearly, Segar's map had diverted them. The downside was, he and his group were making no headway. He put on a good front, never let on that he had no idea where he was going.

In the brief lead-up to the contest, he'd tried to do as much research as he could on the Lost Arch Gold Mine, but had found little more than the traditional story, the one Terry Gold had convinced him was untrue. And then, at the last hour, one of his staff had found a clue.

They had discovered a bible belonging to a Spanish missionary back in the early 1700s. Inside was an odd inscription. At first glance it looked like the twisting branches of a bare tree. But upon closer inspection, it had proved itself to be a treasure map.

There was a squiggly line which they had matched up to a section of what had once been the shoreline of Lake Cahuilla, and then a series of landmarks that led to… Segar didn't know what. At least, he wasn't one hundred percent certain, but the fat, twisting lines on the page looked to him like a series of canyons or arroyos. They'd tried and failed to match it up with satellite images in the short time they had to prepare, but he wasn't giving up. He was certain it was an important clue.

"Where are you?" he whispered to the desert.

He closed his eyes, reached out with his senses,

absorbing the spirits of this place. The desert was alive with mystery and wonder, a place where the spirit world touched the physical. A place of such power that it even drew visitors from other worlds.

"The answers are out there somewhere," he whispered.

"Sir, could you say that again, but louder?"

He nearly jumped out of his skin. "What are you doing, Yoshi? I wanted to be alone."

"I didn't know that. Sorry." Yoshi hesitated. "But as long as I'm here, can we go ahead and get a shot of you meditating?"

"I'm not meditating, I'm communing with spirits. You should know that. Spiritual communion is part and parcel of Chinese mythology."

"I'm American of Japanese descent."

"That's what I said." Segar let out a tired sigh. "Fine, let's do this." He stood and turned to face the camera. Yoshi counted him down and gave the signal.

"It's sunset on the Mojave," he said to the camera, "and as night falls, the spirits rise. This area has long been a hotbed of alien and paranormal activity and a legendary place of power. Spiritual people have long made pilgrimages to this region to connect with the forces that lurk here. Tonight, I am going to do the same. I will reach out to the spirit world and ask them to help us find the treasure."

With that, he returned to a seated position, crossed his legs, rested his hands on his knees, and closed his eyes. He reached out with his aura, letting it stretch toward the horizon in all directions. He felt his body relax as his energy flowed fully into his mind.

What is out there?

"I feel something," he whispered. "A shadow approaches. Darkness."

"Well, it is sunset," Yoshi said.

Segar opened his eyes. "Why do you insist on breaking my connection?"

"Oh, I thought you were making a joke." Yoshi said.

"You want to try again?"

"No. I need to work uninterrupted for a while. How about you give me my privacy for the rest of the night. I'll let you know if I need you." He didn't need to see the way Yoshi's smile slipped for a moment to realize he'd behaved boorishly. "You've worked very hard, my friend. Take the night off."

Now Yoshi really did smile. "Sounds good. Thanks."

After the cameraman left, Segar waited a full five minutes before trying again, but he couldn't achieve the requisite level of focus. He kept expecting to be interrupted.

"I need to get farther away." He climbed down off the boulder and set off into the desert. He hiked for ten minutes until he found the perfect spot— a big, round boulder with sides so smooth it took him three tries to scale it. When he reached the top, he was able to quickly resume his communal state.

"I have to beat Gold," he whispered as calm enveloped him.

"This is not fair. I'm definitely sinking faster than you," Bones said. "I always knew the world was stacked against the big man."

"I don't know about that, but when it comes to quicksand, the odds are definitely stacked against the guy who moves around too much."

"I knew that. I'm just pissed off that I led us right into it. Who the hell puts quicksand in the middle of the desert, anyway?"

"I'm fairly certain this isn't our first encounter with the stuff," Maddock said.

Quicksand was formed when water flowed up from underground and saturated an area of silt, sand, or clay. Consisting of floating particles suspended in water, quicksand yielded easily to any weight or pressure. What made it so easy to stumble into was that, because the water flowed up from underground, it was not unusual for the top layer to dry, forming a thin crust barely distinguishable from the surrounding area. Once stuck in the quicksand, if the person became panicked and started thrashing about, the vigorous movement only served to work the victim deeper into the mire. Most of the time, quicksand pits were shallow and a person touched bottom long before they drowned.

"Have you hit bottom yet?" Maddock asked.

"Knee deep and still sinking," Bones said calmly.

Even if they did touch bottom, the danger didn't end there. They would still need to get out. That would be a difficult task, and a tiring one. Drowning deaths in quicksand were unusual. Deaths from dehydration and exposure were much more common. It was all too easy to dislocate a joint or simply tire one's self out and become stuck.

Maddock looked around. They were too far from the edge to grab hold of anything solid and pull themselves out. This wasn't going to be easy.

Needing to unburden themselves of as much weight as possible, they removed their backpacks, tucked their weapons inside, then heaved the packs back onto dry land.

"You know what we have to do."

Bones sighed. "I thought we were finished with the mud baths after the adventure race."

"One does not simply walk out of quicksand," Maddock said.

"I don't know what you're talking about but from your tone of voice I guess it's something nerdy."

Moving safely through quicksand was a lot like swimming. Maddock gradually allowed his weight to shift forward. Slowly, gradually, he leaned into the mud. It was a bizarre, almost counterintuitive feeling to put more of one's body into the deadly muck. Some people only panicked worse when they tried it. But Maddock and Bones knew it was essential to redistribute their body weight over the greatest possible surface so that the quicksand could support them. The thick, paste-like substance enveloped his chest and torso, seeming to draw him forward.

Remain calm. That's the trick.

"Did I say how much I freaking hate this?" Bones asked. "I feel like I'm voluntarily burying myself in this crap."

"Think of it as a trust fall," Maddock said as he stretched out onto the quaking mud surface.

"I hate those, too. Willis let me fall one time." Bones proceeded to curse their roommate at length as he worked on getting out of the quicksand.

Maddock was now stretched out face first, with his waist bent at a forty-five-degree angle. Now came the tricky part. He began to work his legs up and down and side to side, a little at a time. It wouldn't do to give a great jerk and attempt to heave his bulk out. That would only pull him in further.

He felt his upper body being pulled down. Tired and battered as he was, a small part of him thought it might not be the worst thing in the world to simply lie here for a while. And if he sank, he sank.

His survival instinct kicked in. He was going to get the hell out of here. Forcing himself to remain calm, he raised his head and controlled his breathing. Time slowed to a standstill. Finally, he felt his legs begin to rise. Little by little, like a fulcrum, his body leveled out until he was lying on his stomach with the quicksand supporting his weight.

"How you doing over there?" he asked Bones.

"Race you," Bones grunted. The big man was inching his way forward, moving his arms as if doing an odd twist on the breaststroke.

"Because hurrying is always a good idea when you're in quicksand," Maddock said.

"Never mind. You win." Bones had gone still.

Maddock saw the reason immediately. A beige and

gray snake lay sunning itself mere feet from Bones' outstretched hand. From the dark diamond pattern on its back and black and white bands on the tail, he recognized it as a Mojave rattlesnake. The deadly viper primarily made its home in the high desert or on mountain slopes, but sometimes resided in low-lying areas among Joshua tree forests or cacti. It was also one of world's most venomous snakes and one of the most dangerous of all the rattlers.

"It doesn't seem to have noticed we're here," Maddock said. "Let's try and keep it that way."

"New rule," Bones said, slowly beginning to inch away from the coiled serpent, "if you're going to tell me something I already know, just keep it to yourself."

The snake chose that moment to finally take notice of the intruders into its realm.

"Easy, buddy," Bones said. "You and I don't have a problem."

The rattler apparently did have a problem because its coils began to shift. It raised its head, drew it back prepared to strike. A distinctive rattling sound filled the air.

"Easy, Bones," Maddock said. "Don't make any sudden movements."

"I'm lying in quicksand, Maddock. How fast do you think I can move?"

The snake continued to rattle out its angry warning, showing no sign of fleeing. Bones lay just beyond its striking range, but if the snake came his way, he'd never get away in time.

The buzzing sound reached a high pitch.

"Dude, you've got to chill," Bones said to the snake. "I've got no beef with you. I've got a few cousins who would eat you, but they're disgusting."

The snake uncoiled and began to slither forward. Maddock grabbed a handful of thick mud and flung it at the serpent. It struck the rattler hard on the side of the head. Confused, it paused. Maddock grabbed for more mud, but his fingers closed on something solid—a tough old root anchored in firm ground. He gave a desperate pull and, with a sucking sound, his legs broke free of the quicksand.

He rose to his knees, snatched up a rock, and flung it at the rattlesnake, which was once again advancing. He found his mark again. Annoyed, the snake veered off in another direction and slithered away.

"Nice throw. Greg Maddux has got nothing on you," Bones said.

"I still think it's weird that you're a Cherokee and you root for the Braves," Maddock said as he dragged his friend the last few feet onto solid ground. "Is it really worth it just to annoy your family?"

"Angel is the only one it really annoys, so yeah, totally worth it." Bones stole a glance at him. Angel was Bones' sister and Maddock's ex-fiancée.

Maddock realized that for the first time, the mention of her name didn't bother him. "She doesn't care for your Washington Redskins fandom, either."

"Trust me. Supporting the 'Skins is its own punishment."

They took a minute to scrape off as much of the sticky mud as possible. At least they'd have a little extra camouflage and sunscreen. Nearby, a shot rang out. Two more followed in quick succession.

"I've been listening to that," Maddock said, "and I don't think we were targets."

"Agreed. We were just in the wrong place at the wrong time."

Maddock nodded. "Which would mean you led us right into quicksand for nothing."

"What did I tell you about saying things I already know?" Bones gave the front of his shirt one final, two-handed swipe. "In any case, they're in between us and the ranch. We'll need to find a different way back."

"Let's get our stuff and get the hell out of here."

Maddock turned, taking a moment to get his bearings. And then he froze. "We've got another problem." The packs containing their water, map, weapons, and spare ammunition were gone.

CHAPTER 28

"**This freaking sucks,**" Bones said. "No topographical map, so no way of knowing if we're going the right way. No water. Have I said this sucks?"

"No. You've been a dream come true," Maddock said.

They'd been hiking for an hour, following a path that led away from the sounds of combat, trying to work their way back around toward the ranch. But without their topographical map and no cell coverage, they were experiencing the same sorts of frustrations that had plagued desert travelers throughout history. Whether boxed in by canyon walls or wedged into slots, there was no way to see the broader landscape, to pick out landmarks. And when the desert hiker did find himself on an open vista, the shimmering heat played tricks with distances and the shapes of landmarks.

"I notice you haven't once boasted about your inerrant sense of direction," Maddock said.

"I'm an East Coast Indian. Different magnetic pull out here."

"Well, it looks like it just pulled us into a dead end."

The arroyo they were following ended in a recessed area beneath a high ledge.

"Time to climb?" Bones asked, looking doubtfully at the surrounding hills.

Maddock looked around. Something in the eroded area beneath the overhang caught his eye. A single stone slab that appeared just slightly out of place. It was just a shade darker red than the surrounding stone, its edge just a bit too smooth. And it was just the perfect size to conceal a man-sized opening.

"Maybe not. Check this out." He knelt to inspect the stone. If it was hiding something, it had been a long time since it had last been moved. Maddock brushed aside the detritus that covered it.

"You're right. It does look weird," Bones said. "But unless there's a bottle of water under there, I'm going to have a hard time getting worked up over it."

"I don't need you to get worked up; I need you to help me move it."

"Salty," Bones said.

"The quicksand has dried and now it's crumbling down into my... let's just say I was already miserable from the bumps and bruises."

"Grandpa, what's the worst injury you ever suffered?" Bones affected the voice of a mesmerized child. "Was it in the SEALs?

"No, child," he croaked in a fair imitation of an old man, "I rolled down a hill."

"Screw you, Bones. Help me with this."

They gave it a heave, the effort seeming to tear at Maddock's muscles, and the stone shifted to reveal open space beneath. Maddock peered down to see a smooth, sloping passageway descending at a steep angle.

"See anything?" Bones asked.

"I see daylight. This leads somewhere."

"But is it somewhere I want to go?"

"Somebody went to the trouble of making this stone just to cover up this passage. That's almost always the kind of place you and I want to go."

Maddock scooted feet-first down the passageway and found himself in a tiny cave. He could just see the way out in the distance.

Bones slid down behind him and landed in a crouch. He tilted his head and sniffed twice. "What are you doing, Smeagol?"

"I smell water. Come on." Bones scrambled forward until he came to a halt about ten feet from the cave entrance. Here, a tiny flow of water oozed down the cave wall and collected in a small depression.

"A seep spring!" Maddock said. "Bones, you're a genius."

"Wait until I tell your future brother-in-law that

you drank raw water."

Maddock rolled his eyes and took a tiny sip. It was like nectar of the gods in his parched mouth. The took turns taking small swallows until they were, if not quite refreshed, at least less desperate than they had been minutes before. After they'd rested for a few minutes, they decided to see what was outside the cave.

Down below lay a steep-sided canyon. Its sun-blasted surface was smooth and regular.

"This was once part of the lake," Maddock said, pointing at some shells baked into the sand.

"Cool, but is it the way back to the ranch?"

Maddock took in the breadth of the canyon. His eyes searched for a way out. And then he saw it. He closed his eyes, gave his head a shake, then blinked twice and looked again. It was still there.

A dark hulk lay in late evening shadows. It was sheltered by the steep cliffs, impossible to spot from the sky.

"Look over there and tell me if you see what I'm seeing," Maddock said to Bones.

Bones' eyes went wide.

"Holy freaking crap. It's a ship. The lost ship of the desert is real."

It must have been an hour, maybe more, before Segar returned to full awareness. He had failed utterly. The spirits were out there, but none would speak to him. He had not yet earned their trust. He'd have to try again tomorrow.

"At least the cameras weren't here to see me fail."

He stood, stretched, and breathed in the cool night air. The sky was a delicate shade of purple, the land around him only visible in shades of gray. He looked around for a safe way down, turning slowly.

And then he saw it! Five rock piles were spaced

evenly around the boulder on which he stood.

"It's shaped like a turtle!" He understood! The spirits had spoken to his subconscious when he made what he thought was a false map to mislead Gold. The turtle was real, only he'd been too blinded by this contest to receive the message clearly. Now he understood everything.

"Sorry, Nugget. I found it first." It was no surprise. Terry Gold was no match for him.

He slipped and skidded back to the desert floor and headed back to camp. As he walked, he thought about how to proceed from here.

The turtle was a signpost on the way to the treasure, but which way should they go next? He tried to picture in his mind the map he'd scraped into the rock. What other shapes had there been? Where did the dotted line go? He couldn't remember. Yoshi! Yoshi would have gotten it on camera.

With that problem settled, his thoughts turned to the following day's filming. They would begin at the turtle, the sight of his triumph. He'd need a suitable topic of discussion to go along with it. The spiritual significance of turtles, perhaps. The turtle spirit symbolized determination, persistence, and emotional strength. He could use that! His own determination had led him to this place. And the turtle also symbolized ancient wisdom.

"The wise turtle guides us to the treasure," he whispered. It was perfect!

He was so busy planning his dialog that it was far too late when he finally noticed he'd stepped right off a ledge.

He let out a cry and hit the ground an instant later. His ankle turned beneath him, and he felt more than heard the *pop* as it dislocated. Needles of pain jabbed into him as he rolled over onto his back and let out a low groan. He rolled over, sat up, and examined his foot in the scant remnants of daylight.

He winced at the sight of his foot askew. He had no

choice but to pop it back into place. He grabbed hold, pulled, and twisted. Pain lanced through him and he let out a low groan as he reset it. He made his unsteady way to his feet. His ankle hurt like hell, but he could walk on it.

He had gone about twenty feet when someone stuck a gun in his face. He reacted instinctively, batting the weapon aside and driving a knee into his assailant's groin.

At least, that had been the plan.

His ankle betrayed him, buckling beneath his weight as he attempted the knee strike. That's the problem with instinct, he thought as he fell. It takes no account of injuries.

He felt a knee on the small of his back, the cold muzzle of a gun against the base of his neck.

As he and Bones half walked, half stumbled toward the old ship, Maddock couldn't help but marvel at the sight. It was a caravel, one of the small, highly maneuverable sailing ships used by the Portuguese and Spanish during the so-called Age of Discovery. The sturdy ship with its wide, round, hull, had come to rest in the sand near the base of the cliff. It lay almost level, with only a slight downhill slant. Its masts lay broken, remnants of the rigging still clinging to them, protected by the arid desert climate. Its sterncastle was buried in a massive sand dune, but the forecastle was fully exposed.

"She's a three-master, with a square-rigged foremast," Maddock said. "I put her at about sixty feet in length, beam about eighteen feet. She's a big one."

"The bowsprit's unusual," Bones said.

"I've never seen its like." The spar that extended forward from the ship's bow was intact, but unlike its more functional counterparts, this one had been carved to resemble a sea serpent. Wear and tear of the ropes had worn it down in spots, but it was still a magnificent piece.

"One of the native legends called the desert ship a 'serpent-necked canoe.' I can see why," Bones said.

"And the legends of a Viking sailing ship being found in the desert?" Maddock said. To someone who didn't know much about old sailing vessels, the sea-serpent carving might have resembled the dragon figurehead of a Viking sailing ship.

Maddock took out his phone and began snapping photographs while Bones took out his own phone and began recording a video.

"What's up? This is Bones Bonebrake. The little guy is my assistant, Maddock. I'm here to tell you that we've just discovered the lost ship of the desert. Check this crap out!" He kept up the voice-over as he took video of the incredible find. "All you guys thought it was just a legend, but we proved you wrong. So, all you experts can suck it."

"Very professional," Maddock said.

"I enjoy being right," Bones said. "I'm not going to put this online or anything. It's just for me. And proof that we found it first."

"I don't know how you have the energy for this," Maddock said. "Besides, don't you want to look inside?"

"That I do."

They crawled through a hole in the port side of the hull near the bow then slid down loose sand to what had once been the crew's quarters. The tattered remains of hammocks dangled from hooks. Maddock looked across the open space to a closed door. Scant light filtered through the cracked hull, illuminating the large space. The floor was broken in places, revealing a cargo hold below, its floor covered in sand.

"That leads to the sterncastle and the officers' quarters."

"Let's check it out," Bones said. He took a step and the wood beneath his feet let out a dull crack. He froze. "You go first. I've already fallen through the deck of one rotten ship. It's your turn."

Maddock chuckled. That particular ship had been half-buried in a swamp. He had a feeling the dry desert climate would be a bit more forgiving on the decking.

"Here goes nothing." He stepped out and gradually put his weight on his front foot. The floor complained loudly but supported him. He took another step, then another. "It seems to be holding it up."

"If I fall through, I blame you."

As they gingerly moved forward, step by cautious step, their eyes probed the dim light, searching for any signs of artifacts or treasure. Nothing. The brief glimpses of the decks below weren't promising either.

"I wonder if the crew cleared out the holds at the time they ran aground," Maddock said as he made his way across the creaking, cracking deck.

"Where would they take it all?" Bones asked. "I think they'd scout around first, figure out where they were, locate sources of food and water, look for signs of civilization. Know where you're going before you start hauling cargo in 120-degree heat."

Maddock nodded. "And out here in this desert, if they went scouting, who knows if they ever made it back to the ship?"

They had reached the door. He took a breath, held it, and pushed it open. To his surprise, it swung smoothly and silently on its hinges. The room beyond lay in darkness. Their Maglites had been stolen with their backpacks, so they took out their phones, turned on the flashlights, and shone them inside.

"Holy freaking crap!" Bones said. "What is this?"

"It's not the captains' quarters, that's for sure," Maddock said.

The room was empty, save for a single chest shoved into one corner. An open doorway in the aft bulkhead revealed a ladder leading down into the cargo hold. Only a few broken rungs were visible. But that wasn't what captured Maddock's attention.

Sets of Medieval style iron shackles hung from the

aft bulkhead.

"That's weird," Bones said. "This would be an unusual place to put the brig."

Maddock inspected one of the shackles. The chain and cuff were free of rust, unsurprising in the dry desert climate. Still, something about them didn't look quite right. He let his light follow the length of the chain up to the top of the bulkhead where an iron bracket secured it in place. Four words were stamped on the bracket.

"Property of Paramount Studios," he read aloud.

"Movie props," Bones said.

"We aren't the first to discover the ship." Maddock shone his light down to the floor. A dark stain marred the space beneath the shackles. "I think Kirk Striker found this place and he brought victims here so he could torture and kill them at his leisure."

"You're quite astute, Mister Maddock," a voice said from behind them. They turned to see Shipman standing in the doorway. He held a flashlight and a pistol, the one taken from Maddock. Bones' pistol was tucked into Shipman's belt. "I never dreamed anyone else would find this place. Hopefully you'll be the last."

CHAPTER 29

"**Just keep your** hands where I can see them," Shipman said. His voice was surprisingly calm, his hand steady. "In fact, why don't the two of you have a seat?"

Maddock and Bones reluctantly sat down.

"I don't know what you're worried about," Bones said. "You've got our weapons."

"I want to make certain you didn't hurt anybody. Namely me."

"That's ironic," Bones said.

Shipman frowned. "What do you mean?"

"Was that you shooting at us?" Maddock said.

"Of course not. I don't want to hurt anyone." Shipman's shoulders slumped. "That's why the two of you are still alive. I've been following you, trying to summon up the courage to kill you, but I couldn't do it." Shipman unslung their backpacks which he'd been carrying over his shoulder and tossed them to the seated men. "You'll probably be wanting your water."

Maddock had no idea what the man's game was. Still, he was beyond parched. He took out one of his bottles of water and took slow, measured sips. Bones did the same.

"If you're not the one doing the shooting," Maddock finally asked, "who is?"

"Human traffickers. They've been around for a year or more. They've set up a way station in a section of the system of caverns I so stupidly led you to. I shouldn't have been so paranoid about the race. No one was going to find that place by accident."

"So, the human traffickers are the guys in suits?" Bones asked.

"Capitalizing on local legend. Someone goes to the police to report they've been accosted out in the desert by a man in black, the police aren't going to put too much stock in that. It's not the worst idea. Before I bought the ranch, the UFO crowd used to camp out here, trying to commune with Striker's aliens. You can imagine the stories of men in black that sprang out of those."

"You're aware of human traffickers on your land?" Maddock couldn't believe it. "Have you reported it to the police?"

Shipman shook his head. "Our little police force would be powerless to stop them, and I'd pay the price for opening my mouth."

"But the state and the Feds," Bones began.

"You don't understand how things work. Their sort of operation can't function without the aid and financing of a network of important connections. Buy off or blackmail the right people and you can get away with all sorts. Even if I did report them, the best-case scenario is one of their moles would tip them off and they'd be gone long before the authorities arrived. Hell, they could move deeper into the caverns and probably go undetected. You can't imagine just how expansive they are. Then, when it's all finally blown over, they'd come after me." Shipman sighed. "Also, they pay me."

"That's disgusting," Maddock said.

"I'm keeping my mouth shut either way. Might as well profit from my silence. I just want to be left alone."

"I imagine the women who were killed here felt the same way," Maddock said. "Have you been continuing your father's work?"

Shipman flinched. "What are you talking about?"

"You might be surprised at just how much we've learned," Bones said. "And before you think about killing us to hide your secret, you should know that several of our friends are fully in the loop and are at this very minute digging into your history, and Striker's. You're a dead man walking."

"And speaking of Striker, we've seen the shrine to Megan Keane in your upstairs room," Maddock said. "Was she your first victim? Was that a special memory for you, you sick son of a bitch?"

Shipman shook his head. "No. It's not like that."

"Come on," Bones scoffed. "You're obsessed with Striker. You live on his ranch, drive his car. You're fascinated with him and with serial killers. I take it you inherited the Critzer family madness?"

Shipman tensed for a moment, then seemed to deflate. He sank to the deck, his back resting against the bulkhead. Maddock and Bones were both looking for an opening, but he still held the pistol at the ready, finger on the trigger.

"You two don't understand anything." His voice faded to scarcely more than a whisper. "I never wanted to be like my father."

"Why don't you explain it to us?" Maddock asked.

"Growing up, I knew almost nothing about who my father was. My mother would only tell me he was a bad person and that we were better off without him. He tried to connect with me a few times over the years, but Mother wouldn't allow it. I think she accepted money from him one time so she could move us to a better neighborhood. It wasn't until I came of age that I even learned his name, much less that there was an inheritance waiting for me. He left me everything." He sighed. "I asked her to come and live with me, but Mother wanted no part of anything that had been Striker's."

"What happened between them?" Maddock asked.

"He tried to kill her," Shipman said. "She met him in Hollywood. He was charming, handsome, seemed to be well-connected. She thought he was a good guy who really wanted to help her career along. According to her, things were going great, and then one night he tried to strangle her. But Mother was no hothouse flower. She was a strong girl, raised on a farm. Grew up working side by side with her brothers, and brawling with them from time to time. She managed to fight Striker off and get away from him."

"Did she report it to the police?" Bones asked.

Shipman chuckled. "It was a different world back then. An unmarried woman in the 1940s was not going to call the police to report rough sex with the man she was fornicating with."

"But he was a serial killer," Bones said.

"She didn't know that. She had no idea who and what he was. She was just a young woman trying to survive all alone. She did the best she could."

Maddock could understand that. "When did you find out the truth?" he asked.

"The full picture came together over time. I pieced together clues, learned everything I could about him and the Critzer family. That's why I seemed obsessed with Striker and with serial killers. I was convinced that Striker had indeed inherited his father's madness and I was terrified that the same would happen to me. The last thing I wanted was to be anything at all like him. Yet here I was, drawn to writing and treasure hunting. And if he and I shared those traits..."

"So, what about the treasure?" Bones asked.

"My father was interested in lost treasure of all sorts, but the story that captured his imagination was the lost ship of the desert. It was a hobby of sorts. But when he finally found it, he found very little in the way of coins or artifacts. The ship had been almost stripped bare. But he could find no historical accounts of anyone claiming to have recovered its cargo. And it wasn't only valuables that were missing. Commonplace items were also taken. The galley, the captain's quarters, all cleared out."

"Not the sort of stuff you'd bother carrying across the desert," Bones said.

"Exactly. My father was convinced that the crew must have settled somewhere nearby and had taken everything with them. Finding that place became his obsession. This ship he put to other uses."

"I take it he wasn't searching for the Arch Gold Mine?" Bones asked.

"Not around here, I don't think. He put out lots of cover stories and allowed people to believe he was off his rocker." Shipman grimaced. "Off his rocker as far as treasure hunting is concerned, I mean. But some of his stories drew the wrong sort of attention. Men in black started showing up, following him. Real ones."

"Wait a minute," Maddock said. "The men in black stories were real?"

"According to him they were. Some were interested in his UFO tales. Low-level government types. It was the others who really concerned him."

"Who would those others be?"

Shipman's brow furrowed. "He had put out a story about finding the remnants of an ancient civilization. He claimed to have found powerful crystals and advanced weaponry. That apparently got the attention of some quasi-religious group. He tried to tell them he'd made it all up, but that only made them doubt him. You know how these true believers are. They dogged him all of his life."

"Do you happen to know the name of this group?" Maddock asked.

"Something stupid. Domination, I think?"

"The Dominion?" Bones asked.

Shipman's eyebrows shot up. "That's it. You've heard of them?"

"Have we ever," Maddock said. "Have you ever had an encounter with them?"

"No. I think they poked around and eventually satisfied themselves that Striker really was crazy, and the ancient world legend was nonsense."

"I take it Striker's search eventually led to the caverns?" Maddock asked.

Shipman nodded. "It was late in his life when he discovered them, so I don't know how thoroughly he managed to investigate them. He kept a journal full of weird codes and drawings." Bones covered a low cough at the mention of the purloined book, but Shipman didn't notice. "I haven't managed to decipher more than a few lines. I suspect it's mostly gibberish. Another smokescreen."

"So, you've spent your life following in your father's footsteps," Bones said.

"Only in terms of treasure hunting. But yes, I write for a living, search for treasure in my spare time. As far as I know I was the only person alive who knew about the caverns until the traffickers discovered a back entrance. I still don't think they have any notion of the full extent of it. They don't seem to venture far from their headquarters."

"What's it like down there?" Maddock asked. "We've only seen a little of it."

Shipman didn't catch the subtext of Maddock's question. "You can't imagine the sheer size and complexity. How deep it goes. And the passageways are deceptive. They'll taper off into nothing and just as you're about to give up it opens into a magnificent chamber. And all of it is pitch black save for the light you carry with you. The going is slow. There's water down there, too. I nearly drowned once. Water was dripping down from above. Like an idiot I poked at it with my knife and the ceiling collapsed."

"Tell us about the iron door and the dungeon," Maddock said.

"We can thank the Critzer family for that, too. Frank Critzer had a brother, a prospector, who made his home in these hills. He had a son who was crazy even by the standards of the family. He was little more than an animal, really. Eventually he grew too strong to be controlled, and he ended up killing someone. His father built that dungeon to keep him from hurting anyone else. It worked for a while. But one night he overpowered his father and escaped. Depending on which legend you believe, he either went on a killing spree that ended with his own death, or he continued to haunt the hills, killing when the demons drove him to violence."

"Was he the source of the Mojave Monster legend?" Bones asked.

"The very one."

Maddock realized this was an important moment

for Shipman. The man clearly felt the need to unburden himself. Hopefully they could keep him talking.

"Who made the tunnel from the dungeon room to the caverns?"

"My father had heard the story of the caverns from an elderly Native American woman. To her it was a far-fetched legend but my father had a feeling there was something to the story. One of the consistent threads across the various legends he had collected about the dungeon room was that there was a crack in the dungeon wall and through it the young man could hear the whispers and moans of the spirit of the dead. My father investigated and found the caverns. From that moment on he was certain the crew of this ship had hidden her treasure there."

"What's the name of this ship?" Bones asked.

"If my father found out, he didn't write it down. At least, not in a code I can make sense of."

"It's probably painted on the stern," Bones said. "Anybody feel like doing some excavating?"

Shipman didn't smile, didn't blink. His expression was unreadable, and that unnerved Maddock.

"I don't get it," Maddock said. "If you're so certain there's treasure in the caverns, why did you sell that piece of land to Grizzly?"

"I needed the money and Grizzly was the only one who was interested. His assistant, Ms. Rivera, insisted that area be included. She 'liked the visuals.' I know other ways into the caverns, and I doubted anyone would find the dungeon room." He flashed them a baleful look. "And then, in a fit of paranoia, I inadvertently led you there."

"And when we did find the room, you locked us inside, hoping we'd get lost and die in the caverns?" Maddock asked.

Shipman nodded. "I panicked in the moment. I tend to do that. I couldn't believe someone had found the room. It wasn't a premeditated plan, but yes, that was my thinking at the time."

"And when it didn't work, you tried to protect your secret by blowing the place up," Bones said.

"And by rolling boulders down on me," Maddock added.

Shipman blinked. "I did not blow the place up, although the thought did occur to me. And as for the boulders, I have no idea what you're talking about."

"Right," Maddock scoffed. "I suppose you didn't kill Megan Keane, either."

Shipman cocked his head. "Oh, no. I absolutely did kill her."

CHAPTER 30

"**I think the** yellow bellies have tucked tail and run! That's what happens when you mess with the USA!" Terry Gold leered at the camera. "And let me tell you something. The sound of gunfire? That's just the rat-a-tat-tat of the little drummer boy at Lexington and Concord!"

"I think the little drummer boy was a Christmas thing," Roddy said.

"Brother, there's a little drummer boy beating in the heart of every true patriot." He raised his rifle in the air, lifted his head to the sky, and let out a long, high-pitched howl. He had done it! He always knew he had it in him, but now there was proof.

He and his team had driven off the dirt bags, whoever they were, and had suffered no casualties. Each man had acquitted himself admirably. Not a coward among them. Even Roddy had remained calm and fired off a single shot for the benefit of the camera. And to top things off, Gold had wounded one. He had seen the man go down clutching his leg.

"Are you saying the people you fought weren't Americans?"

Gold shrugged. "I don't know who they are or where they came from, but if they're out here shooting at innocent people, that's as un-American as it gets."

Platt seized him by the arm. "Pops. Somebody's coming."

"Is it Ace?" he asked, raising his rifle and moving behind cover. Ace and another team member had gone out scouting.

"No. It's one dude and he's just walking directly toward us."

Gold spotted him. He didn't look like any of the guys they'd been shooting it out with, but he looked familiar.

Platt raised his rifle. "Put your hands up!" he shouted.

"Lower your weapon, son," Gold said to Platt. "Relax. That's Yoshi. He's Segar's cameraman."

"What the hell, dude?" Yoshi was a fair-skinned young man, but right now his face was scarlet. "You're pointing guns at me? It's just a TV show!" Fists clenched, he stalked toward Platt, who had a good foot and sixty pounds on the smaller man.

"Chill, man." Platt laid down his rifle and held out his hands in a placating gesture. "Some dudes have been shooting at us."

The words stopped Yoshi in his tracks. He scratched his head. "Shooting at you? We just thought you guys were shooting at beer cans or something."

The camera was still rolling, and Gold seized the moment.

"No, son. War was declared, and we emerged victorious." He turned to Yoshi. "Now, what can we do for you?"

"Segar is missing. He said he wanted to be alone for one of his weird spirit sessions. After a while I got worried. But when I went to look for him, he was gone. I'd heard you guys shooting so I came looking for help. At first, I figured he'd just gotten lost."

"It wouldn't surprise me. If it's not a buffet line, Segar has a hard time finding it."

Yoshi looked nervously in the direction of the camera, then back to Gold. He lowered his voice.

"Come on, dude. This might be serious. What if he ran into the guys who were shooting at you?"

A wave of shame washed over Gold. Drunk on his victory, he had allowed himself to act the fool. This was still a serious situation. "I apologize. You're one-hundred percent right. Where's the rest of your team?"

"They stayed back at camp. To be honest, I don't think any of them care very much," he admitted.

"That ain't going to pass muster." Gold gave the

man's shoulder a squeeze. "Our crews are going to team up. We'll find Seagull and bring him back." *And he will be indebted to me for the rest of his life.*

"Shouldn't we call the authorities?" Roddy asked. "I mean, what if we run into those guys again?"

"If they've got Segar then I damn sure hope we run into them."

Roddy threw up his hands. "What the hell, Gold? This isn't television, this is real life!"

Gold fixed the camera with a side-eyed glare, then turned to his co-host.

"This, mi amigo." He poked Roddy in the chest. "Is *reality* television. And let me tell you a little something about the *real world*. We've been trying to contact authorities since the moment hostilities commenced. And if we ever do get in touch with them, they can't just hop in the old prowler and cruise out here. You know why? Because we're in the middle of nowhere. Maybe you've noted there's no green screen behind us."

Roddy's face was beet red. His fists were clenched, elbows cocked. That was good. Better angry than scared.

"It could be days before the manhunt begins. He could be dead by then. In short, it's up to us."

"I get it," Roddy said loudly, trying to save a little face.

"I know you do, brother. I can see it in your eyes. You've got the anger brewing and you're ready to take action." He doubted that last bit, but the boy needed an injection, 20ccs of cojones, stat. A little praise from the alpha dog just might do the trick.

With his left arm draped around Roddy's shoulders and his right hand resting on the top of Yoshi's head, he addressed the camera.

"Our brother has gone missing. Even if foul play is not involved, which we hope it isn't, the desert is still a dangerous place, where even the most experienced among us can get into trouble." He paused to give the camera a long, solemn look.

"Segar, we are coming for you, brother!"

Steven Segar stumbled forward and fell hard to the cold stone floor. He groaned and rolled over onto his side, mentally adding bruised cheek to the list of today's injuries. His wrists were bound behind him, the nylon cord already cutting off circulation.

He still couldn't believe he'd allowed himself to be captured. His body had betrayed him at a critical juncture. Now, here he was, taken prisoner by a punk twenty years his junior. It was almost like one of his movies.

The room was pitch black, the air cold with just a hint of humidity. He was in a cave.

He heard voices from somewhere close by.

"...the hell you think you're doing bringing him here like that?"

"I didn't know what else to do. I couldn't kill him. He's a celebrity, dog!" This the voice of the man who had taken him captive. *"He's got to be worth some serious cash."*

Segar was embarrassed to realize he was smiling at the thought of how high his ransom might be.

"Brian, his movies are so old they don't even get taken down from YouTube. Bro, he's a has-been."

Segar flared up immediately. "No, I'm not. I'm working on a new show as we speak!"

"Will you shut up?" a woman's voice spoke from the darkness.

"Who is there?" he whispered.

"I said, shut up," the woman hissed. "I'm trying to listen."

"...not what we do."

"Come on. The boss has brought in, like three new people this week. One more won't hurt. Look, I don't even want to be here. I thought we were helping people avoid the border patrol."

"Yeah, well the boss doesn't care what you thought you were getting into. And you better not let people think you're not all in. They'll kill you without a second thought. Now, let me see this dude."

A flashlight clicked on, bathing the space in light. He was, indeed, in a small subterranean chamber. There were three other prisoners: a woman with brown hair and red cowboy boots, a blue-eyed blonde who glared at their captors as if trying to decide who's face to bite off first, and a girl with a Rosie the Riveter tattoo who took in her surroundings with an air of impatient disinterest. The latter's eyes fell on Segar and she quirked an eyebrow.

"Well, what do you know?" she said. "They really did capture a former celebrity."

"Former and current. I even have a new book out."

"Did you get a nice advance, or did you publish it yourself?"

Segar didn't reply.

"Listen up," the man with the flashlight said. He was built like a tree stump. Segar was surprised they'd found a suit to fit him, and even more surprised that he'd found enough neck to wrap a tie around. He did them the courtesy of aiming the light at the ceiling to prevent blinding their eyes. "You guys don't give us any problem, and we won't mess with you. That's the deal."

"What do you have planned for us?" the officer demanded.

No-neck shrugged. "The boss is going to have to decide what to do with you."

"Where is Rockwell?" the girl with the tattoo demanded.

"You don't need to know that," he said.

"Can I get some water?" Segar asked. "And some for my friends," he added hastily.

"Sure. I'll get the craft service people right on it."

"Would you mind leaving us a light?" the blonde asked in a tremulous voice incongruent with her wolverine glare of moments before. "It's scary in the dark."

Their captor leered down at her. "Sure, sweetheart. Just for you. But I'm going to tell the boss you owe me." He winked as he laid the flashlight on the floor of the cave, then blew her a kiss as he walked away.

"Neanderthal," the girl whispered. "You don't even realize how easy you are to manipulate."

"Nice work," the woman in red boots said. She turned to Segar. "I'm Franzen. I'm a police officer. Our fake damsel in distress is Spenser." The blonde gave a nod. "And that's Riv." The girl with the tat winked.

"I'm Steven Segar. Now, nobody panic. I've gotten out of plenty of situations like this."

"In real life?" Riv asked.

Segar shook his head. "No, but this is my chance to finally do it for real."

CHAPTER 31

The hour was growing late and the air inside the ship was growing chilly. But the goosebumps on Maddock's flesh had nothing to do with the cold. He was staring into the face of a murderer.

"You admit that you killed Megan Keane? That surprises me," Maddock said.

"Yes, I killed her." Shipman swallowed hard. "I suppose I murdered her, in fact. But not in the way you think."

"What I think is that you spent too much time delving into the minds of serial killers and the lure finally became too great to resist."

"No," Shipman groaned.

"Was it an academic thing? Wanted to see if you could get away with it, like your father did? Or was it just a hunger?"

"That's not it at all."

"Maybe just a little trickle-down Critzer?" Bones asked. "A chip off the old axe murderer." He looked at Maddock. "That last one wasn't funny, was it?"

"Few of them are, Bones."

"Listen to me." Shipman waved with the pistol. "You've got it all wrong." He looked around the dark cabin. "I cared only about the treasure. I did my research, pored over that damned journal, scoured the mountains and the desert. Common sense told me to give up, but I kept on searching. Finally, I found it! The lost ship of the desert." For the first time, he actually smiled. "Imagine my surprise at what I discovered when I got here."

"What was that?" Maddock thought he already knew.

"It was like something out of a horror film. The mummified remains of young women were hanging from those." He waved his gun in the direction of the shackles. "Their bodies showed evidence of the most gruesome sort of torture. And there was a chest containing instruments of torture. No treasure, no priceless artifacts. Only a house of horrors."

"You knew what your father was," Maddock said.

Shipman shook his head. "I knew he had tried to hurt my mother and that she considered him an erratic man with the potential to snap at any moment. Once I learned about his family of origin, I knew we had dodged a bullet. But I never dreamed of the depths of his depravity until that moment."

"Why didn't you report it to the police?" Maddock asked.

"Easy," Bones said. "He wanted to keep the ship a secret until he was sure there was no treasure to be found."

"That's it exactly," Shipman agreed. "That and shame, disbelief, not wanting my name associated with his. It might have been great publicity, or it could have ruined my career. I didn't feel I could take the risk. I frantically searched the ship but found nothing. I rushed home, positively devastated. When I finally calmed down, I took a second look at some of my father's files. Pieces began to fall into place."

"Like what?" Bones asked.

"Pawn shop receipts for old Spanish coins and artifacts. He must have found them inside the ship." For a moment, the gleam of gold fever shone in Shipman's eyes, but then his gloom returned. "The worst was the collection of newspaper clippings about missing and murdered women, including the Black Dahlia. I recognized a couple of the women as those hanging in the ship. It didn't take long to begin drawing lines from each victim to my father. Nothing I could prove, but the conclusion was obvious. He really was a serial killer. It was then I truly began to worry about whether or not I might have inherited certain family traits. That was when I scheduled a session with Megan's mother. I was terribly worried, but trying to hide it. I suppose I didn't do a good job of it because I later learned that she came away from our session feeling unsettled." An expression of regret passed across his face.

"I waited a week before I returned to the ship. I took a shovel so I could bury the remains of my father's victims. If someone else were to also find the ship, better an empty one than a crime scene. Each would bring its own sort of unwanted attention, but only one could lead to my undoing. What I didn't know was Megan Keane had suspicions of her own about me, and my visit to her mother only confirmed them in her mind. She fancied herself a future investigative reporter and decided to apprentice the craft by stalking me. On the day I came to the ship, she followed me. She caught up just as I was burying the first body."

"And she thought you were burying one of your own victims," Bones said.

Shipman nodded. "I don't know how but she crept right up behind me. I heard two shutter clicks, someone snapping photographs. I turned around and there was Megan. She said she'd always known I was a creep and now everyone would know." Silent tears trailed down Shipman's cheeks. "But all I could think about was the ship and the treasure. I couldn't have the world knowing I found it. I hit her with the shovel."

Now he began to sob. Bones glanced at Maddock, a question in his eyes. Maddock mouthed 'not yet.' Shipman still had his finger on the trigger.

"I just hit her. Didn't even think about it. But I suppose my heart wasn't in it. She acted like she hardly felt it. Just turned and ran. I chased her and, in her panic, she tried to climb the cliff wall. I begged her to come back. Said we could work something out. But she wouldn't listen."

"Then what happened?" Bones asked.

"She fell. Died on impact. Suddenly, my idea of burying the bodies beside the ship seemed foolish. If it were ever discovered, all the area around it would be excavated. So, I did what I had to do. One by one, I hid their bodies in the caverns." Tears now dripped from his cheeks.

Maddock couldn't manage any sympathy. Gold fever was common among treasure hunters, but it was no excuse for murder.

"You need to come clean," Maddock said. "Killing us won't stop this. Like we told you. We've shared our knowledge and suspicions with too many people. When you locked us in the caverns, we found Megan's necklace and turned it in to the police. You can't stop this."

Shipman nodded sadly. "You're right in more ways than you know." With a sudden movement, he thrust the pistol into his own mouth.

"No!" Maddock and Bones shouted in unison, but neither man could move fast enough.

The pistol boomed and Shipman slumped to the deck.

CHAPTER 32

Bones couldn't believe it when Shipman pulled the trigger. His hand was inches from the barrel of the pistol when the weapon fired. Might as well have been a mile. There was no need to administer first aid. The bullet had done its job too well. Shipman lay slumped back, blood and gore spattering the bulkhead above him.

"You could have at least answered a few of our questions before you did yourself in," Bones muttered.

"What do you think he meant that you and I were 'right in more ways than we know'?" Maddock asked.

Bones shrugged. "He was already expecting his secret to get out in some other way."

"Maybe these human traffickers know his secret?" Maddock offered. "That would be a very good reason to turn a blind eye."

"Do you think he was telling the truth when he said he didn't try to kill you?" Bones asked.

Maddock shook his head slowly. "I can't say for certain, but I didn't get the feeling he was lying. Why would he? He admitted to causing Megan's death and participating in human trafficking. Why lie about that?"

"Who did it, then?"

"Maybe one or more of the traffickers was poking around the ranch?"

"You realize we're going to have to get the cops in on this? Like, right away." The words were bitter on Bones' tongue. The fact that they had not, in fact, been the first to rediscover the ship, had been a blow. But he realized they wouldn't be able to keep the ship a secret. Nor would they be permitted to keep the journal. The treasure of the Lost Ship of the Desert, if there had been one, would now be fair game. Treasure hunters would descend upon this place in no time. He and Maddock were about to lose their head start.

"We'll do it as soon as we can get a signal." Maddock frowned at Bones. "What's with that expression on your face? You all right?"

"I'm reminding myself that murder and human trafficking are more important than treasure hunting. Even if it's one of the most legendary treasures of the Southwest."

"Let's at least take a quick look around before we head back," Maddock said. "I don't think I'm quite ready to make the hike back."

"Don't bother asking for a piggyback ride," Bones said. "You're way too fat for me to carry." He stood and took a moment to work the kinks out of his spine. "Is there enough of that ladder left for us to climb down or do we need to find a different way?"

With a loud crack, the floor gave way beneath him. Bones let out a shout of surprise as he plunged into the darkness. He hit the deck below him an instant later. The thick layer of sand that covered the planking only cushioned his fall a little.

A light shone down from above. Maddock poked his head through the hole where Bones had been standing only seconds before and grinned.

"Still want me to check the condition of the ladder?"

"Screw you, Maddock. Hand me that light."

Bones stood and Maddock handed down the flashlight Shipman had been carrying. Bones swept the light around the hold. It had been picked clean.

"Looks like the cupboard is bare," he said. "But we might as well check the rest."

Maddock dropped down beside him, and they began their search. As Shipman had said, there was no treasure to be found, and very few artifacts. Wedged in a crack in the deck, Maddock found a hammered silver coin. He held it up so Bones could see the trademark sheaf of arrows.

"An old Ferdinand and Isabella," Bones said. "Late 1400s."

"It's not a treasure but at least we found something."

It didn't take long to complete their search of the ship. Down among what had once been the stores, they dug through loose sand, but uncovered only barrel staves and a few lengths of rope. When they reached the stern bulkhead, Bones felt the last shred of optimism leave him.

"Dead freaking end." He punched the bulkhead. It was only a half-hearted blow, one fueled more by annoyance than anger, but his fist drove straight through the bulkhead and into open space. "Whoa! It's a false wall." He withdrew his fist from the hole and shone his light inside.

The false bulkhead concealed a small area between the rear storage hold and the stern. The space was shaped like a wedge stood on its narrow end and was no more than a meter wide at its highest point.

"Good thing you didn't swing harder," Maddock said. "You might have punched all the way through to the keel."

"Lucky me," Bones said. "Do you think anything was hidden back here or is this just an oddity of the design?" He ran his light all around the small space. He saw nothing but sand and some loose ballast stones down at the bottom. "I'm not seeing anything."

"Hold on." Maddock took a few steps back, cupped his chin, and stared at the bulkhead. "You know what?" This plank down here looks as if it's been jimmied free and then hammered back into place." He yanked the board free and held it out so Bones could see the various scuffs and marks.

"If so, they must done it so they could get to whatever was hidden back here." Without any real sense of hope, he knelt and shone his light through the gaping hole Maddock had opened in the bulkhead.

He spotted something immediately. A shiny, obsidian sphere that seemed to throb with a dark, iridescent glow.

"No freaking way." He picked up the pea-sized object and held it up to Maddock. "A black pearl."

The Tahitian pearl, or black pearl, was one of the rarest and most beautiful of their kind. While most so-called black pearls were in fact, charcoal, silver, or dark green, the true black pearl was exceedingly rare and valuable. They also tended to be much larger than other pearls owing to the size of the oysters in which they grew. This one was small, which must have been how it had escaped notice.

"It's incredible," Maddock said.

"It was down in the loose ballast stones. I couldn't see it until I looked from a different angle."

"Let's see if there are more."

"Already on it."

They worked a few more planks free from the bulkhead. Next, they carefully removed the ballast stones one by one. Finally, they sifted through the sand at the bottom. When they were finished, they'd found the tattered remains of a small canvas bag, and a double handful of pearls. Beautiful pearls in shades of metallic gray. And to cap it off, two marble-sized pearls of pure jet black.

"It's like looking into a black hole," Bones said.

"If Corey were here, we'd be listening to a Spinal Tap joke right about now."

Bones gazed at the pearl in his hand. It was obvious what had happened. Valuable treasure was hidden here. When the crew retrieved it, one of the bags had split. They'd managed to gather most, but not all, of the pearls. His heart pounded. He knew what they had found!

"Do you know whose ship this must be?"

Maddock nodded. "Iturbe."

Juan Iturbe was the name of a legendary Spanish sailor who, in 1615, while attempting to find a shortcut from the Pacific to the Caribbean, found his way into the Salton Sea and ran aground. Decades later, a mule driver named Tiburcio Manquerna claimed to have stumbled across the pearl ship while lost in the desert but was unable to find it again.

"According to legend, Iturbe's holds were brimming with pearls and other treasures of the Pacific," Maddock said. "And there's no record of any such treasure ever being found."

"Which brings us back to our theory that they found a hiding spot somewhere close by, probably the caverns. But we're no closer to finding it."

"Oh, I wouldn't say that." Maddock picked up the first plank he'd removed from the bulkhead. "It occurred to me that Iturbe wouldn't want the crown to lose such a valuable treasure. It would have made sense to leave directions for anyone who might follow. Assuming they knew where to look." He flipped the plank over so Bones could see the underside. A map, complete with landmarks and a myriad of twists and turns, was carved into the back. "I think we just found our treasure map."

Although they were both exhausted from the day's misadventures, the thrill of discovery buoyed them, and they made their way back to the ranch in short order. The sounds of fighting had died down, and they encountered no one until they reached the outskirts of Grizzly's ranch.

"Maddock? Bones?" Grizzly appeared from the darkness up ahead. He wore a pistol at his hip and an unreadable expression on his face.

"Yo!" Bones called back. "Check this out. You won't believe what we've found!" He held up the plank with the map carved on it.

"Tell me later," Grizzly snapped. That was unusual for the perpetually laid-back television host. Bones didn't see him ever looking so intense. "You guys didn't bump into the girls, did you?"

"No, why?" Maddock asked.

Grizzly reached into the breast pocket of his khaki

shirt, took out a folded sheet of paper, and handed it to Maddock. On it was written a brief message in Riv's tight, angular hand.

Made a breakthrough. Gone with Spenser and Rockwell to check out one of the caverns. Don't worry. Will be careful. XOXO

"They went to the caverns?" Maddock said. "When did they leave?"

"No idea. I got home less than an hour ago. Lilith was there looking for Rockwell, all freaked out. Something about work but she wouldn't say what. Said he left the office early this afternoon headed for the ranch, but say why he was coming here. I left her there with instructions to call me if they return or if she hears from them. Not that she's likely to be able to reach me out here, or down there." He pointed in the direction of the caverns. "But giving her a job seemed to calm her down."

Maddock and Bones exchanged a long look of consternation. Grizzly didn't miss it.

"What's going on?" he demanded.

They began filling him in on the day's events, starting with the news that the men in black were involved in human trafficking and had set up shop in the caverns.

"They were shooting it out with somebody earlier today. No idea who," Bones said.

"We have to find them," Grizzly said. "Show me the way."

They set out for the hidden entrance. Maddock led the way while Bones continued bringing Grizzly up to speed. It was a measure of his concern that the discovery of Iturbe's ship and a trove of black pearls elicited only a grunt and a nod of approval. The description of Striker's chamber of horrors was good for a frown, and the news that Shipman had indeed killed Megan Keane earned only a sad shake of the head.

"She had better be okay," he kept whispering.

As they approached the hidden entrance, Bones began to scout around for tracks. He soon found them—three fresh sets, one large, two smaller, leading up to the caverns.

Maddock sagged with obvious relief.

"They made it inside and it doesn't look like anyone else has been here. That's good news."

"How so?" Grizzly sounded hopeful, but his drawn face and tight frown said he was afraid to believe it was true.

"We've already been through this section of the caverns and we didn't run into any traffickers," Bones said. "Just a booby trap that might or might not have been left by them, and we disabled that. The treasure is obviously hidden in a remote area. So, if they really did make a breakthrough that could lead them to the treasure, there's a good chance they won't go anywhere near the traffickers. They're just three fellow idiots searching for treasure."

"Which just leaves all the things that can go wrong deep underground. Riv thinks Rock City in Chattanooga counts as caving. Has Spenser done any caving?" he asked Maddock.

Maddock looked surprised. "How would I know? But never mind that. If they are on the right track, all we have to do is follow Iturbe's map…" He held up the plank. "…and we just might meet them along the way to wherever X marks the spot."

The wooden map was much too large to haul through the passageways, so they spent some time studying it. Then they snapped closeup photographs for later reference.

And then Bones spotted something. Faint letters scratched above the map.

"Look. Something's written here in Spanish."

"Camina con la suerte de los santos," Grizzly read

aloud. "Walk with the luck of the Saints, I think."

"Well, that's friendly." Bones committed the words to memory, just to be safe. Next, he hid the plank underneath a juniper and piled rocks on top of it. They could come back for it later.

"Are you sure you're up to this?" Bones said quietly to Maddock. He'd watched his friend struggle through the pain and exhaustion, and it was obvious Maddock didn't have a whole lot left.

"Don't worry about me," Maddock said flatly, not meeting Bones' eye.

"She'll be all right," Bones said. "She's not an idiot like her brother."

Maddock managed a laugh. "Maybe that's my type."

"What is?" Bones asked.

"You know," Maddock said. "Smart women with idiot brothers."

CHAPTER 33

"We got one!" Platt shouted as he and Ace appeared in the darkness. Between them they frog-marched a young man in a ripped, dirty black suit. He was tall and lean with beady eyes and a wispy mustache. Jesus, he was just a kid. His wrists were bound behind his back and he stumbled as they hauled him forward. The members of the two television crews, all now armed, circled around.

"This foreign invader was trying to sneak up on Ace," Platt said. "But I snuck up on him. Isn't that right, amigo?"

"I'm an American," their captive said, "and I'm not your amigo."

Gold stepped up to the young man and pressed the tip of his rifle to the fellow's crotch.

"You're going to be an amiga if you don't check that attitude."

It took the young man a second to recognize his captor. When he did, his lips began to work rapidly, but no sound came.

"It helps if you say words," Platt prompted. "You got a name?"

"Brian." The young man found his voice again. "What the hell is happening? There's two of you out here?"

"Two of *us*? You've seen our friend, Segar?" Gold asked.

"Yeah. He's back at…" The fellow clammed up.

Gold turned away. "Anybody got a .22 on them?"

"I do." Yoshi drew a snub-nosed revolver from his pocket. Why he'd chosen that particular weapon for this environment Gold had no idea. But it would serve for what he had in mind.

"Great. I need you to shoot this guy right there." He

pointed to Brian's abdomen.

Yoshi nodded eagerly and raised the pistol. Segar's disappearance had flipped a primal switch inside the young cameraman. He was eager for blood.

"What the hell, man?" The wild-eyed prisoner began to thrash, trying to break free from Platt and Ace, who still held him by the elbows.

"Do it at an angle," Gold continued. "I want it to pass through the liver but not rattle around in there. You might want to move in close so you don't miss." It was all a bunch of Grade A bull crap. Hell, there was more truth on a page of the Washington Post, but it had the desired effect.

"No!" Brian shouted.

"You're going to love it. It's like no pain you've ever imagined."

"Why are you doing this? Bro, I've got, like, one of your cassettes. You autographed it for my mom back before I was born."

"Oh, really? Well, if you've got Terry Gold fandom in your DNA, then maybe there's hope for you after all. All right, Brian. I'm going to give you a one-time only special invitation to turn away from the dark side and join the red, white, and by God blue."

Brian's terror dissolved into a nervous, twitchy silence. His breath came in short gasps and his eyes kept flitting from side to side.

"I'll take that silence as a sign that you're interested in my proposition," Gold said. "First of all, you tell me who the hell you people are and what you're doing out here."

"I'm not one of them," Brian said. "A dude I know just brought me in last week. I thought I was going to help people cross the border without getting caught." He flashed a fearful look at Gold.

"I can't blame people for wanting to breathe the sweet air of freedom," Gold said. "So, what are they really up to?"

Brian hung his head. "They got the people across

the border all right, but I didn't know they were going to sell them."

"Sell them?" Yoshi raised his pistol.

"No!" Gold snapped. "I said we'd give him a chance." He turned back to Brian. "You're a human trafficker?"

"I'm not one of them. I'm just stuck. I was trying to run away when you guys found me."

Gold looked Brian in the eye, held his gaze until he was satisfied he had the young man's measure.

"Can you show me the way to where Segar and all the other captives are being held?"

Brian nodded. "I can take you right to them."

"Okay, you lead us to these dirtbags, help us get our friend back, and don't do anything to screw us over, and when this gets reported to the authorities, I'll vouch for you. There's your coupon. Are you gonna redeem it?"

"Yes, sir," Brian said. "I don't like those guys any better than you do."

Gold turned to the camera. "All right, brothers. It's time for the posse to ride!"

"I think I know where we are on the map now," Maddock whispered. They'd arrived at a T-junction, each branch of which split into two passageways. It was a distinctive looking passageway and it aligned perfectly with a similar spot on Iturbe's map.

"The girls are on the right track so far," Grizzly said. "Smart of them to leave the arrows."

Someone had drawn chalk arrows to mark their path into the caverns. So far, the path lined out on the old map matched up with the chalk markings. Whatever their breakthrough was, it must have set them on the same path as Maddock and Bones.

They followed the passageway to the left, then bore right where it branched off. The going soon became easy. The ceiling was high enough that they no longer had to crawl or even crouch. They picked up the pace, always careful not to make too much noise or to let the beams of their Maglites stray too far ahead.

For a moment, Bones felt his spirits lift. And then Maddock called a halt and pointed to a smudge on the wall.

"Someone wiped out the chalk arrow," he said. "They almost managed to cover it up but you can see a little bit of the chalk."

"What does that mean?" Grizzly asked.

Bones could sense panic rising in Grizzly, and rage boiling in Maddock.

"Maybe they were getting close to the treasure and decided to stop marking their path, just to be safe," Bones said. "Or they might have heard someone and didn't want to leave a trail."

Grizzly brightened. "Hell, they might have heard us. We need to be careful. Wouldn't want them mistaking us for the bad guys."

"Hold on! Turn out the lights," Bones said softly. He'd heard something up ahead.

The lights went out, plunging them into utter darkness. A glow appeared in the distance. Someone was coming. Each man drew his weapon. And they backed around the nearest curve in the passageway.

Bones peered around the corner. It wasn't their friend. Two men in dark slacks and white shirts stood a short distance away. Apparently, the traffickers weren't required to adhere strictly to their dress code down here in the caverns.

"Dude, I think we should turn back. There's no way he came this far," a voice said.

"Works for me. Maybe we can spend a little time with those chicks we brought in."

Bones' heart skipped a beat.

The men turned and headed in the opposite direction.

No one needed to speak. Bones, Maddock and Grizzly stood as one and crept off in silent pursuit.

CHAPTER 34

There it was again. The staccato beat of gunfire. The human traffickers were shooting it out with someone. Whether that was good or bad news, Segar and his fellow captives couldn't say. One thing was certain—no one was keeping an eye on them. This would most likely be their best chance to escape.

Segar's heart raced as he twisted and thrashed about. The cord cut into his sweat-slicked wrists, but he kept fighting. The spirits had put him in this place for a reason. He was here to save the day. The other captives were holding up well, although he doubted they would be much help. Franzen, the cop, had obviously gotten herself captured. Spenser was one of the new generation of social media celebrities, and Riv worked for Grizzly Grant, which spoke for itself.

"How did they get you?" Franzen asked. She was doing something behind her back, vigorously moving her arms. Segar wasn't sure what she was up to.

"I was beating the crap out of one of these dirtbags when my ankle betrayed me," he said. "And you?"

"I was out looking around. Somebody snuck up on me and bashed me in the head," she said through gritted teeth.

"Were you trying to bring down these traffickers all by yourself?" Segar asked. "That's not a job for one cop. You're not an action hero."

"I was looking for a way into the caverns, but I didn't know there would be traffickers here. I was searching for clues. A friend of mine who went missing years ago. Some men brought in something of hers they'd found in the caverns."

"Maddock and Bones," Spenser said.

"You know them?"

"We do," Spenser said. "And if we get out of this

alive, they're going to be very unhappy with us."

Franzen appeared to be only halfway listening. "Human traffickers. How could they be operating here without us knowing?"

"Don't feel bad. We knew there was danger and we walked right into it." Spenser said. "And they took our friend, too."

"That Rockwell fellow? We'll get him. No one needs to worry. I'm going to work myself free." Segar twisted and worked his wrists even harder.

"You're going to hurt yourself, is what you're going to do," Riv said.

"I'll be out in a minute. I know the trick."

Riv raised her eyebrows. "Oh, yeah? What trick is that?"

"When they tied me up, I inflated my chest as much as I could. That way, when I breathe out, the ropes are looser."

"How does that help with your wrists being tied?" Spenser asked.

Segar let out a long, impatient breath. "It all works together. It's a Zen thing."

"I'll tell you what does work," Franzen grunted. Like the others, her wrists were bound behind her back. She'd been working her arms vigorously for a few minutes. "A sharp edge and friction!" With a twist, her hands came free. She didn't waste time removing the cords from her wrists, but immediately set to freeing the others.

"I don't suppose any of you know the way out of here?" she asked as she untied Riv.

"I still have the map we were working from," Spenser said. "If we can find our way to the place where they captured us."

"Good." Franzen untied Segar and helped him to his feet. "Let's get the hell out of here."

"But what about all the captives? What about their friend?" Segar couldn't believe an officer of the law would consider fleeing the scene and leaving innocents behind.

Another gunshot rang out somewhere in the darkness.

"I hate to say it, but I think she's right," Riv said. "They have guns. We don't. Our best chance of helping them is to get out of here safely and find help."

"But we have to try," Segar protested.

"We're going to take things as they come," Franzen said. "If there's an opportunity to safely free more victims, we will. At the very least I want to get the three of you out of here safely."

Segar looked down at her and grinned sadly. "I appreciate you untying my wrists, but you don't have to worry about things from here on out. I'll take the lead." Rolling up his sleeves, he turned, picked up the flashlight their captor had left behind, and led the way out of the chamber.

He limped along on his injured ankle, trying to mentally block out the pain. He was so focused on it that he turned the corner and walked right into one of the traffickers. Startled from his trance, Segar threw a right cross with all his might. It caught the surprised man clean on the jaw. His knees buckled and he flopped to the ground.

"Nice shot!" Spenser said. "Did you even know he was there?"

"The secret is to act, not to be. Or maybe it's the other way around. It's a line from one of my films."

Meanwhile, Franzen had relieved the fallen trafficker of his pistol and was in the process of tying his wrists and ankles. Riv took the man's belt knife.

"Are you trained to fight with a blade?" Segar asked.

"Does growing up in a really bad neighborhood count?"

"It's a start. If you need any pointers, let me know." He winked. "Pun intended."

Riv mumbled something that sounded like, "Goddess give me strength," and turned away.

While Franzen searched the man's pockets, Segar

peered around the next corner. Up ahead lay a large cavern. Weak, battery powered lanterns cast the space in jaundiced yellow light. Segar gasped. The room was filled with captives. A single guard stood with his back to Segar.

Big mistake, compadre!

Segar took off like a sprinter from the starting blocks. Slowed by his injured ankle, he didn't quite get there before the guard whirled around and reached for his weapon.

Segar bowled him over. They landed in a heap and began to struggle for the gun. Segar quickly found himself at a disadvantage. His opponent forced him onto his back and struggled to bring his weapon to bear. He seized the man's wrist in both hands, trying to keep the pistol at bay. This freed up the attacker's other hand for punching. He managed to land a few before someone grabbed the man from behind and drew a knife across his throat. Segar covered his face but didn't quite avoid the blood.

Riv dragged the trafficker's still-twitching body off him and helped him to his feet. Segar gave a nod of thanks, then turned to look around.

The captives were nearly all young women, mostly teenagers and early twenties, but a few who looked close to Spenser's age. All were cuffed with zip ties. The chains of their ankle shackles were looped around one heavy chain that was anchored to the rock wall on one end. The other was secured to an iron ring with a massive lock.

One boy about twelve years old looked up at him. His eyes went wide and he gasped.

"Steven Segar!" he exclaimed.

The captives began speaking all at once. Mostly in Spanish, but a few in English.

"Please help us," one young woman said in heavily accented English.

"That's what I'm here for," he assured her.

Riv began barking orders in Spanish and everyone

quieted down. Franzen dug a key ring out of the fallen guard's pocket and began searching for the one that would open the lock that held the captives.

"Set them free," he ordered.

Franzen turned a frown in his direction. "What does it look like I'm doing?"

He turned to look for the guard's weapon, but Spenser had already claimed it.

"You should probably give me that," he said.

Her big blue eyes flitted toward Franzen, who gave a tiny shake of the head.

"I can't defend myself hand-to-hand like you can," Spenser said.

"That is true. You may keep the weapon."

"Thank you." As he watched, she ejected the magazine, counted the remaining bullets, popped it back into place, and chambered a round.

"Don't forget the safety," Segar reminded her.

"Thanks!" Her smile did not reach her eyes. Must be nervous.

Franzen had unlocked the chain and was now working to unlock the individual shackles, while Riv was carefully cutting the zip ties that bound their wrists.

"Are there more captives?" Segar asked the young man who had recognized him moments before.

"Many more," the youth said. "Are you going to set them free, too?"

Segar smiled and nodded. "That I am, my young friend."

CHAPTER 35

Maddock and Bones heard the sound of distant fighting. The men they followed heard it too and picked up their pace. The dark tunnel opened into a large cave. All around were signs of human habitation and modification. The floor had been smoothed, and the chamber was ringed by cells that had been hewn into the natural rock. Crates and boxes were stacked haphazardly in some of them. Inside a few others lay blankets, sleeping bags, and stray clothing.

"I think we've found their lair," Grizzly whispered.

Maddock nodded and waved for his friend to be quiet. But it was too late.

"Did you hear something?" a voice from up ahead said. "Somebody back there."

"Aw, bro! Brian must be back there. Dude was probably asleep behind some boxes and we missed him," another voice replied.

"I'll check." Footsteps approached.

Maddock and Bones moved to either side of the cavern entrance and waited.

"Brian? You in here?"

The trafficker stepped into the cavern. Maddock and Bones sprang. Maddock seized him by the wrist and controlled his gun hand while Bones struck him hard on the jaw. The man's knees buckled, and he slumped to the ground, Maddock ripping the pistol free. Bones covered the man's mouth.

"You yell, you die. Understand?"

The man made a jerky nod.

"Where are the girls and Rockwell? And don't pretend you don't know who I'm talking about."

"You keep going through one more cave and then go right."

"Are they still alive?" Maddock asked. The man

probably took no more than a split-second to reply, but to Maddock it felt like an eternity.

"Yeah. They were a little while ago, anyway."

"We keep hearing shooting. Who are you guys fighting?" Bones asked.

"Nobody knows. They just showed up. Must be trying to move in on our territory."

A beam of light sliced into the dim cavern. They had taken too long. The other trafficker had returned.

They all scrambled in different directions as the boom of gunfire erupted, deafening in the confined space. The man's companion didn't manage to get out of the way. The bullets tore through him as he stumbled to his feet. He let out a surprised grunt and fell again to the ground.

Maddock squeezed off a single shot that took the man in the heart.

"Let's go!" Armed with the trafficker's pistol in one hand and his own in his right, he charged down the corridor and into the next cavern.

They hadn't had time to ask what lay ahead. The answer to that question was a dozen bound women, plus a handful of armed guards seated at a table. They were playing Texas Hold 'Em to the light of a small lantern. Maddock didn't give them the opportunity to react. Every shot found its mark. Bones only managed to squeeze off a pair of shots, though he didn't miss either.

"Leave some for me, Maddock," Bones grumbled. He glanced down at the cards one of the dead men had been holding and gave a shake of his head. "Aces and eights. He should have expected it."

Maddock barely heard him. He was operating on sheer rage right now, and if he slowed down, he might suffer an adrenaline dump. He wasn't sure his body had enough left to carry him through should that happen.

"¡Callense!" he barked to the surprised captives. Everyone fell silent.

"You guys untie them and tell them to hide until someone comes for them." He stopped long enough to replace his weapons with two fully loaded ones. The fallen traffickers wouldn't need them anymore.

"Hold on," Bones said. "We'll only be a minute."

Maddock kept walking.

Moonlight dusted the landscape with silver. Somewhere very close by, a coyote began to yip. His pack soon followed, filling the night with their unearthly howl.

"That's music to my ears," Terry Gold said to the camera. "The sweet sound of free spirits that can never be tamed."

They'd tracked Segar and his captor to a box canyon, at the end of which lay the entrance to what must have been a decent-sized cave considering how many men came boiling out to take a shot at Gold and his crew.

The fight had been intense, with the defenders putting a hailstorm of lead in the air, and Gold's squad countering with carefully aimed shots. Little by little they'd whittled the enemy down, but he couldn't imagine any way they could overcome such a position without suffering loss of life.

The sound of running feet caused him to turn around. Roddy came jogging forward. Blood soaked his t-shirt and he had a bandage around his left bicep.

"What happened?" Gold said.

"Winged me." Roddy said. "I'm embarrassed to even call it a wound."

Gold looked into the young actor's eyes. Really looked. The man didn't seem afraid, or even upset.

"You all right?" he asked.

"I'm alive."

Gold turned to the camera. "Hey, turn that off so we can talk."

"No, keep rolling," Roddy said. "I know what you're going to say. That I've done enough and I can sit the rest of it out. I'm not going to do that." He turned to the camera. "We captured one of them. He says they've got at least thirty women and children held captive in those caverns."

As the young man spoke, Gold seethed with rage. Men like these were the lowest of the low. Their victims would most likely end up forced into sex work, doomed to what would likely be short lives filled with abuse and misery.

"They're holding Segar captive, as well as a local police officer," Roddy went on. "The man we've caught has no idea what's planned for either of them. This is just a way station for them. They planned to leave in the morning."

"They're not going anywhere," Gold said. "We've got them hemmed in. And it would be nice if we could get just a little support from law enforcement." Communication had been a challenge out here in the middle of nowhere. They'd finally managed to contact local police. The officer who had answered the phone sounded doubtful but promised to have someone check it out as soon as possible. They were still trying to contact other authorities, but they had to face the fact that time might be running short. If that were the case, Segar's life depended on them.

"Let's move in for a closer look," Gold said to the camera.

Roddy led the way, but they could have followed the sounds of sporadic gunfire. When they arrived at the front line, as it were, things were at a stalemate.

The human traffickers had taken up a solid defensive position among the boulder piles that hid the entrance to the caverns. That would be a difficult line to break.

"We need some grenades," Roddy said. "Something we can throw in behind them to drive them out."

Gold absently tugged at the stubble on his chin. They had no grenades, but they had good old American ingenuity. Time to improvise.

"We have a couple of emergency flare guns, don't we?"

CHAPTER 36

Spenser and the others were already gone when Maddock reached the chamber. The place was empty, save for one man. He was built like a tree stump, with powerful arms, a shaved head, and no neck to speak of. He was standing with his hands on his hips, turning slowly around as if he had never seen its like.

"Where the hell did they go?" he said to himself.

Maddock crept up behind him and waited for him to turn around. Their eyes met. The man had a moment of confusion, which turned to agony when Maddock kicked him in the groin. He let out a throaty grunt and collapsed like soft butter. Maddock pressed his pistol to the man's temple.

"Where are they?"

"I don't know, man. They were supposed to be here. Them and the police lady." He began to babble. "Everything was cool. We were going to leave in the morning. And all these random-ass people start showing up. Attacking us from outside and inside. Who are you?"

"The guy who's already squeezing the trigger unless you make yourself useful."

"I know they didn't head toward the main cavern. I just came from there and I didn't see anybody."

"Where do I go next? And I'll know if you lie." That itself was a lie, but Maddock thought this blubbering coward would believe it. Perhaps a life of bullying the weak made a man soft.

The man sputtered out hasty instructions along with a generous spray of saliva.

"What happens to the people you transport?"

"I don't know, man. I'm just a middleman, bro. I get the illegals into the country without the Feds catching them. Whatever business arrangements they make after that, you can't put that on me."

The mental list of punishments that were too good for this man was too lengthy for Maddock to peruse. Instead, he settled for confiscating the man's pistol. He had no use for three, so he popped out the magazine, cleared the chamber, and tossed the weapon away.

"Get up. You're going to lead the way," he said.

"Okay, okay. I'll help you find them, I promise." Big baldy climbed to his feet. "Like I said, it's back the way you came."

He took two steps and then dashed out of the cavern at a dead sprint, where he ran into Bones and Grizzly.

The results were predictable.

"I'm in here," Maddock called.

Bones and Grizzly came running in. Grizzly scanned the empty chamber with panic-filled eyes.

"Where are they? Where's Riv?"

"Relax. He told me which way they went. Come on."

They dashed out of the cavern, careful not to trip over the body of the fallen trafficker. They followed his directions until they stumbled into a cavern where a large group of confused-looking young women sat huddled in a tight circle. They were not restrained, but a heavy chain and a large pile of loose shackles lay nearby. Someone had set them free.

They all began talking at once. Maddock understood enough of what they were saying to understand that a man and three women had passed through here. That must be Spenser, Riv, Rockwell, and the police officer. The captives pointed in the direction in which the quartet had gone.

Maddock thanked them and ordered them to stay put. He took off at a fast jog, the best he could manage in his state. Up ahead, shots rang out and he heard a woman scream.

Something was happening at the mouth of the cavern. Through his binoculars, Gold could see movement in the darkness but not much else. At least twice as many figures as before scurried around behind their defensive position.

"Perfect timing." He put down the binoculars and looked around at his team. Everyone was in position. He picked up the flare gun and leveled it at the bunker. Ace, next to Gold the most experienced of the group, had the other. "If this works, be ready for those dirtbags to come buzzing out of there like a swarm of hornets."

"Do it, Pops," Platt replied.

Gold counted it down.

"Three… two… one…."

They fired in unison. The flares soared into the darkness, lighting up the desert floor. Both found their marks. The cavern mouth lit up like the Fourth of July. The traffickers scattered. Some fled back into the cavern, but most came spilling out.

Gold and his team opened fire. For a moment Gold thought his men had wiped them out with the first salvo, but then voices began to call out.

"No mas!"

"We give up!"

Gold turned to the camera. "With apologies to John Denver, that, my friends, is what I call a sweet surrender." He turned and addressed the traffickers. "Everybody lay face down and put your hands behind your backs." Platt translated into Spanish. "If anyone reaches for a weapon, we shoot!"

They quickly disarmed the traffickers, bound them, and set a few men to guard them.

"All right," Gold said. "Let's run them to ground." With a quick glance to make sure the camera was still rolling, he raised his rifle high. "Charge!"

CHAPTER 37

Maddock tried to pour on an extra burst of speed, but the human body had its limits, despite the movies that would have viewers believe otherwise. Bones passed him, then Grizzly. The sounds of gunfire grew louder. He couldn't be too late.

Maddock caught a whiff of fresh, dry air. They were nearing an exit. Up ahead, a well-lit chamber beckoned. Inside, a ragged-looking group of men were shouting at one another. More shots rang out and one man fell.

And then all was chaos. One of the traffickers spotted Bones and fired in their direction. Grizzly returned fire. Three jerky shots, one of which hit its mark.

"Calm down," Maddock barked. "Stay behind cover and make your shots count."

Another shot from an unseen assailant took out another of the traffickers. Who else was shooting at them?

"Who the hell is shooting at them?" Bones shouted.

"I don't know but I'll take all the help I can get," Maddock said.

One of the traffickers cracked under the pressure. Screaming like a wild man, he made a mad dash in Maddock's direction, firing wildly.

Maddock took aim, but before he could squeeze the trigger, Bones' pistol boomed.

"Got him!" Bones cried as his shot took the man between the eyes. "Sorry, Maddock, but you haven't exactly been sharing."

Their numbers down to three, the traffickers surrendered. Bones and Grizzly disarmed the men and bound their wrists and ankles while Maddock looked around.

"Where are they?" Maddock said.

"Hiding from the traffickers, I hope," Bones said.

"If something's happened to Riv…" Grizzly said.

"We haven't seen a single captive harmed," Bones said. "They're too valuable to waste like that," he added with a bitter note in his voice.

"Somebody else was shooting at them," Maddock said. "Could it have been one of them?"

"If they were resourceful enough to escape, they could get a hold of a weapon," Bones said. "They might have run, not knowing who we were."

"Spenser!" Maddock shouted.

"Riv!" Grizzly called.

Footsteps and then a powerful voice boomed, "Everybody freeze!"

On this most bizarre of nights, Maddock wouldn't have believed anything could shock him. But when he turned around, there stood actor Steven Segar crouched in a martial arts stance.

"Now, let's all remain calm," Segar said.

"Holy freaking crap," Bones said. "You're Steven Segar. I own both of your movies on VHS."

Still holding his defensive stance, Segar frowned. "I've made a lot more than two movies."

"I meant the two good ones," Bones said.

"Is this your operation?" Maddock demanded. He didn't care how famous the man was. He wanted to find Spenser and he wanted to know what was going on.

"Of course not." Segar stood up straight and smoothed his clothing. "I was filming a show out in the desert when I was kidnapped. They were going to hold me for ransom, I assume. But I escaped and rescued three damsels in distress while I was at it."

Just then, Riv and Spenser burst into the cavern, followed by an angry-looking Franzen.

"Maddock!" Spenser ran forward and leaped into his arms. In his diminished state, she nearly bowled him over, but he managed to remain on his feet. She pressed her forehead to his, her eyes so big and blue. "I always knew some day you'd come walking back through…"

She didn't quite manage to finish the quote before Maddock's lips were planted firmly on hers. When they finally broke the kiss, she made an angry face.

"It's rude to interrupt a girl when she's quoting Indiana Jones."

"Sorry," he grunted. "By the way, I'm about to drop you."

She slid nimbly to the ground and slipped her arm around his waist. Nearby, Grizzly was holding Riv tight.

Segar looked at Franzen and winked. "Don't you think the hero of the day deserves a kiss, too?"

Franzen's lips moved but she couldn't find the words before they were interrupted by a commotion on the far side of the chamber. Everyone hit the ground and drew their weapons, with the exception of Segar, who flowed into a crane stance for no apparent reason.

And then the night got even stranger.

A line of traffickers walked in single file, hands behind their heads. They were escorted by a group of armed men. They were followed by a confused-looking police officer and, bringing up the rear, Orry Rockwell. His face was battered and bloody, but he appeared to be moving okay.

Their leader wore a battered cowboy hat with a red, white, and blue band. He was tall with a long face, a big-toothed smile. He wore his stringy hair pulled back in a ponytail.

"Well, God bless America!" the man boomed when he saw them. "Looks like somebody saved old Seagull's bacon."

"I saved myself, Terry Nugget," Segar replied. "Along with these ladies and a number of captives." He glanced down at his blood-spattered shirt. "And this is not my blood."

Bones turned to Maddock and mouthed, "Terry Gold?"

Franzen and the newly arrived officer, a tall, curly-haired man named Brown, quickly took charge. Gold and Segar put their crews, except for Gold's camera and audio team, at the officers' disposal. Rockwell, after checking on Riv and Spenser, joined them as they rounded up and secured the remaining traffickers and made plans for the care of the captives.

Meanwhile, Gold introduced himself and actor Roddy Green. Maddock hadn't heard of him, but Spenser looked mildly impressed. Gold and Segar, with an occasional interjection from a diminutive young man named Yoshi, explained the premise of their television show and how they came to be here. Segar provided only vague details of his capture and Gold followed with a detailed account of their rescue mission.

"And I refuse to believe that Seagull, here, was the hero of anything," Gold said.

Riv spoke up. "I can't lie. He did knock one of those dudes out cold."

"And he led the way every step," Spenser added. "We figured he was most expendable," she added to Maddock in a whisper.

"I'd like to get these ladies on camera right away," Segar said to Yoshi. "Make a note."

"Your treasure hunting show. I don't suppose you're looking for the Arch Gold Mine?" Bones asked.

"We are. It must be somewhere in these caverns," Segar said.

"We could make an entire season out of exploring these caverns," Gold agreed.

"Hold on," Grizzly objected. "A significant portion of these caverns lie on my property, and we're already in pre-production for a similar program."

"I'm sure we can work something out," Gold said. "For now, Segar and I need to do a little filming." The two men took up a position in front of some of the captured traffickers and began discussing their combined victory.

"Hollywood," Bones deadpanned.

With the others distracted, Bones and Maddock recounted the day's events to Grizzly, Riv, and Spenser. All were stunned that they had, in fact, discovered

Iturbe's lost ship.

"The treasure is long gone," Bones said, "but we found a few artifacts, so it's not a total bust."

Shipman's tale, and the revelation that he had, in fact, killed Megan Keane, was a sobering one.

"I'm going to tell to Franzen," Riv said. "She knew Megan and will want to hear the true story right away." She took Grizzly by the hand and led him away.

When they had gone, Spenser grabbed Maddock by the elbow and steered him out of the chamber and into a side passage.

"Listen," she said as soon as they were out of earshot. "This place will soon be swarming with police and then the feds. And after that comes the television show and then it's fair game for treasure hunters from near and far."

"I know. I didn't get the chance to tell you all, one of the things we found in the ship…"

"There's no time." She reached into her pocket and took out two folded sheets of paper. "We figured out the journal. There was no hidden code, aside from notes jotted in here and there in Morse code. The whole thing was a map." She unfolded them and handed one sheet to him. "This is where we are right now." She tapped a spot on the map. "And this is where you need to go."

Maddock knew in a glance that Spenser's map was consistent with Iturbe's. He couldn't believe it. He'd been stumped by the journal.

"A map? How?"

Spenser fidgeted, tugged at her hair, not quite managing to conceal her look of triumph. "It's one of those things you can't see until you see it, and then you can't unsee it."

"But you figured it out?"

"Riv and I worked on it together. But I made the breakthrough. Does it sound bad to say that?" She bit her lip.

"Not at all."

She batted her eyelids and flashed a coy smile. "I'm

an Indiana Jones girl at heart. I want you to find the treasure. Take advantage of the confusion and get out of here. If anyone asks, I'll say you're looking for more captives or traffickers the others might have missed."

"Come with us." Maddock couldn't believe what he was saying. "You deserve to be there."

"Not this time. I'd only slow you guys down and the clock is ticking. Besides, Segar and Gold want to get me on camera. Good publicity."

"Thank you." The words seemed so inadequate to Maddock that, on impulse, he fished into his pocket, dug out the largest of the black pearls he had found, and pressed it into her palm. "Here, you hold onto that until I get back."

She marveled at it, then flashed a sly grin. "If you don't come back, I'm keeping this."

"In that case I guess I'd better make it back."

CHAPTER 38

"**Looks like Striker** was on the right track," Maddock said as he and Bones followed the path laid out by the map. "Hopefully he didn't actually find the treasure."

"Of course he didn't," Bones said. "That's what you and I are for." He was limping a little. Maddock wasn't the only one who had been through the wringer.

With a map to guide them and no fear of running into human traffickers, they moved quickly. Although the directions were easy to follow, many of the passageways they entered were well-hidden. It was easy to see how they had gone largely undiscovered.

The way grew steep, plunged them deep beneath the earth.

"It's going to be one hell of a climb back out," Maddock said.

"Maddock," Bones said seriously as he ducked beneath a low-hanging stalactite, "I'm too tired to deal with your negative take on everything."

"Fair enough." Maddock glanced down at the map, then looked around. The caverns down here were pristine. They were likely the first people to pass this way since Striker. And before him? Maybe Juan Iturbe.

He looked around, got his bearings, and shone his light on a meter-wide crack in the wall. "The next chamber is that way. According to Striker's map, this is the end of the line."

They slipped through the narrow opening and found themselves in a chamber that was more like an art gallery than a cavern. The stalactites had been sculpted to resemble the tentacles of the kraken. Stalagmites and boulders were shaped like coral, eels, and even a mermaid. It was like being deep beneath the sea. They shone their lights all around, marveled at the sights.

"Somebody must have spent a lifetime on this

place," Bones said. Maddock couldn't disagree.

They made a quick inspection of the small cavern but found neither treasure nor another way out.

"Are you freaking kidding me?" Bones complained. "Tell me this isn't the end of the line."

Maddock took out his cell phone and reviewed the photos of Iturbe's map. He quickly located the chamber in which they stood.

"Look at this! Iturbe's map doesn't end here. There should be a passageway leading out." He looked up. "Should be right about one o'clock."

"Doesn't look promising," Bones said as they moved in that direction.

Sure enough, there was nothing there. Just a blank wall. No stray boulders hiding a passageway, no obvious trapdoors, not even a crack.

"Could the map be wrong?" Bones asked.

"No, there's no way," Maddock said, shining his light around. "Can you imagine the time and effort that went into making this place? And why put it way the hell down here unless it's a place of significance."

"That was my thinking, too. So, what did Striker miss?"

"The map is two-dimensional, which could mean that the passageway could be, I don't know, above or below us. But, if that's the case, how do we get in?"

They looked around. Maddock marveled at the wonders of this very strange place. He ran his hand across a starfish. The texture was perfect.

"I don't think Iturbe and his men ever tried to find civilization. I think, like you said, they stayed here and made this place their life's work."

"All of that work for a cargo of pearls?" Bones said. "That doesn't make a lot of sense."

"I know. Which suggests this is more than just a treasure vault."

Bones folded his arms. "Isn't that always the way?" He reached up and touched the tip of one of the stone tentacles. "Any bright ideas?"

"This place was built by sailors," Maddock said. "Men who, above all else, loved the sea."

"I hope you're not expecting praise for that brilliant insight," Bones said. "Considering what we're surrounded by."

"That's what I'm saying. Striker was a prospector at heart. So, what did he overlook down here that a true man of the sea would recognize immediately?"

Bones shrugged. "I recognize everything in here. Doesn't help."

"Start over with an open mind. There's got to be something here. Iturbe went to the trouble of leaving the map. What would be the point if it didn't lead somewhere?"

Finally, Bones spotted something.

"This thing over here is weird-looking. At first, I thought it was a tentacle wrapped around something, but now that I look at it up close, it's not quite right."

Maddock looked at the odd sculpture. It rang a bell. And then he remembered. "That's because it's not a tentacle. Those are the entrails of Saint Erasmus. The thing they're wrapped around is a windlass."

"Explain," Bones said.

"Erasmus of Formica, commonly known as Saint Elmo, is the patron saint of sailors and of abdominal pain."

Bones cocked his head. "How in the hell do you become the saint of upset stomachs?"

"By pissing off the Roman Emperor over and over until he has your guts tied to a winch and cranked out of your body. Which is why this is one of the symbols associated with Saint Erasmus."

Bones absently rubbed his belly as he reassessed the oddly carved stone. And then he stood stock-still.

"We forgot something."

"What's that?" Maddock asked.

"The message included with Iturbe's map. 'Walk with the luck of the saints.' Could that be a clue?"

Maddock instantly knew Bones was on to

something. "That would make sense. This is the only sculpture we've seen that obviously relates to one of the saints. It's also the sort of thing a seventeenth century sailor might identify as significant in a way a prospector like Striker wouldn't."

He took out his knife, knelt, and prodded at the base of the object. The stone was different, more porous than the other sculptures. He dug in and twisted the knife and a large chunk of stone broke off.

"It's fake," Maddock said with a note of triumph in his voice.

Bones took out his own knife and they chipped away at the mortar until they struck metal. Some more work revealed a hexagonal iron rod set in the floor.

"Holy freaking crap," Bones said. "The sculpture is covering an actual crank."

"So, even if Striker recognized this one shape as being unusual, he wouldn't have been able to turn the crank unless he cleared all the mortar away from the base."

Bones grinned. "What are we waiting for?"

They worked for a few more minutes until they'd cleared the mortar from the base of the crank. Maddock's heart raced. What were they about to find?

"You found it, you do the honors," he said.

Bones stood and gripped the windlass in both hands. He paused and looked to Maddock.

"Righty tighty, lefty loosy, you think?"

"It's got to be one or the other. Just don't break it."

"Here goes." Bones grunted as he put all his strength into the effort. Slowly, the handle began to turn. "Help me out, here."

Maddock lent his strength and they rotated the crank a full turn.

There came a series of clicks and bangs from somewhere below them as the gears of some unseen machine began to turn for the first time in centuries. The floor vibrated and a low rumbling filled their ears. Dust floated down from up above and Bones eyed the ceiling nervously.

"I hope we didn't just activate a booby trap."

"I think we're good." Maddock pointed.

A few feet away, a hole opened in the floor. From somewhere below came the sound of running water. Maddock shone his light in to reveal a narrow stone staircase winding down into the darkness.

"What did I tell you?" Bones said. "Finding the treasure is what you and I do."

CHAPTER 39

At the bottom of the staircase they found themselves at a bridge. It was a narrow affair and spanned a gap of twenty feet. Maddock shone his light down into the gap.

"I can't see the bottom," he said.

"In that case, we'd better not fall." Bones folded his arms and inspected the odd bridge. There were no railings, only a narrow bridge, two tiles wide. "I'm guessing it won't be as easy as just walking across."

"Doubtful. Maybe we should come back with a rope or two." He put up a hand when Bones rounded on him. "I'm joking. Besides, even if we had a rope, there's nothing to secure it to."

"We'll just have to get it right the first time," Bones said.

Maddock knelt and inspected the first row of tiles. One was carved with the image of a whale, the other a dolphin.

"Walk with the luck of the saints," Maddock said, echoing Iturbe's message. "They were sailors, so if this whale symbolizes Jonah…"

"Then it's bad luck," Bones said. To a sailor, a 'Jonah' was a passenger who, like their biblical namesake, carried bad luck with them on a voyage.

"How certain are we about this?" Maddock asked.

"Sure enough that I think you should test your theory. I'll hold on to you in case the whole thing comes crashing down."

"That's comforting." With Bones gripping his belt in both hands, Maddock put one foot onto the tile where the aquatic mammal was carved. It seemed solid, so he put his entire weight on it. It held.

Bones let out a sigh of relief. "One down, six to go."

The next choice was cat versus dog. A cat on board a ship was considered good luck, so Maddock made that his next choice.

"Two for two," he said.

"Don't get cocky," Bones warned.

Maddock didn't. He next chose the lucky cormorant over an eagle, and an apple over an unlucky banana. Each step held, but he couldn't escape the uneasy feeling that crept over him. He didn't know how the bridge was constructed or what condition it might be in. What he did know was that it would be a relief to reach the other side.

The next choice gave him a moment's pause. Two beautiful women, each sitting on a rock in the water, gazed up at him. At first glance they appeared to be identical, but it only took a moment to realize that one of them had the tail of a fish. That made her a lucky mermaid. The other women, the one with human legs, was obviously a siren—one of the mythical creatures whose beautiful singing voices lured sailors to their deaths against the rocks.

"What's next?" Bones called.

"Two birds. One is flying. The other is just standing there." He paused, gave it a closer look. The eyes were closed, the legs uneven, and a wing out of place. "Scratch that. It's not standing; it's dead."

"Got to be an albatross."

"I think you're right," Maddock said. The seabirds were thought to carry the souls of dead sailors. Seeing one was a good omen, but to kill a cormorant was to invite bad luck of the worst sort.

He stepped onto the flying seabird.

"One more to go," Bones said. "Unless you want to jump from there."

"I'd rather not." Maddock still didn't trust the bridge. "Besides, the last one's simple."

The tile on the left was engraved with a mariner's cross—an amalgam of a Christian cross and a boat anchor. To the right was a compact, stylized version of the mariner's cross. This one had long, curved arms with sharp flukes. The stock was set low on the shank, its arms wider at the ends than in the middle, similar to a Coptic cross.

"Saint Clement's Cross," Maddock said. "The patron saint of mariners."

He realized his mistake just as his foot touched the tile. The stone crumbled and he lurched forward.

"Maddock!" Bones hopscotched across the bridge as Maddock clung to the ledge in front of him. His grip was slipping, his strength waning.

And then Bones was there. He hauled Maddock out of the gaping hole and up onto solid ground.

"I don't get it," Bones said. "Why would the patron saint of mariners be bad luck?"

"It wasn't him who was bad luck. I should have remembered that the Erasmus cross is sort of an ironic symbol. After all, he was executed by being tied to an anchor and thrown into the sea."

"Ouch. So, what would your ironic personal symbol be?" Bones scratched his chin. "I suppose it could be your very small organ, but then we'd need to include something else for scale. Like an M&M."

"I've already designed your symbol," Maddock said.

"Really, what does it look like?"

"A lot like this." Maddock held up his middle finger, then turned and headed down the corridor.

"That hurt, dude."

They came to another deep chasm. This one was spanned by what looked like a section of culvert ten feet wide. A lip at the end fitted into a deep groove that ran along the edge of the precipice.

"What the hell is this?" Bones asked.

"I think it rolls back and forth," Maddock said. "This keeps it on its track."

"I can see why." Bones shone his light across the chasm. They faced a blank wall. About thirty feet to the right, a single passageway was the only opening. "So, we get inside this thing and roll it to the side?"

"Beats getting on top of it and riding it like a log."

Maddock inspected the interior of the giant stone

pipe. It was carved to resemble the skeleton of a fish, with a spine running down the top and parallel rows of bones running along its length.

"I hope it's not a whale," Bones said.

"We're about to find out." Like Jonah, Maddock stepped into the belly of the fish. He set his feet wide apart and shifted his weight to the right. The pipe barely budged.

Bones climbed inside. "Do we cross first and then roll it?"

"Let's try moving it first and see what happens." Maddock eyed the carved bones. He didn't trust them. "Back up. I want to try something." He scooted back until the pair were barely standing inside the pipe.

"You get any closer to me, we're going to have to get married," Bones said.

"Just shut up and roll the pipe."

They set to, putting all their weight into it. It wobbled and then slowly it began to roll. Slowly, slowly. A quarter of a turn and then…

A spike suddenly jutted out from the first of the stone vertebrae. It hung there, gleaming, its tip inches from Maddock's nose. He stepped back, knocking Bones out of the tube.

"What the hell was that?" Bones asked.

"I was afraid of that. It's booby-trapped."

"Because of the whale bones?"

Maddock shook his head. "One of the trials endured by Saint Erasmus was to be rolled down the hill in a spiked barrel."

"The entrails-on-a-stick dude? I hope in his next life he got to come back as something awesome, like a rich playboy or a bonobo."

Maddock closed his eyes and took a moment to clear that image from his mind. "Have you ever wondered what you're going to come back as, Bones?"

Bones shrugged. "Awesome begets awesome. I'll be fine."

"The good news," Maddock continued, "is Saint

Erasmus survived."

Bones arched an eyebrow. "Unharmed?"

"Well, he was healed afterward. I assume that if we continue to roll the pipe, we'll trigger more traps. So, if we're careful, we should be able to work our way through."

"Screw that. We'll roll the freaking thing into place from out here. That will trigger the traps. Then we can make our way through."

Maddock blinked twice. "Makes a hell of a lot more sense than doing it my way."

The two weary men but their shoulders into it, heaved at the great pipe and, with a deep grinding sound, it began to roll. Each quarter turn another spike shot out until all the traps had been triggered. They formed a spiral pattern running down to the other end.

"I think we can navigate that fairly easily," Maddock said once they had the tube set in place. "Just keep your eyes open in case there are more nasty tricks waiting for us."

They picked their way around the spikes without much difficulty. At the other end lay a dark tunnel. The sounds of running water surrounded them. Water dripped from cracks in the ceiling and trickled down the walls and ran in rivulets down the sloping passageway.

"That would have made for a much more interesting adventure race," Bones said. "Imagine B-list celebrities, one-hit wonder musicians, and a few aging ex-athletes running through a spiked barrel that's rolling down the hill."

"Are you describing a television show or a public execution?"

Bones made a noncommittal bob of the head. "A little of this, a little of that."

The sound of running water grew louder. Maddock let his light play across the ceiling. Moisture clung to the stones, droplets sparkling like gems in the artificial light.

"I think there's an underground river above us," Maddock said.

Bones eyed the leaky ceiling. "As long as it stays up there, we're good."

Drops of ice-cold water rained down on them as they walked. To Maddock's weary body, each was a stinging pinprick. It almost felt like a warning.

The passageway leveled out. Up ahead stood an arched doorway. It was flanked by a pair of tridents mounted to the wall. One pointed up, the other down.

"Tridents. That's a promising sign." The trident was the Special Warfare symbol of the Navy SEALs, and both men felt a certain attachment to it.

"Unless they're like the trident we found a few years ago," Maddock said.

"Don't remind me."

The floor of the chamber was covered in water. The walls were carved with rolling waves and sea birds, but Maddock and Bones found themselves captivated by what stood before them. Atop a pedestal stood a twelve foot-tall statue of a powerfully built man. He wore only a cloak draped over his shoulder and wrapped around his pelvis. He stood atop the waves, guarded by a dolphin and a hippocampus, the mythological horse that could ride the sea. A crack had formed in the ceiling and water tumbled down onto the figure. Over the years, it had worn away the crown of his head all the way down to the simple band of celery that held back his hair. But his bearded face was still handsome. In his right hand he held a trident.

"Poseidon," Maddock said. "God of the sea, rivers, and horses." He ran his light up and down the length of the statue. "Something bothered me about the main caverns. There were signs that people had lived there, but no trappings of religion."

"Good point," Bones said. "No crosses. No place of worship."

"I think that's because they had to keep their true religion a secret."

"Which was?" Bones asked.

"The Cult of Poseidon. These men loved the sea

above all else. The only Christian icons they memorialized were those directly associated with sailors. Everything else was about the sea itself."

"They got stranded in the desert, found the caverns, and moved in," Bones said. "I can buy that. But why did they come all the way down here to build this temple?"

"Not a temple, a vault. They knew they might not live to see a rescue. The treasure needed to be in a place no one could accidentally stumble across it, and it needed to be secured in a way that the uninitiated couldn't access it. Finally, they had to consider that it might never be found. In which case, such a magnificent treasure of the sea needed a final resting place. I'll bet when they found their way down into these deep caverns and found water flowing from stone, it seemed like a fitting place to make a tribute to Poseidon."

"That's awesome," Bones said. "But what about the treasure?"

Maddock shone his light around. Down at the base of the statue, along the lip of the pedestal, lay the broken remains of wooden chests. Here and there he saw the sparkle of a gemstone or the gleam of a pearl.

"I think I might know. But you're not going to like it."

"What the hell are you saying to me, Maddock?"

"It looks like they laid the treasure at the feet of their god. Sometime after they were gone, the ceiling started leaking. Over time, I guess the chests rotted and fell apart."

"Holy crap," Bones grumbled, then he brightened up. "Could the treasure be here, under the water?" He made a sweeping gesture. "Just waiting for us to pick it up?"

"Maybe," Maddock said.

"What do you mean, maybe?" Bones had descended the steps into Poseidon's chamber and now waded toward the statue. "We can at least collect the stuff that's up here on the pedestal. Come help me." Bones began sifting through the detritus, pocketing any valuables he found.

Maddock moved slowly through the water. It was all he could manage. He could feel a gentle flow of water. There was an outflow somewhere. His toe came down on something solid. He reached down into the dark water and his fingers close around a gemstone. When he shone his light on it, he whistled. It was the largest, purest sapphire he'd ever seen. It refracted the beam of his Maglite, splitting it into a myriad of blue beams that shone upon the form of Poseidon.

And in the god's left hand, something began to glow a deep red.

"What did you just do?" Bones eyed the object nervously.

"I need to see what that is."

Maddock heaved his bulk up onto the pedestal, then clambered on top of a hippocampus so that he was eye level with the object in Poseidon's hand.

It was a baseball-sized sphere, its surface black and crusty. Fossils were embedded in its surface—tiny crabs, crayfish, and seashells. Red light streamed from invisible cracks in its surface.

"In some works of art, Poseidon carries a stone encrusted with sea creatures," Maddock said.

"What's up with that red light?"

"I don't know," Maddock said, watching the flickering red light. "The sapphire seemed to turn it on."

"Must be female, then."

Maddock rolled his eyes. The strange object continued to glow. He reached for it, hesitated. Was it as benign as it appeared?

"I just wish I knew what this was."

"Oh, I can tell you exactly what it is," a voice said from behind them.

Maddock turned to see a man carrying an automatic rifle standing in the doorway. Smiling, he raised the weapon.

"Please get down from there. And if either of you makes a move for a weapon, I'll turn you into hamburger."

"Orry Rockwell," Bones said. "What the hell do you think you're doing?"

CHAPTER 40

"**That is a** *pōhaku o ka hekili.* Thunderstone for short." Rockwell stood in the doorway, made no move to come closer. His expression was relaxed, but he still held the rifle trained on them, finger on the trigger.

"Never heard of it," Maddock said. He had climbed down from the pedestal and stood beside Bones, knee deep in frigid water. His only remaining pistol was in his backpack. He'd secured it there when they began their search for the vault. Even if it were within easy reach, he had only two bullets left. He'd need a golden opportunity to take Rockwell down.

"A Mormon missionary in the Pacific gathered accounts of them during his travels. If the legends are true, they form in submerged volcanoes and are exceedingly rare and incredibly powerful. In the hands of someone who knows how to wield it, it can cause earthquakes, even volcanic eruptions."

"Did Poseidon have one?" Bones asked.

Rockwell pursed his lips, narrowed his eyes in thought. "If he actually existed, I suppose he could have wielded one."

And then Maddock remembered something. "Poseidon was also the god of earthquakes."

"In which case, one of these thunderstones would come in handy," Bones said.

"If Iturbe and his crew heard the legends, obviously they'd concluded that it belonged to Poseidon. It matches the artwork and legends perfectly."

Rockwell's eyes flitted to the stone, but only for a split-second. Not nearly enough time for Maddock and Bones to make a move. "The missionary claimed he once witnessed a shaman use one of these to protect a village from a lava flow."

"I'm surprised the LDS church allowed that story to

get out, considering it suggests pagans can wield godlike powers."

"Oh, the church absolutely suppressed his story," Rockwell said. "But the Dominion has ways of finding things out."

Maddock twitched at the mention of the name. The Dominion was a pseudo-Christian clandestine organization who sought world domination and a return to what they considered "traditional" values. A few years earlier, the Dominion had been exposed in the United States thanks to the work of Maddock, Bones, and Tam Broderick's Myrmidon Squad, and many of their leaders rooted out. But the organization continued to operate in the shadows, primarily in the United States and Western Europe.

"You're one of the Dominion?" Bones said.

"I guess you can say I'm of the Dominion even though I'm not a member. I grew up in Utah in a conservative Mormon family. I'm descended from Porter Rockwell, friend and bodyguard to Joseph Smith and Brigham Young."

Maddock knew the name. "The Destroying Angel of Mormondom?"

"That's what they called him. I kind of like it, but it's too long to fit on a t-shirt, and if you try and go with an acronym, you get DAM. Mormons won't go for that." Rockwell forced a laugh at his own joke. "He was even the subject of a prophecy from Joseph Smith himself: *So long as ye shall remain loyal and true to thy faith, need fear no enemy. Cut not thy hair and no bullet or blade can harm thee.* And it proved true. He remained faithful and time and again he came out of situations unscathed."

"Maybe he was just good at killing," Bones said.

"Probably. But he genuinely believed it was due to his devotion to the prophecy. But even so, he once cut off his hair so that it could be made into a wig for a woman who had gone bald from typhoid. He had many facets, but ultimately he was a man who cared for his people and his cause."

"He was also a murderer many times over," Maddock said.

"That all depends on a person's perspective, doesn't it? He was a lawman and a true believer. He was abiding by his conscience."

"Religion is always a convenient excuse for horrible behavior," Bones said.

"Where would the world be without true devotion?" Rockwell's eyes went wide as he spoke. The red glow from the thunderstone bathed his face in sinister light. "And I don't mean religion. The same single-minded zeal that drives the religious zealot also burns in the hearts of the greats in every field. You can't push boundaries without deep devotion, true belief. Think about advances in science, the greatest works of art." He paused, looked directly at Maddock. "The greatest discoveries in history."

That one hit Maddock hard. Of the many people he admired, how many would have accomplished what they had without extreme or even complete devotion to their passion?

"How about the guy who invented fake boobs?" Bones asked.

Rockwell's smile didn't reach his eyes. "I'm going to miss you. I really do like you guys. You're believers, too."

"That's true," Bones said. "I believe in the three B's: bros, babes, and beer. Not necessarily in that order."

Maddock grinned. He knew Bones was stalling for time, looking for an opportunity to make a move. But some of the things his friend came up with…

"That actually will fit on a t-shirt!" Rockwell said. "Thanks for that. I'd give you credit, but that might lead to awkward questions." He flashed an apologetic grin. "But you and I both know none of those are your true passion." He returned his gaze to Maddock. "You two are driven by the love of the hunt. But it's not about the treasure. It's because you have to know."

An invisible hand gripped Maddock by the throat.

Bones raised his hand like a pupil in class. "So, what

is it I supposedly want to know, because blissful ignorance has worked pretty well for me."

Rockwell laughed again. "Deflection won't work on me. You know what I'm saying. You have to know." He said it slowly, injected the words with deep meaning. "What's at the top of the mountain. What's at the bottom of the sea?"

"Snow. Sand. Both of them suck," Bones said.

"No lasting relationships, no kids, loose attachments to your extended families," Rockwell said.

"How do you know that?" Maddock said.

"I listen, read between the lines. And you've confirmed everything I thought about you."

Out of the corner of his eye, Maddock saw Bones begin to inch forward. He knew he needed to keep Rockwell focused on him.

"I can't wait to hear what you thought about me," Maddock said. "I'm sure you're every bit as clever as you think you are."

"You should have left after the race, gone back to your regular lives. But just a whiff of a new twist on an unsolved mystery was enough to make you interrupt your regularly scheduled programming. And the Arch Gold Mine? Please. That was no reason for you to stay."

"Is that it? We took an extended vacation?" Maddock laughed.

"There was no good reason for you to go out into the desert the day after I rolled those boulders down on you. But you did, not only putting your own health at risk, but leaving people you care about behind, because you wanted to search for the Lost Ship of the Desert."

Maddock swallowed hard. He couldn't manage a reply. Bones moved a little closer.

"Don't come any closer, Bones," Rockwell warned.

"It's cool. I just thought you'd like to know that we found the ship. Like, not even kidding."

"Did you? Well, that makes what happened tonight even more interesting. Your friends are up there, in the company of strangers and human traffickers. There's a clever, intelligent, beautiful girl up there." His gaze bored into Maddock. "Yet, even though you had just solved one of the greatest unsolved mysteries of the Southwest, you still left them behind. Why? One find of a lifetime in a day isn't enough for you?

"I followed you down here. Watched you put your lives at risk multiple times. You could have gone back for equipment, returned, and done it safely. But you were willing to risk being impaled on spikes in order to get there just a little sooner. Why?"

"The treasure," Bones said. "We had to at least try and find it before the government takes control of the place."

"Had to," Rockwell echoed. "That's exactly what I'm talking about. But I don't think it's about the treasure. Any legend would have been enough for you, because you have to know."

They lapsed into silence. It was true.

"So that's what drives us," Maddock said. "So what?"

"It doesn't just drive you. It owns you. You will always choose it over everything and everyone else you value. It will always be first among firsts. You will do anything. Just like me."

"Are you trying to say you're a victim of your deep belief in human trafficking?" Bones deadpanned.

Rockwell smiled. "That's just a way to pay the bills. This is my passion." His eyes took in the entire chamber. "Water! Clean, pure water. This is the true gold."

"Slow down, Bobby Boucher," Bones said. "What are you talking about?"

"Why is that surprising? Human traffickers can't care about clean water? I desperately want enough clean water for everyone. I sincerely wish that your future brother-in-law could safely sell his raw water."

Maddock blinked. "Wait. What?"

Bones and Rockwell laughed.

"I have to say, I actually do like this dude," Bones said to Maddock. "He's got you pegged."

"I'm sincere about this," Rockwell said. "I believe in the Salton Sea project. I hate the Pacific Garbage Patch. I truly believe that the human race is in deep trouble if we don't change the way we deal with water."

"So that makes it okay to enslave people?" Maddock said.

"It makes it necessary. The difference between my devotion and yours is that yours does not have global ramifications."

"That's not necessarily true," Bones said. "You've heard of Atlantis, right?"

Rockwell's eyes went to Bones. He stared. "I almost believe you. But the reality is, the world must change. And I can't change the world without wealth, and success. I will clean up the Salton Sea. And in doing so, I will show on a small scale what the word could accomplish on a grand scale. It has got to be done. I'm the only one who can do it."

Maddock understood the passion, was even sympathetic to the cause, but could not condone the methods.

"I get it," he said to Shipman. "But think about it. How does killing us change anything for you? Won't the traffickers identify you as their boss?"

"They think my name is Bryce Shipman. That's who the police will go after, not the guy who was captured by the traffickers. Spenser and Riv saw it happen. Once things went to hell up there, I hid and tried to pick off a few of them from behind cover. Dead men tell no tales, you know."

"So, you pointed the police in the direction of the guy who killed Megan Keane," Bones said.

"Did he?" Rockwell's eyebrows shot up. "That's funny. I was blackmailing him for the murder, but I didn't know for certain that he did it. Seems the type, doesn't he."

"His treasure hunting was bringing him too close to your operation?"

"Exactly. Couldn't have him poking about, and

certainly couldn't have him telling stories. That's his job, after all."

A piece fell into place in Maddock's mind. Something Shipman had said. "It was you who blew up the dungeon room."

"Circle gets the square. Couldn't have a back door into my operation." His face fell and he let out a sigh. "Damn it! I hate this! If you had just waited a week to start searching around, everything would have been different."

"How so?" Maddock asked.

"We'd still be friends. The cargo would have already moved along. It would have been weeks until the next shipment. If you were still searching, I could have found a temporary site. Hell, I would have joined you. I'd have loved to have found this with you guys."

Maddock was growing tense. Their options were limited. The water numbed their legs, slowed their movement, and although he appeared relaxed, even friendly, Rockwell showed no sign of losing focus or removing his finger from the trigger. And Maddock had run out of topics of conversation.

"You know what, Rockwell?" Bones said. "You're not right, but you're not wrong." He turned to Maddock. "Know what I mean?" He raised his eyebrows in an exaggerated fashion and mouthed *Lights Out*.

"I do know what you mean." And Maddock did understand. The light from the thunderstone had faded to almost nothing. The only light was that provided by their Maglites. What they were about to try was risky, reckless even. But he had no better idea. There was nothing to do now but wait for Bones to give the signal.

"Maddock and I have done plenty of things we're not proud of, but we did it with Uncle Sam's stamp of approval, so that made it okay. We really freaking hate what you're doing, but we understand what it means to get blood on your hands in pursuit of a greater cause."

"And we agree with you about clean water. Always have," Maddock said.

"What are you saying?" Rockwell asked.

"We could be assets to you," Bones said. "Well, I'm an asset. Maddock's just an asshat. You trust us to keep your secret, we join your cause." He put out his hands, imploring. "Maddock and I love the water. We're men of the sea. Let us be your seamen."

Rockwell chuckled. Visibly relaxed. The moment had to come soon.

"You almost got me. But I could never trust you. See, that's the thing about true devotion. It's not transferable."

"Speaking of devotion, what about Lilith?" Bones asked. "Is she involved in your little scheme or have you kept her in the dark?"

The last thing Maddock saw before the lights went out was Rockwell's face twisted into a snarl of rage. At the word 'dark' Maddock and Bones turned out their lights and dove to the side.

Rockwell let out a yell of anger and opened fire. The strobe-like flash of muzzle flare turned Poseidon's vault into a macabre slide show. Images flicked past Maddock's vision almost too fast to take in. Dark water. The hulking figure of Poseidon, bullets chewing through him as Rockwell sprayed the chamber with gunfire. Ducking behind the safety of the pedestal. Bones surfacing from beneath the dark water like the world's brownest merman. Grabbing his pistol.

And then the gunfire ceased.

"What the hell did you do?" Rockwell yelled.

"Greenhorn," Bones muttered.

"Let me guess," Maddock said. "You're the smartest guy in every room, but with all the stress you've been under lately, you forgot to grab a flashlight."

"And your cell phone is almost out of juice." Bones turned to Maddock. "Goat porn," he said confidentially.

"I'll be fine," Rockwell said. "I've got you outgunned. I'll just kill you and take your flashlights."

"We dropped them in the water," Bones said.

"You wouldn't. Even if you did manage to kill me,

you'd never find your way out."

"That's how petty we are," Bones said.

"And I'd find my way out," Maddock said to Bones.

"Oh, so would I."

"Stop it! Both of you!"

"The cracks are beginning to show," Bones said quietly.

Being this far beneath the earth did something to a person. There was keen awareness of exactly how much rock hung above them. And few environments were more terrifying than absolute darkness. It affected even the most experienced caver, but few were equipped for the added duress of a life-and-death battle.

"I need that stone, Maddock!" Rockwell shouted.

"What do you want with it?"

"There's a fault line running up through Palm Springs and the Coachella Valley and it's a ticking time bomb. If I can harness the power of the stone, I can do anything I want. Spoiled one-percenters will find out it's a long fall from atop their high horses."

"We won't let you do that," Maddock said.

"You know what? To hell with the both of you." Rockwell stepped through the doorway and fired again.

Maddock and Bones were ready. Operating on limited ammunition, each fired a single shot at the first flash of muzzle fire, then ducked back behind the pedestal.

And then all was quiet again, save for the sound of falling water.

"Think we got him?" Bones whispered.

And then Rockwell cried out.

"Ow! One of you bastards shot me in the leg!"

"It was me," Bones said.

"No, definitely me," Maddock replied.

"It's not funny. This hurts."

"Let me make something clear to you," Maddock said. "There's a great difference between hunting a rabbit and hunting us. You are out of your depth here. Give up the rifle and we'll see you safely up to the surface."

Rockwell laughed. "I said it hurts, not that I'm dying. You grazed me. And if you think I would allow you to leave when I just confessed to human trafficking and blackmail, and after I just tried to kill you, you are nowhere as smart as I think you are."

"He poses," Bones said.

Rockwell fired off another burst. It went wide. Maddock and Bones ducked beneath the water and prayed they wouldn't be caught by a ricochet.

They resurfaced and Maddock spoke to Rockwell through the darkness. "You do know what happens when you use burst-fire. You only get a few squeezes of the trigger before you run dry. And if you run out of ammunition, I think you know what happens next."

"You're right. I can't fight you guys." Rockwell paused, and when he spoke again, his tone was conversational, with a touch of cockiness. "You experienced treasure hunters missed a couple of things."

"Such as?" Maddock asked.

"These tridents outside the chamber. The one on the right is anchored to the wall, but the one on the left is attached to some sort of mechanism."

Maddock's heart was suddenly in his throat. He hadn't noticed, but he sensed Rockwell was telling the truth.

"What's the other thing?" Bones asked.

"The water that's spilling down onto Poseidon. That's not a crack in the ceiling. It looks like some kind of valve or stopper that's failing."

"Oh, crap," Bones said.

He and Maddock sprang to their feet and began splashing through the water.

"Did you know powerful things happen when Poseidon's trident touches the ground?" Rockwell taunted.

They followed the sound of his voice, not daring to turn on the flashlights now that they were no longer behind cover.

"I wonder what this trident on the left does."

"Which trident was the one on the left?" Bones asked.

"The one pointing down."

A rusty squeal pieced the air. A loud thud and the floor vibrated as something heavy clunked into place.

"No!" Bones fired off a shot in the direction of Rockwell's voice. The muzzle flash revealed a massive stone seal rising from the floor closing off the archway.

"That's bad," Maddock said.

And then the ceiling fell in.

CHAPTER 41

Orry Rockwell lay on his back on the wet stone floor. All he could hear was the rush of running water and his own ragged breathing. For a moment he imagined he could hear Maddock and Bones crying out on the other side of the wall, but they were sealed away forever. A shame really. He had liked them.

He rolled over onto his side and a lash of pain sliced through him. He let out a cry of anger.

"I can't believe how much this hurts." He tore his shirt into strips and bandaged the wound the best he could. It didn't seem like a serious wound. What was more, he could claim he'd encountered a human trafficker and been wounded in the struggle.

The sound of running feet startled him. Flashlights bobbed in the darkness. And then Terry Gold was standing over him.

"What the hell did you just do?" Gold demanded as he snatched up Rockwell's rifle.

"What are you talking about? I came down here looking for Maddock and Bonebrake."

"You trapped them in there is what you did." Steven Segar was struggling to lift the trident handle. It was the wrong handle, so his struggles, though ferocious, were in vain. "We heard you."

Rockwell felt as if he'd suddenly been doused with cold water. How could they know?

"I don't know what you're talking about."

Gold shoved Segar aside and raised the trident handle on the left. Rockwell held his breath. He was ninety-nine percent sure he had opened a floodgate into the chamber. What would happen if the sealed doorway opened now?

They didn't have to find out. Nothing happened.

"I don't know what that does," Rockwell said. "This

is as far as I got."

His cheek burned as Segar slapped him across the face. The indignity and positively surreal experience of being slapped by a B-List celebrity rendered him mute.

"You wouldn't believe how well sound travels down here," Segar said. "We could hear you all the way on the other side of that spiky tube thing."

"I don't know what you think you heard, but I didn't do anything."

"It's not what we think we heard," Gold said. "You see, I habla a little Espanol, and one of those dirtbags fingered you as the big boss."

"That's crazy."

"I don't think so," Segar said. "Just as your compadre was ratting you out, we saw you sneak away. And we knew you were up to something— something that was worthy of a reality television show."

Gold took up the narrative. "We couldn't bring a crew down here and hope to keep pace with you, but we brought our buddy Yoshi with his handheld camera." He pointed with his thumb to a young man standing just behind him. Yoshi, who held a camera trained on Rockwell, waved. "We fell behind at first, Segar isn't as young as he used to be. But we kept coming. Of course, we heard you long before we caught up to you, and Yoshi started recording the moment we heard your voice. Did you catch any of what he was saying, Yoshi?"

"Let me see." The young man made a show of playing back a portion of what they'd recorded. The screen was dark, but Rockwell's voice came through clearly.

...if you actually think I would allow you to leave when I just confessed to human trafficking and blackmail, and after I just tried to kill you...

Yoshi turned off the recording. "Is that enough, gentlemen?"

"That's perfect," Gold said. "By the way, I was recording with my phone. You should see the look on your face." He flipped the phone around and showed

Rockwell a freeze frame image of himself looking poleaxed.

"That isn't me."

Segar punched him in the face.

When Rockwell's eyes cleared and his ears stopped ringing, he tried to stand, but his legs were wobbly.

Segar raised a finger in warning. "The sensei will only tolerate a certain amount of prevarication."

Water poured from the ceiling in a primal flood. Maddock danced to the side as a hunk of stone the size of his head fell from the ceiling. The water was rising at a rate he could not believe. Already it was at his armpits.

"Get to the statue!" he shouted.

Gripping their flashlights in their teeth, he and Bones swam through a hailstorm of falling rocks, swept along in the maelstrom. Bones reached the statue first. He grabbed on to Poseidon's right arm. A moment later, Maddock caught hold of the left.

"What's our play?" Bones said around a mouthful of Maglite. He squinted his eyes against the downpour.

"Any ideas on where there might be a release lever?"

Bones pulled the flashlight out of his mouth so he could gape at Maddock. "Do you think I've been here before?"

"I asked for ideas, because I'm fresh out."

Bones thought. "I've got it. Trident goes down, door goes down. Trident goes up…" He grabbed hold of the trident and pushed up. Nothing. Again. "Never mind. You got any ideas?"

"Maybe we can float to the top," he offered. He knew it would be no good. Water was pouring in from the underground river faster than it flowed from the chamber. Unless they could somehow pull the plug, the water would back up and they would drown.

No sooner had that thought entered his mind than a massive upsurge of water lifted him high. He lost his grip on the statue, made a desperate grab for it but came away with the thunderstone.

He almost dropped it, so surprised was he to find it in his hand. It was both thrilling and unnerving, but at least it wasn't something that killed at the first touch. He had enough to contend with at the moment.

He and Bones were rising fast.

"What happened?" Bones asked.

"I think the rubble from the falling ceiling must have clogged the outflow."

Bones looked up. "Now I know how that kid from Willie Wonka felt."

Maddock had an idea. He reached into his pocket, not an easy task while treading water and holding the thunderstone in the other hand.

"Just so you know," Bones shouted over the pouring water, "I do care about other stuff, not just the hunt. And other people."

Maddock's hand closed on the sapphire. He pulled it out and held it against the thunderstone. "Shut up and shine your light on the sapphire!"

"Think you can use that thing?"

"We'll find out."

CHAPTER 42

By the time Gold, Segar, and Yoshi had escorted Rockwell back to the main caverns, the scene was a very different one from when they had left. Law enforcement had arrived in full force: local police, sheriff's deputies, even a few rangers from nearby Joshua Tree National Park.

The traffickers were nowhere to be seen. All the cargo, Rockwell had never allowed himself to think of them as humans, were gathered in the main chamber. They had been provided food, drink, and blankets.

Spenser spotted them first. Her flicker of a smile faded into bemusement and then concerned when she saw that his wrists were bound. She said something to Riv, who called for Grizzly and Franzen. The four hurried over.

"Where's Maddock?" Spenser asked.

"There's been an accident," Rockwell said. He flinched as Segar raised an open hand.

"Another lie," Segar warned. "Rockwell has trapped them inside of some chamber. We couldn't get there in time to stop him, but we've got it all on tape. Enjoy jail, amigo."

"What kind of chamber?" Grizzly asked.

Gold gave a quick shake of his head. "We couldn't get the door open, but we will. We'll cut through it, blast it, whatever we've got to do."

"Damn right we will," Grizzly said. Spenser nodded approvingly.

"But they're all right?" Riv asked.

Rockwell barked a laugh. He was finished. Might as well land a parting shot.

"All right? They're dead! That was a flood chamber. As soon as I pulled the lever it sealed and filled with water."

"They can swim," Spenser said.

"You might be the best swimmer in the world, but I hold your head under water long enough. Well, use your imagination."

"Is this true?" Spenser asked Gold.

He couldn't quite meet her eye as he replied. "We're not sure."

Grizzly let out a roar of pure rage and made a charge for Rockwell. It took the combined efforts of Franzen, Segar, and Yoshi to hold him back. They dragged him to his knees where he finally collapsed against Riv's shoulder, eyes squeezed shut, his body trembling with rage.

Rockwell turned and gazed down into Spenser's blue eyes. Strangely, he saw no fear there, not even concern.

"Sorry about your new boyfriend," he said. "You're pretty. You'll find another."

Spenser tilted her head and fixed him with a pitying smile.

"If you believe Maddock is dead, you're not nearly as smart as you think you are."

They were almost out of time. Maddock kicked with all his might, trying to keep his head, and more importantly, the stones, above water.

"Here goes!" Bones shouted.

"Ready." And then a falling rock struck Maddock on the head. The sapphire slipped from his grasp.

Moving with the quickness of a striking viper, Bones snatched the gem.

"Got it. Don't freaking drop it again."

They tried again. As he fought to tread water, Bones directed the light at the sapphire. The light passed through the gem, split into many beams. One struck the thunderstone and it began to burn in his hand, filling what little remained of the chamber, and what was left of the chamber shone with a blood red glow.

Past experience had taught Maddock that controlling a stone of power required a connection with the force within the rock. After all, the human mind was driven by electrical impulses. He reached out with his mind, trying to connect with the stone.

The water lifted them ever higher. Maddock still kicked, now scarcely able to keep his nose and mouth above water.

He closed his eyes, pictured the stone in his mind. He invited the light to envelop him, its energy to fill him. His skin tingled with its warmth.

He tried to take a breath, but water filled his mouth and nose and he came up sputtering.

"Come on, bro! You can do it!" Bones shouted.

Maddock tried again. He imagined the power of the thunderstone pouring through him. In his mind's eye he pictured the vault below. He reached out with the power, imagined balling it into a fist and striking the door with all his might. Imagined it shattering.

And suddenly he was no longer the one in control. The pictures in his mind turned shades of red and gold. He didn't understand, couldn't explain, but he saw through the stone that surrounded them. Saw the empty chambers as inky blots. And then he saw the fault lines.

They ran through everything, their lines burned like fire. The thunderstone was acting of its own will now. Its scorching red energy poured out of the chamber and along a deep fault line. Where it ended, Maddock couldn't say.

He went under again. Felt Bones grab him by the belt and lift him up.

"I think the closing credits are about to roll."

"Let's hope there's a post-credit scene." With one last desperate grab he reached for the power and nudged it toward the door. A whip-like strand of energy curled out from within the thunderstone and cracked against the door.

Beneath the dark water, Maddock could sense the door crumbling, felt the fault line shift.

Wham!

His head struck the ceiling. He opened his eyes and was surprise to realize they were in an air pocket.

"What happened?" Bones asked.

"I guess it didn't work."

And then the bottom dropped out. Maddock and Bones found themselves being carried down into a whirlpool as the water drained from Poseidon's Vault.

"I think you just flushed us down the toilet," Bones yelled.

"Yet you haven't said 'holy crap' once," Maddock shouted back, still holding on to the thunderstone.

"I was saving that for last," Bones said.

They were being swept along at a dizzying clip. Poseidon's trident appeared above the rapidly falling surface of the water. Then his head and shoulders.

"Here it comes!" Bones yelled. "Holy crap!"

Maddock just had time to hold his breath before he was sucked down below the water and into the darkness. And then a thought came to him.

If the water is taking us back the way we came, that means it's going to carry us right back into…

Visions of the spiked tube through which they'd come filled his mind. There was no time for fear. He felt himself being swept upward, felt the familiar twist of oxygen deprivation. His throat burned. Lights flashed before his eyes.

And then he was flung from the passageway like a cork from a champagne bottle. He flew through the air and much sooner than expected landed flat on his stomach. His body was beyond feeling any pain by this point, but the salty taste of blood in his mouth told him he had not stuck the landing.

Miraculously he still held on to the sapphire and the thunderstone. The latter still burned bright red. He raised the stone and felt the world shift crazily beneath him.

"What the hell?"

He quickly took in the scene. He was lying on top of the spiked tube. The tremors from the shifting fault line and the powerful surge of water had caused it to shift to the side. Down below, water still poured out of the passageway and down into the abyss below. His heart dropped.

"Bones?" He tried to push himself up to his hands and knees, but that caused the tube to shift.

"Holy freaking crap, Maddock! Stay still. You're going to roll that thing right over me."

Bones clung to the groove in the stone that formed the track in which the tube rolled. It was all he could manage to hang on as the water poured in all around him.

"Get out of the flow of the water!" Maddock shouted.

"That's what I'm doing." A minute later, Bones had worked his way out of the path of the water and had managed to climb up onto the ledge. He now sat with his back to the wall, catching his breath.

"We've got a big problem," he finally shouted. "You can't pull me up onto that thing without it rolling over and taking us both down."

Maddock looked around. Bones was right. They needed to find another way.

"Look, Maddock," Bones said. "I can climb out of here. I'll just work my way down to the end and climb across. I've made plenty of climbs like that."

"It's a blank wall. No hand holds."

Bones took a deep breath and let it out slowly. "You like her, don't you?"

Maddock nodded. "A lot."

"Then get the hell out of here. Go find her. I'll catch up."

Maddock shook his head. "It's like Rockwell said. A true believer only knows one way to do things. We leave together."

He closed his eyes, tried to reconnect with the

thunderstone. Its power was fading, but he could just manage to touch it. As he had before, he saw the stone in his mind, searched for a fiery line that would indicate a fault. He didn't find one, but what he did find was a jagged crack beneath the surface of the wall where Bones sat. Someone had plastered over it. If he could just...

He imagined the crack becoming wider. It pulled apart. The plaster crumbled and fell onto Bones' head. He looked up in surprise and his eyes were suddenly alight.

He immediately turned and clambered to his feet. Maddock had opened a jagged crack in the wall, perfect for climbing. Bones set to, scaling the wall with surprising vigor. When he had reached the top, he looked back.

"Your turn. Just make sure you get over here before I fall."

Maddock tensed. He had never been any good at this sort of thing. He rose unsteadily to his feet, the tube shifting crazily beneath his feet.

"I can't look at this," Bones said

Faltering step by faltering step, Maddock struggled to maintain his balance atop the pipe as he slowly rolled it toward Bones.

A tremor shook the chamber and Maddock slipped. He regained his footing and his balance just in time.

"Any time this week!" Bones shouted. His feet had slipped and he was holding on for dear life.

Maddock wanted to hurry, but he knew that could lead to a fatal mistake. He steadily worked the pipe to the side. The gap between himself and Bones continued to close. He was getting the hang of this.

Twenty feet.

Fifteen feet.

Ten feet.

"Losing my grip here!" Bones shouted.

"Almost there." Maddock couldn't take his eyes off his friend. "Hold on."

"Can't! Gotta jump." Bones pushed out to the side.

He flew through the air, arms and legs splayed out like a skydiver. He seemed to hang in the air for a moment.

The force of his landing arrested the pipe's movement and sent Maddock staggering to the side. He waved his arms, felt that fluttering sensation that comes when you've tilted your chair back just a bit too far. And then he regained his balance.

"You all right?" he asked Bones.

"Yep. Had to save myself as usual. Now, you think you can maintain your balance while I stand up?"

"I think that depends on how awkwardly you stand." He braced himself while Bones pushed himself up onto his hands and knees. The pipe wobbled.

"Don't tip us over," Bones warned.

"Same goes for you."

"Ready? Three… two… one." In one quick motion Bones sprang to his feet. The pipe rolled to the right.

Maddock felt like Fred Astaire, nimbly moving his feet to keep himself balanced. Bones was struggling to get into sync with his partner.

"Dammit to hell, Maddock. How many times have I tried to get you to go to Beerfest with me?"

"What does that have to do with anything?" Maddock shouted, desperately trying to maintain his balance atop the rolling pipe. Down below the deep chasm beckoned.

"They have log rolling contests! We could have been practicing!"

"I think you mean a lumberjack contest," Maddock said as the rolling pipe began to slow.

"What did I say?" Bones asked as they finally came to a stop.

Maddock's shoulders sagged with relief. "Now let's get the hell off this thing and head back to the surface. There are several beers and one blonde with my name on them."

"That's what I'm talking about," Bones said. "But don't let Spenser hear you say that. I want to tell her myself."

"You know I was just…" Maddock didn't get to finish the thought. Another tremor rocked the chamber. Stalactites plummeted down from the ceiling to smash against the pipe. The very foundation trembled and the pipe came out of its groove. Slowly, it began to roll.

"It's going to fall!" Bones shouted as he tried to shield his head from falling rock.

"Run!" Maddock yelled.

They ran. Maddock felt the world tremble, felt the pipe rolling out from underneath him. He leaped into darkness.

They ran.

CHAPTER 43

They had almost reached the surface when they heard voices. Footsteps approached. Flashlights bobbed in the darkness.

"What's that red light up ahead?" It was Spenser's voice.

"It's us," Maddock called.

Spenser let out cry and hurried to him. She didn't bowl him over this time. Instead she pulled him close and kissed him deeply. Maddock pulled her close, sagged against her.

"We were on our way to find you," Spenser whispered in his ear. "I knew you'd make it."

"That makes one of us." Maddock closed his eyes and enjoyed the feeling of her arms around him. He couldn't remember ever feeling so utterly drained.

He heard Bones let out a grunt of pain, and opened his eyes to see Grizzly, arms wrapped around Bones, squeezing him tight.

"Aww. He's like a kid who found his lost dog," Spenser said.

Bones looked down in bemusement at Grizzly, then looked at Riv. "What do I do?"

"He's just got a case of the feels. You should see him when we watch the finale of *The Office*.

"It gets me every time," Grizzly said, breaking off the hug.

"It's cool," Bones said. "You should see Maddock cry when Indy lets go of the grail and takes his father's hand."

"Yeah, well I've got good reason for that," Maddock said. "And I don't cry. I just get a little… reflective."

"Not judging it, dude."

Someone cleared their throat. Maddock had not noticed the others. Gold, Segar, and Yoshi stood nearby.

"You know what makes me cry? Every single film in Segar's catalog."

"I'm just glad you guys are all right," Grizzly said. "Very few people will listen to my far-fetched theories without dismissing them outright."

"We get it," Maddock said. "You're a true believer, just like us."

Spenser pursed her lips. "What's this true believer stuff?"

"Something Rockwell said. I'll explain later."

"I've got a question," Riv said. "What is that thing you've got in your hand?"

Maddock had forgotten about the thunderstone. He began to explain, but Spenser stopped him.

"Hold on. You'd better start from the beginning. Or at least from wherever things get interesting."

"It's a long story."

She took him by the hand. "It's a long way back to the ranch."

The sun was high overhead when they finally made it back to the ranch house. There they cleaned up, tended to injuries, and enjoyed a quick meal. Maddock and Spenser spent the afternoon in bed, most of it sleeping.

They gathered that night in the big room. No one had the energy to prepare a meal, but Grizzly had a surprise in store. Jashawn, who had been their teammate in the practice race, showed up with four large pizzas from "the best pizza joint in LA." They were no longer hot, but he insisted they were even better when reheated. Nigel Gambles arrived around the same time bearing a bottle of brandy and a cooler filled with imported beer.

They spent the evening drinking, laughing, and filling one another in on the events of the previous week. Jashawn was amazed at all that had transpired, and begged to be included whenever Grizzly took a crew down into the caverns.

"I'm sure I can arrange some sort of sponsorship with my company," he said.

Predictably, Gambles was hungry for every scrap of information on Striker and Shipman. He devoured Striker's journal, then peppered them with questions, jotting their answers down on a legal pad in neat cursive.

"You really found it? The Lost Ship of the Desert?" He turned and stared out the window as if he could see the ship from here.

"We'll take you to see it as soon as the police will allow it," Maddock said.

Someone found an old Steven Segar movie on television and they enjoyed a few laughs at its expense.

"What's going to happen with Gold and Segar?" Bones asked.

"Are you kidding? Both are destined for career comebacks," Spenser said. "They've obviously found a place with fast Internet, because they've been uploading teaser clips to the web all afternoon. They're trending all over social media."

"What about you?" Bones asked Grizzly. "Have your plans changed at all?"

"We won't be able to do the treasure hunt show exactly as we planned, since you guys have already found it. But we can still do a series on Iturbe, the ship, and the Poseidon vault. Gambles is going to work with me on a Striker documentary."

Gambles raised his glass in salute. "Cheers!"

"And we've still got the adventure race. We'll be keeping busy."

Jashawn turned to Spenser. "Speaking of the race, where's your brother?"

Spenser rolled her eyes. "He's in the hospital. He contracted a waterborne parasite from his 'raw water.' He's going to be fine, but he'll be in for a few more days. Our mom is in full helicopter parent mode. He's miserable. Punishment fits the crime. I love the guy, but he's just so..." Lost for words, she made a palms-up gesture.

"I got you," Jashawn said. "I got a cousin just like that."

Franzen dropped by late that night to inform Maddock and Bones that, although they were not suspects, they would be required to give statements, and probably to the FBI.

"I'm going to have to ask you not to leave the state for the time being. And keep me informed of your whereabouts."

"Fine by us," Maddock said. He suddenly realized he was in no hurry to leave California.

Maddock slept in the next morning. Spenser was already awake. She was sitting on the bed, clad in one of Maddock's shirts and nothing else. She closed her book and greeted him with a smile when he awoke.

"Good morning. How did you sleep?"

"Fine," Maddock said, a note of suspicion in his voice. Her smile was too big, and there was a twinkle in his eye. "What's going on?"

"Oh, not much." She set her book down and reached for her tablet which lay on the bedside table. "Just current events."

Maddock sat up, feeling every bump and bruise. He wondered which part of the story had gotten out. "The ship? The human trafficking? The revelation of the identity of the Black Dahlia killer?"

Spenser shook her head. "None of those."

"What then?"

"Remember you told me about the fault line? How you could feel the power running along it? How you felt it split open?" She turned on her tablet and opened a browser. "Check out this video."

Maddock could tell by her sly grin that she'd been waiting for him to wake up just so she could show him this.

It was a television news report. Beneath the headline, RIVER FORMS OVERNIGHT IN SALTON, chopper footage showed a river pouring into the sea. As the chopper gained altitude, the camera followed the flow back into the hills. Maddock scanned the article. Residents had been surprised to find themselves cut off from the interstate highway by a river that had appeared seemingly out of nowhere. Experts were puzzled. Everyone was pointing to unusual seismic activity in the area the previous day. All agreed that a river of fresh water was a boon to the Salton Sea and increased the likelihood of its survival.

"Did I do that?" Maddock asked.

"If not, it's one heck of a coincidence, don't you think?" She kissed him on the cheek. "You performed a miracle and didn't even know it. That's pretty awesome." She leaned back, stretched, and arched her back. "God, I'm so jealous that you got to see that vault. Next time, you're taking me with you. Promise me."

Maddock was preoccupied admiring her legs and didn't answer right away. "Oh, yeah. About that. I've been thinking." He proceeded to tell her about the things Rockwell had said. "So I was thinking, maybe it's time to put other things first in my life."

Spenser turned to face him, propped up on her elbow, and looked him in the eye. He could only endure five seconds of her blank stare.

"What?" he demanded.

"You would change your whole life because of a human trafficker's TED talk?"

He felt his ears burning. "That's not exactly fair."

"Wouldn't it be easier to surround yourself with people who get you? I mean, your friends understand, don't they? And your sister?"

"I suppose."

"That really only leaves the woman in your life, and if she's on board…"

Maddock wasn't sure how to reply.

Spenser's eyes bored into him. "You didn't ask me which movie scene always makes me cry. Too late!" She held up a hand. "It's the final scene of the last Indiana Jones movie. Indy's just gotten married and it looks like he's about to walk off into the sunset. Mutt picks up his fedora and everyone in the theater thinks there's going to be a passing of the torch…"

"And then Indy grabs it away at the last second, puts it on and gives him a look that says, "There's only one Indiana Jones."

"That's the one. Think about it." She abruptly changed the subject. "Look, this has been awesome, except for the part where I got abducted. But I've got to get back to work this week."

"Oh," Maddock said. He wasn't sure what he'd expected. Of course she would go back to her life of luxury resorts and fine dining and he'd go back to doing what he always did— searching for treasure and waiting for things to get complicated, as they inevitably did. "Well, if you're ever in Key West…"

"I'll be spending a few days at one of California's oldest resort hotels," she went on in a rush, as if he hadn't spoken. "They've just completed extensive renovations and are anxious for some influencers to spread the word. And since my brother is still on an IV drip, I find myself in need of a plus one." She scooted in close and rested her head on his shoulder. "Fancy meals, hot tub and sauna, couples massages, and every bit of it comped."

"You know, I might could be persuaded." He put his arm around her and gave her a squeeze.

"And did I mention," she whispered, "it's haunted?"

Maddock threw back his head and laughed.

"Count me in!"

The End

FROM THE AUTHOR

One of my favorite things about writing the Dane Maddock Adventures is the research that goes into the books. (Don't tell my younger self that). I love making use of "real" mysteries and legends, as well as actual people and places. Contest is loaded with these, and I would be remiss if I did not acknowledge the work of author M.L. Behrman, whose book, *Mojave Mysteries*, provided a wealth of story material.

ABOUT THE AUTHOR

David Wood is the USA Today bestselling author of the Dane Maddock Adventures and several other books and series. He also writes fantasy under the pen name David Debord. He's a member of International Thriller Writers and the Horror Writers Assocíon, and also reviews for New York Journal of Books.

Learn more about his work at www.davidwoodweb.com or drop by and say hello on Facebook at www.facebook.com/davidwoodbooks.

Made in the USA
Las Vegas, NV
20 August 2023